Footprints in the Butter

Footprints in the Butter

An Ingrid Beaumont Mystery
Co-Starring Hitchcock the Dog

Denise Dietz

Delphi Books
Lee's Summit, MO

ISBN: 0-9663397-2-X

Published by:
Delphi Books
P.O. Box 6435
Lee's Summit, MO 64064
Fax: 816-478-2156
E-mail: DELPHI BKS@aol.com
http://www.theauthorsstudio.org

Website: http://www.eclectics.com/denise
E-mail: Calliope97@aol.com

First printing September 1999
Printed in the United States of America

This book is dedicated to CHEROKEE (1986-1998) who was, and always will be, Hitchcock.

I'm a rough dog, a tough dog, with the soul of a pussycat;
I'm a growly dog, a howl-y dog, and I'm neither thin nor fat;
I'm a fickle-ish dog, a ticklish dog, who really likes to snoop;
I'm a bite-y dog, a fight-y dog, and my size implies that scoop;
I'm a nice dog, a feisty dog, with a windshield-wiper tail;
I'm a shoeless dog, a clueless dog, but my instincts will prevail.

—Cherokee (with help from Denise), *I'm a Tough Dog*

Acknowledgement

*I would like to thank Fran Baker and Jody LoGrasso
for their help, encouragement, and sense of humor*

Footprints in the Butter

Chapter One

My name is Ingrid Anastasia Beaumont. My ex used to say that my initials stood for "I'm a bitch." True.

I was delivered by an usher at the Chief Theatre. My mother had been watching Alfred Hitchcock's Notorious when she went into labor, and she wouldn't budge until the movie ended. I can't really blame her. You see, Ingrid Bergman, beautiful and rich, had been poisoned by her insensitive husband, and Cary Grant was about to come to her rescue. I mean, we're talking Cary Grant—suave, cleft-chinned, urbane, aristocratic.

Except for my cleft chin, I don't possess Cary's attributes. Nor Ingrid's. My mother always tells everybody that my middle name, Anastasia, was for Ingrid Bergman's Academy Award performance. Baloney! When Bergman won her Oscar I had just turned nine. The Anastasia was for my grandmother, who's half Russian, half Chinese. From Nana Ana, I inherited eyes that tilt slightly North, and I was born in the Year of The Rat. Which, says Nana Ana, means that I'm ambitious, honest, and compatible with Dragons, Monkeys, and other Rats. I should have heeded Nana Ana's words. My ex was a Cock.

Just for the record, I'm not a detective or even an amateur sleuth. I adore riddles and crossword puzzles, but I despise mysteries. So I guess God was playing one of his/her practical jokes when Wylie bit the dust.

"Kill the bastards!"
It was Sunday afternoon, the day after my high school reunion dance. I was at Mile High Stadium, watching the Denver Broncos get massacred by the Dallas Cowboys.

In Colorado Springs, seventy miles away, Wylie Jamestone took his last breath.

Wylie's severed pate spurted blood while I screamed bloody murder: "Kill, kill, kill! Blitz, damn it, *blitz!*"

The Broncos blitzed. The Cowboys fumbled. The Broncs recovered. I roared my approval, then performed a high-five with the fat man sitting next to me. He fumbled for my breast, I don't know why. I'm not a ravishing beauty, quite the opposite, yet men always try to ravish me. I've been told I look like Bette Midler. When people tell me this, they usually stare at my bust, then, embarrassed, raise their eyes to my slightly crooked front teeth, which are frequently clenched. You see, I've heard that Bette Midler bullshit a thousand times, and honestly, I don't see the resemblance.

I slapped the fat man's hand away. Undaunted, he asked, "What's your name, darlin'?"

"Hannibal Lector," I growled. "The Purple People Eater."

It went way above his head, like a hail-Mary pass.

"But... but you're a girl," he stammered, his vodka-spiked cocoa sloshing from his thermos, puddling on his khaki pants.

"I am woman, mister, hear me roar." Although my door-prize ticket sandwiched me somewhere between Heaven and Mile High Stadium's manicured football field, I leaned forward, jiggled the orange and blue pom-pom somebody'd handed me at the gate, screamed, "Bite the dust, you motherfriggin' Cowboys," then thrust my middle finger skyward. Admittedly, it was a childish gesture for someone facing decade five.

The Broncos' offense, bless their eleven hearts, responded to my badmouthing with a vengeance. Trampling Cowboys beneath their cleats, they scored three times and won the game.

Talk about an air-tight alibi! My friends later informed me that TV cameras had panned in close. My blondish curls, they said, had spilled over my forehead, hiding my hazel eyes. Beer had geysered, landing in the shape of a giant turkey's wishbone across my lucky orange sweatshirt. My cardboard sign read: HI BEN AND PATTY. WELCOME TO COLORADO. But it was my middle finger gesture that provoked applause from patrons at the Dew Drop Inn.

Subsequently, I found out that Lieutenant Peter Miller had

missed the last two minutes of the televised game, the part where Coloradans have heart attacks and nobody goes to the bathroom. Lieutenant Miller, a homicide detective, was much too busy inspecting the crime scene, searching for clues. Unfortunately, Wylie was much too dead for questioning, even if, as usual, he had all the answers.

The AFC playoffs, not Wylie, was on my mind as I navigated Interstate 25, driving toward Colorado Springs. There's a long stretch between Castle Rock and Monument where my radio broadcasts the cold hiss of static, so I turned it off. Therefore, I missed the first news flash about the murder, the one where they keep the victim's identity a secret, pending notification of his immediate family. In this case, Wylie's immediate family was a sister in Houston, and his wife Patty.

"We're number one!" I kept shouting through my jeep's open window. My voice, already raspy, was almost guttural by the time I reached my cozy turn-of-the-century house and discovered that my significant lover's rental car was missing. Damn! I wanted to celebrate the Broncos victory with a few ticklish tackles of my own. Vaguely, I remembered Ben saying something about kidnapping Wylie and buying him dinner.

Hitchcock greeted me with a joyful whimper and a gyrating butt. I returned the salutation, then found my remote where he had buried it. Tonight it was easily discovered beneath a lime green couch cushion. Sometimes it's wedged beneath my ersatz Oriental carpet. Mostly, it's in the back yard, just outside the doggie door. Wiping away dog drool with my thumb, I turned on the TV and clicked to ESPN.

There had been a brief electrical outage, so my answering machine looked even more inanimate than usual. Every Sunday its red button blinks in a mesmerizing rhythm of continuity since a certain Hollywood producer likes to call during football games, when he knows I'm not home or won't answer. That way he can leave caustic messages without repercussions.

Hired to compose the score for a pending slasher flick, my deadline loomed closer and closer, and my bad guy's theme still sounded like melting ice cubes. I'm not a procrastinator, quite the opposite, but I had been totally distracted by my high school reunion.

Anyway, I was in the process of recording a new "leave your name and number at the sound of the beep" when my doorbell rang.

Part Irish Setter, part Lab, part Great Dane, and bigger than my couch, Hitchcock issued forth his warning bark, which usually sent solicitors, not to mention potential rapists, scrambling for distance. Not this time. The doorbell rang again. Between barks, a man shouted, "Is Ms. Beaumont home?"

"That all depends. Who wants to know?"

"Lieutenant Peter Miller. C.S.P.D."

"Police?"

"Yes, ma'am."

"Just a sec. Sit, Hitchcock! Stay!"

The man who stood on my front porch was attractive. About my age, he had dark hair and a silver-streaked mustache. He also possessed an identity packet.

"Are you Ms. Beaumont?" he asked.

"Yes. Delete the Ms, okay? It sounds like its short for misanthrope. I distrust mankind, but I don't hate it."

"Sorry," he said, and even though it was nice of him to apologize, he sounded as if my Aunt Lu had just been steamrolled by a San Francisco trolley. Except my Aunt Lu, who lives in San Francisco, is a rather hefty woman who could probably steamroll a trolley.

As I stared at Miller, it suddenly occurred to me that I hadn't had a confrontation with uniformed authority in twenty-plus years, not even a speeding ticket. On the other hand, Miller wasn't wearing a uniform, and that bothered me. When I'm bothered, I usually say the first thing that pops into my head, which in this case was: "Am I under arrest?"

"Why would you think that?"

"You're not wearing a uniform."

Puzzled by my reply, Miller's eyes touched upon his charcoal suit jacket, gray slacks, and Hushpuppies. "Right," he agreed. "I'm in Homicide, Ms. Beaumont. Sorry."

This time, I wasn't sure if his sorry referred to homicide or Ms. Then it struck me. "Oh, shit. Did something happen to Ben?"

Puzzlement gave way to perplexity. "Who's Ben?"

"Ben Cassidy, an old friend." I heaved a sigh of relief. If Miller didn't know Ben, Ben was okay. Unless, of course, Ben had lost his wallet and his voice. But I didn't want to ponder that happenstance, so I did what I do when I don't want to ponder nasty happenstances. Looking down at my bare feet, I seriously considered polishing my toenails.

"It's cold," Miller hinted, huffing on his fingertips.

"Come in, Lieutenant. Hitchcock, *friend!*"

Despite the recent lack of police opposition, I felt both jittery and defiant. Habit.

"Do you have a weapons permit, Ms... uh, Miss Beaumont?"

"I beg your pardon?"

"The dog," he said, entering.

"Hitchcock? His bark's worse than his bite. If I don't scream, he'll sniff your crotch, then roll over, begging to have his belly scratched." I snatched up my remote and pressed MUTE. "What brings you to Ingrid Beaumont's neighborhood, Lieutenant?"

"I'm here because..." Miller glanced toward my TV screen, where Vikings were sacking defenseless Raiders. "Football fan, Ingrid?"

"Fanatic."

"You saw the Broncos play today."

Was that a question? "Yes, Lieutenant. In fact, I was at Mile High Stadium. That's why my voice sounds so hoarse. During the game, I cheered. After the game, I shouted at fellow fans, you know, through the window of..." I swallowed the rest of my babble and looked down at my toes again. For some dumb reason I felt like bursting into frustrated tears, probably because I suspected that Miller's switch from Ms. to Ingrid had something to do with a nasty happenstance.

"Why are you here, Lieutenant?" I challenged, lifting my cleaved chin and trying to square it. "I've scored enough buddy-cop movies to know that your visit's unofficial. Otherwise, you'd have a cohort standing by your side, for instance Wesley Snipes or Jodie Foster."

"Were you alone?" asked Miller.

"Huh?"

"Alone," he repeated patiently. "At Mile High Stadium."

"No. There were probably sixty-thousand peop——"

"I meant——"

"Look, I usually watch with my friends at the Dew Drop Inn. I'm not a fair weather fan and I love my Broncos, win or lose. I won the ticket during my high school reunion dance. Door prize."

"Hey, I didn't mean to sugges——"

"Yes, you did! Alone?" I mimicked. "Christ, you sound like my ex husband."

"I won't take up much of your time," said Miller, seemingly unperturbed by my hostility or the unflattering comparison. "You probably want to be left in peace so that you can——"

"Damn it! Get to the point! What's this all about?"

"Wylie Jamestone, of course."

The perplexity was back. In fact, Miller looked as if he had memorized a script then forgotten his lines.

"Wylie hates football," I said irrationally. "He doesn't *do* sports. He even made fun of jocks in high school."

"Is that where you met? High school?"

"Yes. I just told you. The reunion. Oh, God! Did something happen to Wylie?"

"Ingrid, I thought you knew." This time Miller looked stricken, as if he had begun to sing *The Star Spangled Banner* and suddenly realized he couldn't reach the rockets-red-glare high notes. He glanced around for his invisible cohort. Then, with a cop's subtlety, he stated, "Wylie Jamestone's dead."

I wanted to scream no, no, that can't be true, but it emerged as one long, drawn-out moan. "Noooooooooo."

Hitchcock rushed forward, fangs bared.

Miller retreated until his butt pressed against the front door. "Ms. Beaumont, Ingrid," he begged, "please call off your... Hitchcock, *friend!*"

My ganglionic mutt immediately flopped to the floor. He was well trained but had never been able to distinguish voices, just smells. Which didn't bother me since I seriously doubted that any intruder would have the smarts to shout "Hitchcock friend" during a busy rape or pilferage. Also, a burglar would smell sweaty. Lieutenant Miller smelled like Oreo cookies and Juicy Fruit gum.

"I'm sorry, Ingrid, I thought you knew," he repeated, and I realized that his original sorry had referred to Wylie, not Ms.

"If I knew about Wylie, why would I ask about Ben?"

"Your question caught me off guard," he admitted somewhat sheepishly. "But people say strange things when confronted with the death of a loved one."

It was a lousy excuse, a typical police-goof-justification. Loved one? Where did Miller get the impression that Wylie was a loved one? If he had said buddy, pal, or even kindred spirit, I might have bought it.

Stumbling backwards, my jean-clad rump found then dented a couch cushion. "I assume Wylie died today since he was in perfect health last night. How did he die? Oh, God! Homicide! Wylie was murdered, wasn't he?"

"Yes. Naturally, I assumed somebody called you."

"I've been home fifteen, maybe twenty minutes, and my answering machine... elec... electrical outage," I stammered, then burst into tears.

An agitated Hitchcock tried to lick my face while Miller fumbled through his jacket pocket until he retrieved a clean handkerchief.

My crying jag was volatile but brief. I blew my nose. "Is that why you asked if I was alone at Mile High Stadium?"

"No. If I thought you had anything to do with Wylie Jamestone's murder I would have brought my partner along."

"For your protection?" I asked sarcastically.

"Yes, ma'am," he replied, and I realized that he meant legally, not physically. "In any case," he continued, "you have an alibi."

"Baloney! I could have won the ticket and decided not to attend. I could have sold the damn thing and watched the game from any watering hole in town."

"You could have, but didn't."

"What led you to that conclusion?"

"The, uh, victim's wife, Patty Jamestone, swears she saw you on TV. You were high up in the stands. You made an obscene gesture. There was even a crudely lettered sign that said——"

"Why'd you ask Patty about me?"

Miller reached into his pants pocket and retrieved a pack of Juicy Fruit, then an obese knife, the kind with corkscrew and nail file, then, finally, a piece of paper. Thrusting forth the paper, he said,

"This is from Jamestone. It's a hand-printed copy. Forensics has the original."

I scanned Wylie's brief message. "'Give this to Ingrid,'" I read out loud. "'Let the treasure hunt begin.'"

"Do you know what it means?" asked Miller.

I shook my head. "Give what to Ingrid?"

"A painting."

"Who's on the painting?"

"I thought *you* could tell *me*."

"How? I never visited Wylie's studio. Jesus, Lieutenant, are we playing 'Murder, She Wrote'?"

"A famous blonde."

"What? Oh. The painting. Is it Bette Midler?"

"I thought Bette Midler had red hair." Hunkering down, Miller offered Hitchcock a couple of Oreos, retrieved from yet another pocket. Although he had been trained never to accept food from strangers, Hitchcock eagerly slobbered, chewed, swallowed.

"Bad dog," I chastised. Despite the white cream on his fuzzy black chin, Hitchcock looked both guilty and smug, and I recalled that Wylie had worn that very same expression last night at the dance.

"Ingrid," said Miller, "I'm curious. Why did your sign read 'Hi Ben and Patty, welcome to Colorado'?"

"That's a stupid question." I dabbed at my eyes with Wylie's note, caught myself in time, and switched to the snotty handkerchief. "Ben and Patty are both from out of state. They came for the reunion. If TV cameras happened to scan the stands, I thought maybe they'd get a kick out of my sign."

"Okay. But why wasn't your sign lettered Ben, Patty and Wylie?"

"I... I told you. Wylie hates... hated football. He... he'd never watch the game."

Which, even to my own ears, sounded like a lame excuse.

Hitchcock rolled over on his back and waved his paws like shaggy black pom-poms while Miller continued asking questions.

Unofficially, of course.

Before he left, I questioned Miller. How did Wylie die? Where?

Were there witnesses? Fingerprints? Clues?

Miller wouldn't give me any detailed information, but the ten o'clock news did. Wylie Jamestone, world-renowned artist, had been murdered inside a friend's studio. The weapon was a small bronzed statue of Rodin's *The Thinker*, rendered to Wylie's bald pate. And the only witness was a calico cat.

Wylie's draped cadaver had already been conveyed to the morgue, so the TV cameras honed in on the bewildered puss. She had a name—-Sinead O'Connor. And an owner—-Kimberly O'Connor. Teenage Kim lived next door and had discovered Wylie's body while searching for her cat. The cat was finally located in Wylie's studio, standing next to a bowl of spilled milk. No, Kim didn't faint or scream or puke or anything; jeeze, her parents had cable and she watched gory movies. No, she didn't see anybody "freaky-looking" enter or leave the house.

I knew something the TV reporters didn't. Wylie's note had been thumbtacked to the wooden stretcher of his latest canvas. But I didn't know who dominated the canvas. An evasive Miller had successfully avoided my queries.

A sickly child, prone to earaches and high fevers, Wylie Jamestone had begun school late, so he was older than the rest of us, born in the Year of the Dog. Which meant that he was generous, stubborn, often selfish. He wasn't a lazy dog and he hadn't gone to the dogs, but he did possess this perpetual I'd-like-to-lick-my-balls expression. If there's an afterlife, Wylie was probably licking his balls right now.

Because he'd had the last laugh. *Give this painting to Ingrid. Let the treasure hunt begin.* Why me? It had been thirty years since my high school graduation, thirty years since my senior prom, thirty years since I had sung with the Clovers.

Searching through coffee table paraphernalia, I found Patty's phone number. She was staying at a borrowed house, located in the exclusive Broadmoor area.

"The owners migrate to Arizona for the winter," Patty had explained, after I met her at the Colorado Springs Airport.

I recalled our post-hug conversation.

"I'm just a hop, skip, and jump away from the Broadmoor Hotel," Patty had said. "Does it still have that lovely lounge where you sing along with the piano player?"

"The Golden Bee? Yes. But I don't sing any more, Patty."

"I suppose," she said, "you prefer to write the songs that make the whole world sing."

"No. I prefer to write the songs that make the whole world cringe. At least I did."

Patty had insisted on taking a cab. "You're busy, Ing," she had said, "a workaholic, just like Wylie. That's why he arrived a few days early, so he could set up his studio."

"Okay, Patty-Cakes, thanks. See you later, alligator."

"After a while, crocodile."

"Never smile at a crocodile."

Bringing my attention back to the present, I found myself heaving a deep sigh. *Our standard high school good-bye,* I thought somewhat nostalgically. Without further hesitation, I reached for the phone, glanced at the torn-out deposit slip from my checkbook, memorized Patty's address and telephone number, then touch-toned seven digits. Busy. I had a feeling her receiver was off the hook. An exclusive Broadmoor residence would have call-waiting, right?

So I touched-toned Alice Shaw Cooper.

"Patty's sedated," Alice said, her voice sounding like an emery board against a fingernail. "Dwight and Ben are both with her. I saw you on TV, Ingrid. Everybody did. We were at the Dew Drop Inn. Oh, Lord! Gotta' go. Sick."

As I hung up, I pictured Alice's neatly coiffured head bent forward over the commode, not a pretty picture. But I understood her reaction. Once upon a time, before she married Dwight Eisenhower Cooper, Alice had been engaged to Wylie.

Next, I called my friend Cee-Cee Sinclair.

Elderly but ageless, Cee-Cee looks like Barbara Stanwyck during her *Big Valley* days. Having inherited a rather large sum from her deceased husband, she works with a local agency called Canine Companions, where she helps train dogs to service the handicapped. Her own dog, an Australian Shepherd named Sydney, could never qualify as a Canine Companion. She—Sydney, not Cee-Cee— is a real bitch; independent, possessive, and growly.

Cee-Cee had found Hitchcock for me, at the Aminal Shelter. A tiny, six-week old Heinz 57, he gazed up at me adoringly and wagged his windshield-wiper tail.

Who could resist that tail?

Cee-Cee loved mutts, me included, and she devoured mystery novels, so I told her about Wylie's message. "I need your help, Ceese. I don't have a clue. You're good with clues."

We agreed to meet for breakfast.

I thought about calling Patty again. *Phone's off the hook,* I reminded myself. I thought about driving to her house. *She's sedated,* I reminded myself. Indecisive, I tossed my lucky orange sweatshirt into the wicker hamper and donned a Grateful Dead T-shirt. Wylie had been a Dead fan.

I shuddered at the irony of my last thought, then tried to watch the football game. Eventually I fell asleep, delinquent tears pasting my lashes to the very tops of my non-prominent cheekbones.

When I awoke the next morning I was sprawled across my mattress. I don't suffer from somnambulism so Ben had carried me to bed. Hitchcock adores Ben so my diligent watchdog had swallowed his warning bark.

My significant lover's sandalwood scent permeated the pillow next to mine, but he was gone. Rats! I wanted to ask Ben about Patty, for instance why he had paid her a visit last night. He had obviously arrived after Miller left since Miller hadn't recognized the name. But why? *Stupid, Beaumont!* Ben had heard about Wylie's murder and driven over to comfort Patty.

Following Lieutenant Miller's unofficial investigation I should have done the same thing, except I can't handle death.

No, not death. Grief. I sweep anguish under the carpet, along with other deep emotions. Ever since Stewie's macabre wake, I've developed that... shall we say character glitch?

Where was Ben now? Had he eighty-sixed Wylie and skipped town? Nope. Ben's suitcase still decorated the floor boards, and his thick wallet lay on top of my antique bureau. A murderer might flee without luggage but he definitely wouldn't leave his wallet behind.

I raced toward the window and peered through its pane. Ben's rental car squatted alongside my curb. Then I remembered. Ben jogged every morning, rain or shine. Today's autumn sun shimmered brilliantly, which didn't surprise me, because Ben was sun-shine.

Just for grins, I checked his wallet. Credit cards. Cash. Okla-homa drivers' license. A condom. Three snapshots of his ex wife and daughter. One senior prom picture of Our Gang——Wylie, me, Ben, Patty, Dwight, Stewie, Alice——-all looking as if we'd just shouted "Cheeeese." Nestled between the photos was a plastic-laminated four leaf clover.

I remembered how Wylie had originated our singing group, The Four Leaf Clovers. Now Wylie was dead, murdered, and prac-tically everybody had a motive, including me.

Especially me.

Staring out the window again, I thought about the reunion dance. *What a friggin' fiasco!*

Chapter Two

Dracula would have loved my reunion dance.

Spreading his modified forearms, he'd have swooped down from the gym's rafters, then metamorphosed into one of the waiters who balanced trays filled with glasses of Sauvignon Blanc, White Zinfandel, Beaujolais, and Spumante Ballatore.

Furthermore, except for the occasional face lift, fleshy necks presented perfect dart boards.

"What happens when an elephant steps on a grape?" asked a familiar voice. The voice belonged to a man who had altered my life. Maybe alter was a tad resolute, but he had certainly compassed it. Right now, the magnetic needle wavered on north. No, south. No, east. No, west. Obviously, I wavered too.

"What happens when an elephant steps on a grape?" he repeated.

"The grape gives a little whine," I replied, making an about-face. Ordinarily, I hide my trepidation with sarcasm. But I had been caught off guard, visualizing vampires, so I hadn't heard Wylie Jamestone sneak up behind me.

Fortunately, I had already encountered him last night during Alice Shaw Cooper's cocktail shindig. That lavish event had been held at the Colorado Springs Cheyenne Mountain Resort, which has a truly spectacular view, comfortable party rooms, and a lovely ladies' lounge. I had spent a great deal of time in that lovely lounge, chanting a mantra to the lovely toilet bowl and lovely sink-mirror: "You can handle this, Beaumont. No big deal."

So now, tonight, I didn't stiffen my fingers into talons or retreat toward the nearest girls' bathroom, which, if I recalled correctly, always smelled of lipstick, cigarette smoke, pot, and something akin to kitty litter.

Wylie's gaze took in my ankle-length ivory skirt, a pure silk charmeuse column of pleats, then my ivory sweater, bedecked with multicolored beads. "An ensemble," he said, "to celebrate glorious Colorado nights. You look like a gay football player."

"Gay as in gay?" Self-consciously, I adjusted my sweater's uplifted shoulder pads while noting that even a Woody Allen clone could resemble Arnold Schwarzenegger when he wore a superbly tailored tux. "Or do you mean my gay, garish beads?"

"The beads. Hail Ingrid, full of grace." Wylie looked around, as if searching for the wad of bubble gum he had once stuck beneath the bleacher seats. "Where's Ben?"

"Playing veterinarian. A neighbor's prize Collie went into labor and she panicked."

"The Collie panicked?"

"No. My neighbor. Ben should be here soon."

"Can I fetch you some wine, Beaumont?"

"No." I wanted to draw back, perhaps even soar toward Drac's rafters.

"Your wife looks beautiful," I said, thinking: *If we discuss trivialities, I'll maintain my composure.* What composure? Most of the time I assume an assertive attitude, cocky even, but tonight I felt as fragile as dry Shredded Wheat.

"Patty always looks beautiful," Wylie said wryly. "It's her trademark."

"What the hell does that mean?"

He finished his champagne and, for a moment, seemed to contemplate tossing the crystal goblet toward some imaginary fireplace. "Only Alice Shaw Cooper would serve cheap bubbly in expensive goblets," he said. "I'd rather sip Dom Perignon from a plastic cup."

"What exactly did you mean by trademark?"

"Cher's famous for her tattoos, right?"

"Among other things."

"Well, Patty's tattoo is perfection."

"Jesus, Wylie, you're such a smartass. Or maybe you'd prefer 'metaphysical philosopher.'"

"There's nothing abstract about perfection, Beaumont."

"I beg to differ. Perfection is conceptual."

He laughed but it sounded slightly off-key, almost nasty. "If perfection equals conception, Alice has certainly fecundated the quintessential reunion dance."

"Fecundated?"

"You're the crossword puzzle addict. Fecund means——"

"Intellectually productive or inventive."

"Right." He summoned a waiter with an arrogant finger snap. "Study the decor, my darling," he said, exchanging his empty goblet for a full one, a sneer curling his lips. "Contemplate the cracks, then tell me what rhymes with fecund."

I raised one eyebrow and glanced around our old high school gymnasium. It hadn't changed much in thirty years, except for the people who stood clustered together, exchanging handshakes, kissing the air, or simply *tsking* their tongues against the roofs of their mouths.

Everyone was dressed to kill. Everyone had dabbed perfume behind their multi-studded earlobes, above their breasts and/or pectoral mounds, under their armpits, between their thighs. Yet the hint of athletic sweat lingered, and that impregnable odor, Eau de Lockers, wafted like a chlorinated shadow.

Alice had opted for live music rather than a Disc Jockey, but some dipshit must have remembered our senior prom deejay's thing for Clint Eastwood and cued the band, because they were actually playing that motivational tune from *Rawhide*.

An over-the-hill cheerleader yelled, "Whip me, Rowdy, spur me on, Clint, oh yeah."

An over-the-hill jock yelled, "Hey, girl, pull down your britches an' show us your heinie. Raw hide, get it?"

My eyes continued roving. Alice had decked the halls with boughs of tissue roses. Red, white, and blue crepe paper hung from basketball hoops, the scoreboard and bleacher seats, looking very patriotic, very Republican convention-ish. Why Republican? Because there were elephant cut-outs dangling from the crepe paper like charms dangling from the end of a bracelet. Funny. I hadn't noticed the elephants until now. I hadn't noticed the banner over the gym's double doors, either. Probably because, after entering, I hadn't looked back. The banner's large red block letters proclaimed Alice's damnfool theme: **AN ELEPHANT**

NEVER FORGETS

"Well," said Wylie, "What rhymes with fecund?"

"Nothing. Wait." Mentally, I traveled through the alphabet. "Second?"

"Good guess."

"It's not a guess. There's nothing else, except beckoned or reckoned, which are both a tad farfetched."

"It's fun to watch your creative juices flow, Beaumont. However, we are straying from the subject."

"Which is what? Second? As in guess? Sight?"

"Nope. Chance."

"What do you mean? Oh, I see. Except for the elephants, Alice has duplicated our senior prom's motif."

"I think she wants her youth back."

"Who doesn't?"

"If you had a second chance," he said, toeing the gym's floor with one spiffy cowboy boot, "what would you change?"

"Dwight's accident and Stewie's death. I'd marry Ben, have a kid, and last but not least, I'd change New York."

He winced. "Please forget New York."

My first finger gestured toward Alice's banner. "I'll never forget, Wylie."

"Okay. But can you forgive me?"

"No!"

"What did the elephant say to the rose?"

"Go to hell, Wylie!"

"Not even close. The elephant said, 'Forgiveness is the perfume the trampled rose casts upon the foot that crushed it."

"You just made that up."

"Of course. Do you forgive me?"

"I'm not exactly a trampled rose."

"Please?"

"Maybe."

"A definite maybe?"

"Yes, Wylie, a definite maybe.'"

"Ingrid," he said, an enigmatic smile creasing the corners of his lips. "When you talked about second chances, you didn't mention the Clovers."

"Are you kidding? I was the white equivalent of Diana Ross, minus her talent. Do you honestly believe the Clovers could have sung 'baby baby where did our love go' and topped the charts?"

"Yes!"

"No way! We were a conglomeration. We wanted to be The Supremes and The Marvelettes and The Pips, even, to a certain extent, Tom and Jerry."

"Who the fuck were Tom and Jerry?"

"Simon and Garfunkle. First they were Tom and Jerry. Then they were Art and Paul, folk singers. Tom and Jerry sang like the Everly Brothers," I added, scratching my memory.

Wylie gave me a lop-sided grin. "Patty used to call the Everly Brothers the Everlasting Brothers."

"Why?"

"Because she thought little Susie would be everlasting, that she'd wake up through eternity. I'd like to wake up through eternity, no shit."

"But you'd be a vampire, or a Stephen King corpse."

"Right."

I stared into his eyes, trying to gage his sincerity. Damn! He looked totally sincere. Nonplused, I stammered, "Tom and Jerry fizz-fizzled but Simon and Garfunkle developed their wistful melancholy and distinctive style. What would you change, Wylie? I mean, if you had a second chance?"

"I'd give your voice a wistful melancholy and a distinctive style."

"Dammit, you're fixated on the Clovers. Could it be that you want your youth back, too?"

"I'm hungry. I wonder what time Alice plans to serve her elephant sandwiches."

"Elephant sandwiches?"

"Yup. She said she food-colored ten loaves of white bread gray, filled them with cream cheese and tuna salad, used black olives for the eyes, then cut the bread with a Dumbo-shaped cookie cutter. How can you tell if an elephant's been inside your refrigerator, Beaumont?"

"By the footprints in the butter."

"Jello."

"Butter."

"Jello."

"Butter."

Wylie usually won our riddle wars by sheer perseverance, but before he could Jello me again, we both heard Ben's footsteps whap-whapping across the gym's wooden floor boards. Clothed in a conservative navy-blue suit, Ben had negated the effect with his usual sockless Nikes. Smiling, waving at fellow reunionites, he headed straight toward us, then straightened the HELLO, MY NAME IS **INGRID** tag pinned directly above my left breast.

My breast responded while my gaze took in Ben's craggy features. Until recently, I had always mistrusted the adjective craggy because it brought to mind abandoned coal shafts and Jack Palance, the quintessential villain. Now craggy conjured up Ben's masculine features, dominated by a rather prominent, some might even say stubborn, jaw. Ben's father was Irish, his mother Cherokee, so he had genetically inherited red-brown hair and brown eyes so dark they looked like the coal hidden beneath Colorado's rough, rugged, craggy landscape.

"How's the new mom?" I asked.

"Fine." Ben chuckled. "But your neighbor's pissed. Apparently she paid high stud fees, then neglected to bolt her backyard gate shortly thereafter, so Lassie strayed and—-"

"Hitchcock!"

"Yup. One Collie and three miniature Hitchcocks."

Ben shifted his gaze and I could feel his good humor freeze. Damn! Why had I mentioned New York?"

"How's it going, Jamestone?" Ben's inflection made my bank teller's have-a-nice-day sound sincere.

Wylie's eyes immediately sought mine. I nodded, shrugged, and looked down at the floor.

"Listen, Ben," he said earnestly, "I've apologized to Ingrid and she forgave me, so why don't we shake hands and bury the hatchet?"

"I'd like to bury it in your balls, you son of a bitch."

Wylie burst out laughing.

I raised my eyes and stared, totally aghast, then shouted, "Ben, no!" because my significant lover looked like he was about to release an uppercut that would send our famous artist flying toward the band. "Dammit, Wylie, what's so funny?"

"You guys were talking about the Collie's pups. Son of a bitch struck me as funny, a veterinarian's epithet, sorry." Turning abruptly, he walked away.

Ben's craggy brow creased. "Did you really forgive him, Ingrid?"

"Yes. I don't want to hold grudges, and New York will never happen again."

"That's for sure!"

Patty Jamestone strolled toward us. Her dress was a stunning winter white matte jersey; sensuous and elegant from its plunging neckline to its rushed bodice and hanky hem. Around her slender wrist was a finely etched bangle bracelet. Lustrous pearls adorned her ears while a sparkling diamond-emerald ring almost obscured her knuckle. Though her small feet were encased in gold satin, high-heeled evening pumps, she neither wobbled nor click-clicked, and I wondered, not for the first time, if pretty Patty walked on invisible clouds.

"They're playing my song," she stated, nodding toward the band. "The theme from Patty Duke's old show."

I listened, then said, "'But Patty's only seen the sights a girl can see from Brooklyn Heights.' Have you ever been to Brooklyn Heights, Patty?"

"No, hon. We live on Long Island, a spit away. Hi, Ben."

"Hi, beautiful."

I watched Ben's icy demeanor melt. Patty had that effect on men. They stood when she entered a room, offered her their seats on an overpopulated bus, and scurried to open doors for her. And she never did a damn thing. I mean, she just was.

"Where on earth did Alice find this band?" I tried to keep my voice conversational, hide the bitchiness I felt. Patty's seductive mystique was overwhelming. If I was a rose, she was an orchid. Furthermore, one never trampled orchids; they were too expensive.

"The musicians," said Ben, "have played every old TV tune from A-Team to Zorro."

"What a lovely outfit," said Patty, staring at my skirt and sweater. "Anne Klein?"

"Nope. Isaac Singer."

"I don't think—-"

"My sewing machine, Patty."

Her ring glittered as she patted her ebony hair, drawn back from her forehead and plaited in one long, thick, French braid. "I suppose you knitted that angora lambswool sweater, pet."

"Sure. I whipped it up while watching Monday Night Football. The Broncs versus the Chiefs."

"You're kidding!"

"I'm kidding. It was on sale at the mall. Unadorned. But I succumbed to that stupid TV ad and ordered a beading gizmo. After I finished beading the sweater, which wasn't as easy as it looks on TV I might add, Hitchcock ate my thread, spangles, sequins and beads. Shiny wampum showed up in Hitchcock's poop for a full week."

Patty wrinkled her perfect nose at the thought of poop.

Ben grabbed us around our waists and waltzed us to the middle of the floor while the band played the theme from *Peter Gunn*.

I stumbled, Patty floated gracefully, the music died.

"Pre-senting the Four Leaf Clovers!" Wylie shouted.

Positioned atop a raised platform, he held a mike to his mouth. The band stood at attention, like musicians awaiting the arrival of some visiting dignitary. Soon they'd play for he's a jolly good fellow which nobody can...

"Oh, shit," I swore, trying to deny the sight and sound. I knew what would follow, and of course it did.

"This is your lucky day!" shouted Wylie, completing the introduction which had haunted me for twenty-plus years.

Ben hefted me up onto the platform, whereupon I gazed out over the expectant crowd.

"We can't sing." Despite my backward lurch, the microphone echoed my squawk of dismay. "Stewie's dead. We're not Clovers any more."

Wylie winked at me, then turned toward the audience. "Pre-senting the newest member of our talented group," he said. "Dwight Eisenhower Cooper."

The reunion gang applauded wildly.

I studied Dwight's face as three men lifted his wheelchair up onto the stage. His lips twitched in what could have been a grin or grimace. His dark hair was short, thick and wavy, while an Elvis curl formed an upside-down question mark above his right eyebrow. But his faded blue eyes... well, let's just say that he could have auditioned for a part in *Night of the Living Dead*.

My gaze shifted to Alice Shaw Cooper, who blotted her lips on invisible tissue. *Her* eyes shot microscopic daggers toward Wylie. Why? Did Alice still want to sing with the Clovers? Hey, she could take my place. There was a frog in my throat, an ugly, warty toad, and I knew my voice would be rusty, like furniture left out in the rain.

Rain! I remembered Stewie's words, just before he left for Nam: "I'm gonna' carry a lucky clover, Ing, and when you sing about familiar faces you'll think of me."

"Hey, what a fab idea! We'll all carry lucky clovers, Stewpot. You, me, Benji, Wylie Coyote, and Patty-Cakes. But I won't sing again until you come home, and that's a promise."

God, I was so young! We were all so young!

I turned my back to the mike. "Ben, please listen. I promised Stewie I wouldn't sing until he came marching home again."

"But he'd want you to sing, honey, to honor his memory, especially tonight."

"Maybe you're right. Maybe he would. Okay, I'll try."

I saw Wylie consulting with the band. He reminded me of my beloved mutt; a waggish Hitchcock planning to trash the trash and retrieve some forbidden chicken bones. In other words, Wylie looked both guilty and smug.

"This is for you, Stewpot," I murmured under my breath, just before we began to croon our standards. *I Believe,* followed by Creedence Clearwater's rolling rocker, *Proud Mary,* then Debbie Reynold's simple-minded ballad, *Tammy.*

Dwight wasn't bad, actually, He crewel-stitched his voice through Ben and Patty's harmony like eggs sizzling in butter, yet he didn't disturb the syncopated rhythm.

My performance was robotistic, a knee-jerk reaction, until the audience called for our theme song. Tears blurred my vision as I sang the introduction. "Farewell every old familiar face. It's time to stray... it's time to stray. Only wait till I com-mu-ni-cate... here's what I'll say..."

"I'm look-ing o-ver a four leaf clover," we all trilled.

When we finished, reunionites clapped and whistled. Were they nuts? This was a generation who had attended concerts by the Dead, and Dylan, and Manfred Mann; a generation who had insisted that Puff the magic dragon was drug-related. How could they applaud I Believe Proud Tammy?

The band segued into movie themes. *You Light Up My Life* was their first selection. Ben's sneakers whap-whapped again as we began to dance.

"Before you arrived," I said, inhaling bleach from his collar, "Wylie reminisced over the Clovers. Do you think that's why he instigated our pathetic performance?"

"It wasn't pathetic."

"Yes it was, Ben, and Wylie did it on purpose. He's acting so weird, as if he wants to tell each person here to go stick an elephant tusk up their ass. The Clover bit was my tusk."

"Patty said it was Alice's idea. Maybe she wanted to get Dwight away from his dark corner, light up his life."

"Baloney! When they lifted Dwight onto the stage, I saw Alice. Her mouth got so tight, her lips disappeared. Making Dwight the fourth Clover was Alice's tusk."

"And Dwight's tusk?"

"Dwight didn't want his life lit. The limelight hurt his eyes. They looked zombie-ish."

"How could Wylie possibly know—-?"

"Wylie's intuitive."

"Assuming you're right, and just for the record I don't agree, why hasn't Wylie done anything to me?"

"Because you're not the singer who reneged and spoiled his grand plan. And you've never been a jock like Dwight."

"Dwight hasn't been a jock for thirty years, and why the hell would Wylie want to piss off Alice?"

"I don't know, Ben. It's just a hunch."

"I thought Wylie was the intuitive one."

The object of our conversation waltzed by, then halted. "Let's switch partners," he said.

Before I could object, Patty melted into Ben's arms. "Why did you resurrect the Clovers?" I hissed into Wylie's ear.

"It was Alice's idea," he replied quickly.

Too quickly. Wylie was lying through his teeth. All of a sudden I had a revelation. It was like watching a movie and admiring the handsome hero until he smiled, revealing fangs. Wylie was lying through his fangs.

Because this whole event—the decor, the elephant cut-outs, the banner theme, the Clovers— every detail, except possibly the choice of champagne and the gray Dumbo sandwiches, had been Wylie's scheme. An attempt to regain his lost youth?

"Wylie, why are you playing Peter Pan?"

He didn't even pretend to misunderstand. "I like Pan," he said. "Pete could boff Wendy, tinker with Tinkerbell, and he never had to assume responsibility. Adolescent hormones and all that shit."

"Except for Disney's animated, penis-less version, Peter Pan is always played by a woman," I shot back.

"Are you saying that I'm gay?" His eyes narrowed. "Are you suggesting that my marriage to Patty is a sham? That my thing with you was merely an attempt to prove my manhood?"

"No! I'm suggesting that you grow up."

"Look around."

"We've already played this game."

"Study the people. What do you see?"

"Friends. Familiar faces."

"Strip away the beautiful clothes. What do you see?"

"Naked bods," I replied sarcastically.

"No, my darling. Naked souls."

Releasing my waist, Wylie stomped toward the platform, leaped up, grabbed the mike, then whistled. The sound hurt my ears, and everyone else's, but he had our attention.

"Hey!" he shouted. "We were supposed to be the generation that saved the world through love. Instead we opted to become Peter Pan's lost boys. Our homes are status playpens, our favorite toy a cellular phone."

"Shut up, Jamestone," growled Junior Hartsel, the ex football jock.

Wylie ignored Junior's menacing bellow. "Ponder this, my friends. What would happen if you stripped the Lone Ranger's mask from his face? I think you'd find a wrinkled, toothless, senile man."

"Are you crazy?" The ex cheerleader stepped forward. "The Lone Ranger wears an itty-bitty mask. It just covers his eyes. You can see his nose, mouth and chin." She ran her fingertips across her own nose, mouth and chin, as if trying to ascertain their ageless reality. "And his hair," she added desperately, "when he's not wearing a cowboy hat."

"His hair's a rug, his false teeth bleached, polished, shiny with petroleum jelly." Wylie grinned. "I think the Lone Ranger dons a rubber mask. Pull away the rubber and you'll discover a monster."

"Ick!"

"Boo!"

"Shut up!"

"Get off the stage, Jamestone!"

"Did you honestly believe you could hide those saggy chins and boobs?" he continued. "Alice plans to crown a Reunion Dance Queen. Any volunteers? C'mon, who wants to be queen? How about you, Junior? *You've* aged well, except for that bald forehead, humongous butt, and bony chicken chest. We could choose Dwight. He's handicapped... sorry, physically challenged... and if we chose Dwight, we'd all feel so friggin' good inside."

Wylie gestured toward the cheerleader. "Gimme an S, gimme an H, gimme an I, gimme a T. What d'ya got? Look at her, folks, trying to put the letters together. It spells hits, you airhead! Speaking of hits, what male vocalist won the Grammy in 1966?"

Most of us just stood there, speechless, but one *Jeopardy* addict shouted, "Who is Glen Campbell?"

"No, you asshole. That was '68. Anybody else? C'mon, Ingrid, you're the expert."

I knew the answer. Sinatra. But I simply shrugged my padded shoulders.

"Frank Sinatra," said Wylie. "It was a very good year. Wasn't it, Beaumont?"

Okay. I hadn't fooled him. I never *could* fool him.

"Seriously, folks," Wylie said seriously, "we tsk-tsk over the homeless, then spend billions on plastic surgeons and products that promise eternal youth."

Wylie continued his harangue, only we couldn't hear him, because Alice had yanked the microphone's cord from its socket. Angry tears streamed down her face, and you could practically see the steam vaporizing from her ears.

Reunionites buzzed like a swarm of angry hornets while the ex cheerleader screamed, "Who the hell do you think you are anyway? Why don't you eat shit and die!"

Fondling his crotch a la Michael Jackson, Wylie jumped down from the platform. I grabbed his arm and led him toward an empty bleacher section. "Dammit," I said, "what brought that on?"

"Your Peter Pan remark."

"I only meant—-"

"They say a dying person's life unfolds before his eyes. Once we had ideals, Beaumont! Once we stopped a war!"

Surprisingly, despite everything, I wanted to hug him, nurture him, and I wondered why he and Patty didn't have any kids. An heir would have helped Wylie regain his lost youth.

I was bothered, to put it mildly, so I responded with the first thing that popped into my head. "Are you dying, Wylie?"

"We all die by bits and pieces. How do you make a statue of an elephant?"

"By bits and pieces?"

"Wrong. Try again. How do you make a statue of an elephant?"

"I don't know. I give up. How?"

But Wylie was running toward Patty. Draped across her arms were two coats—-one a fur-lined tweed, the other a full-length mink. Patty's chin appraised the basketball hoop's backboard, and I felt like cheering her regal stoicism. Gimme an F. Gimme a U. Gimme a C. What d'ya got?

Following Patty and Wylie's abrupt exit, I searched for Alice. She was standing near a white Styrofoam cooler, empty except for melting ice cubes.

Alice's hair had once been dishwater blonde. Then she watched celebs talk about how they were worth it. Alice decided she was worth it, too. After all, she was worth plenty. So every month she hopped a plane to New York and paid a visit to some exclusive beauty salon. From a distance, Alice looked like a platinum Q-tip.

Up close, she looked mournful. "The wine's all gone," she muttered, nodding toward the cooler. "And everybody hates the champagne."

"Everybody doesn't hate it, Alice."

"Wylie hates it. I hate Wylie."

"No, you don't."

"He looked nice tonight."

"Who? Wylie?"

"Yes. He looked nice, but sounded nasty." She sucked in her lower lip. "What a bummer. Wylie was always a beatnik."

"Hippie, Alice."

"Remember his pad?"

"Apartment, Alice."

"Would you do me a big favor, Ingrid? Pretty please with sugar on top? Cheer up Dwight and Junior? Dwight's sulking and Junior's fuming. Gosh-darn. I wanted everybody to feel groovy tonight."

It suddenly occurred to me that Alice's marriage to Dwight Eisenhower Cooper was appropriate. Alice sounded as if she had just stepped out of a 1950's movie. She never swore, and she probably thought that sex was an abbreviation for sexton, the church employee who, among other things, digs the graves.

"What about the cheerleader?" I asked sarcastically. "The one who told Wylie to eat shit and die. Should I cheer her up?"

"She's already bright-eyed and bushy-tailed." Alice pointed toward the end of the basketball court, where the cheerleader, skirt held high, was dancing to what sounded like the theme from Clint Eastwood's *The Unforgiven*. "Dwight and Junior have always admired your spunk, Ingrid."

"I don't give a rat's spit if..." Pausing, I studied Alice's red-blotched cheeks and brimming eyes. "Okay, what the hell... heck. Where's Dwight?"

"Outside."

"And Junior?"

"Over there, standing by the bandstand."

He's not standing, I thought, he's slumping. Junior Hartsel had once been a pretty decent football player. Unfortunately, he was short, barely five-nine. He had never grown into his bulk, nor his dreams, but he had used his athlete's status to boff a goodly number of our graduation class.

On my way to the stage, I stopped to adjust one shoulder pad, and felt Ben's voice tickle my ear. "You light up my life, babe," he whispered, hugging me from behind. "Let's go home."

"I wish. But I promised Alice I would cheer up Dwight and Junior. Dwight's outside, sulking. Or maybe he's planning some murderous revenge scheme against our dear departed Wylie. Would you soothe the savage beast, Ben?"

"Sure. Afterwards, I'll soothe your savage breast."

I gazed longingly at Ben's broad shoulders, then hastened toward Junior, who was now on top of the stage.

The band was taking a break, and Junior was drunk. He slid onto the drummer's stool, then looked up at me with bleary, blood-shot, basset-hound eyes. "Wylie said I had a big butt," he whined. "Do you think I have a big butt, Beaumont?"

"You have a very nice butt, Junior." It was a fib, but why quibble? "Maybe you should put that nice butt inside a cab and head for home."

"*Your* home?"

"No. *Your* home."

Junior thumped the snare drum with the flat of his hand. "You have nice boobies," he said with a wink that failed.

"Thanks." I had never seen a wink fail. I mean, you just shut one eye, right? Wrong. Junior's upper lip crept toward his nose, which twitched like a rabbit. But the damn eye remained at half mast.

"Let's find the locker room," he said slyly. "You can show me your boobies and I can show you my heinie."

"No, thanks." I shuddered, considered retreating, then remembered my promise to Alice. "Maybe some other time, Junior."

"Wylie said I had a bony chicken chest."

"Junior, Wylie didn't mean——"

"And a bald forehead."

"Junior, I think you should lie down some place until you

sober——-"

"Okay."

He thumped his bald forehead against the drum, rebounded slightly, thumped again, then lay motionless, eyes closed, arms dangling, his "nice butt" overlapping the stool.

I found three reunionites, who promised to carry Junior away. But when we returned to the stage, he was gone.

Ben said that Dwight had been sitting in his wheelchair, staring nostalgically at the football field. Ben said that Dwight looked as if he didn't want to be disturbed.

We stayed for the door-prize drawing, which I won. Then we left. It was kind of like winning a big poker pot and leaving immediately thereafter, but I didn't care. I wanted Ben to light up my life, a rather scintillating euphemism for screwing one's brains out.

Ben drove his rental car. I drove my jeep. Careening round corners, I decided to call Wylie. Unfortunately, I didn't have one of his playpen toys, a cellular phone.

By the time I arrived home, my breasts were unbeading my sweater, anticipating Ben's soothing caress, so I didn't call Wylie, and he didn't tell me the answer to his elephant-statue riddle.

No big deal, I thought.

But it was. Because those were the last words Wylie ever said to me.

Chapter Three

"I saw you on TV," said Cee-Cee Sinclair.

Twisting her ponytail free from its rubber band, she pulled her Looney-Tunes-populated sweatshirt out from under her rump. A perpetual jogger, she looked healthy, wealthy, sweaty, and wise. Correction. Cee-Cee didn't sweat. She perspired.

"TV," I said with a groan. "The whole damn state caught my middle finger gesture. I got at least ten phone calls, including one from my mother. She ignored my finger and suggested that the next time I attend a televised football game I might consider combing my hair. That's why I'm late. Not my hair, my mother. I listened patiently while she rambled on and on."

Cee-Cee grinned. "Patience is the ability to remain silent and hungry while everyone else in the restaurant gets served."

Although I wasn't really hungry, I nodded agreement. Then, watching Cee-Cee sip her coffee, I thought about how I didn't have many close friends. Oh, I had accumulated *acquaintances,* starting with the small nub of dissidents who attended my high school. We thumbed our noses at the conservative system, grew our hair down to our butts, wore peace symbols, and listened to Joan Baez. After graduation, I tried waiting tables and writing songs. Then I traveled to Washington and "Marched Against Death" with thousands of other anti-war acquaintances.

Moving to California, I formed brief lasting relationships with men I don't remember. Women confidants were rare.

Throughout this turbulent era, Patty was my one constant. She was stable, reliable, law-abiding, and loyal. Unlike my parents, Patty forgave my transgressions. She applauded my successes and listened sympathetically when lasting relationships didn't last. Then she changed, became the quintessential Jewish American

Princess, even though she's not Jewish.

Cee-Cee hefted her coffee mug toward my copy of Wylie's note. "Okay," she said. "Tell me about Wylie Jamestone."

"First, I want to thank you for being my friend."

"That's not necessary. I'm proud to be your friend."

It was difficult for me to accept much less acknowledge compliments, so I asked, "What year were you born?"

"You've got to be kidding. Nobody knows my real age, not even Bill."

Cee-Cee still has warm feelings for Bill, her first husband. Her second, a bad poet, lives in Paris. Her third developed some kind of computer chip. Upon dying, he'd left her a fortune.

"I'll bet you were born in the Year of the Tiger, Ceese. Tiger people are courageous, candid, and sensitive. Look to the Horse and Dog for happiness. Beware of the Monkey."

"Okay. No monks. No chimps. No yabba-dabba-dabba. Why are you procrastinating, Ingrid?"

"I'm not."

"Sure you are. Look, we can have breakfast together and call it a day. But if you want to pick my brain, you'll have to discuss Wylie Jamestone. No matter how much it hurts," Cee-Cee added perceptively.

I took a deep breath. "Wylie once quoted Picasso. 'There are only two kinds of women—- goddesses and doormats.'"

"How did Wylie treat women? Like doormats?"

"No, goddesses. You have to understand, Ceese. Wylie was a dead ringer for Woody Allen, at least he was before he bought contacts and shaved his head."

"I think Woody's sexy, charismatic."

"So was Wylie. In high school, he always wore greenish corduroys, a white T-shirt, and a long great-coat straight out of a World War Two movie. He attracted girls like a magnet. You'd have adored him because he loves... loved a good mystery."

Cee-Cee nodded, and I knew her reaction was due to the fact that she loved mysteries more than raw oysters, her favorite food. While I'm crude and hard-edged, Cee-Cee is soft, like a pillow. She even looks soft, with her dove-gray hair, turquoise eyes, and a figure that no amount of dieting can ever change to angular.

Years ago, we had formed a bond, a friendship based on mutual respect. I respected her unique ability to mother mutts while she respected my musical talent. She even remembered my alias, Rose Stewart.

The waitress finally placed our omelets and bagels on the table. "Be careful," she warned, "the plates are hot."

We waited until she walked away. Then Cee-Cee said, "Speaking of hot, Ingrid, was Wylie your boyfriend?"

"No. A hunk named Ben was my boyfriend, but we broke up after high school. Wylie and I were kindred spirits. He drew pictures, I wrote poetry. One day he heard me, Ben, my best friend Patty, and a guy named Stewie, harmonizing. I think it was 'Baby Love.' Anyway, Wylie decided that we could out- synchronize the Supremes. Ben strummed a guitar. I played the piano. Stewie was our percussionist. Patty looked pretty."

"Patty Jamestone? Wylie's wife?"

"Yes. Do you know Patty?"

"Not really. Wylie's murder made this morning's front page. They mentioned his widow. Please go on."

"I adapted a few of my poems to music, but mostly we updated songs from the late fifties and early sixties. I can still visualize myself, wagging my first finger like a Dachshund's tail, shouting 'Stop, in the name of love!' Ben and I were in love."

"Dachshund's tail. What a great image."

"Wylie created our publicity posters. I believe they're collectors' items now, worth a fortune. I didn't keep any; who knew? Wylie painted our portraits, blending them into one humongous clover. He wanted to call us The Beaumonts, but decided it sounded too much like The Belmonts, so he named us The Four Leaf Clovers. 'I'm looking o-ver a four leaf clover that I overlooked be- fore.'"

"'One leaf is sunshine, the second is rain.'"

"Right. Ben was sunshine, Stewie rain. In retrospect, it fit. Ben was optimistic, Stewie patriotic. Stewie spit out government slogans like a sprinkler system. 'Third is the roses that grow in the lane.' I was a rose. 'No need ex-plain-ing the one re-main-ing; it's some-bod-y I adore.' That was Patty. She was Wylie's somebody I adore."

"Why did Wylie choose that song?"

"It had something to do with luck. Ben suggested that we call ourselves The Rabbit's Feet, and our theme could be Gracie Slick's 'White Rabbit,' which was more in... shall we say tune?... with the times. Rabbit's feet, said Ben, are lucky. Wylie said there were four of us, four clover leaves. Ben said rabbits had four paws. But Wylie was always so stubborn. Once he got something into his head, he..."

"He what?"

"He played puppeteer, manipulated our strings. 'Let's be democratic,' he said, 'and take a vote.' So we did. It was a tie. Patty and Stewie opted for Clovers. Ben and I chose Rabbit's Feet. Wylie broke the tie. *Voila!* Clovers."

"I take it Wylie didn't sing."

"Correct. He was our manager, our spiritual leader. Within a few years, he vowed, we'd have a bullet on the charts. Unfortunately, several bullets found Stewie over in Vietnam. His body was shattered into so many pieces, they couldn't even ship it home. Wylie's heart murmur kept him out of the war. Ben got himself a student deferment... Cornell University... veterinary medicine. I tried the left coast and finally hit it big with one song."

"You evolved into Rose Stewart," Cee-Cee said wistfully, fingering the embroidered Bugs Bunny above her left breast, "and I bought your album. That was *my* rebellion against the war."

"When 'Clowns' hit number one on the charts, Wylie sent me a letter of congratulations. He doodled all over the margin; roses and doves. One dove had Jane Fonda's face."

"So you and Wylie kept in touch after graduation?"

"Yes, even though he moved to New York."

"Did you see him often?"

"No. Wylie occasionally visited Colorado, but we never got together. I was always in Hollywood, firing my latest agent or pitching a score. Last year I flew to Manhattan to doctor a new musical. Nice paycheck, but they ignored my suggestions, and the show closed after one week. I met the Jamestones for dinner and theater. 'Phantom of the Opera.' Wylie was still charismatic. Patty was still beautiful, except her eyes looked sad."

"Why do you think she looked sad?"

I shrugged. "Patty always wanted an acting career. For some dumb reason, she thought fame would simply fall into her lap so she never really pursued stardom. My guess is that Patty can't handle rejection."

"Who can?"

"Me. I'm an armadillo, tough skinned, a rat with armor."

Cee-Cee looked as if she might refute that last statement but she merely said, "Tell me about the reunion, Ingrid. Who arranged it?"

"Alice Cooper."

"The Alice Cooper?"

"No. Sorry. It's a tad confusing. A woman named Alice Shaw was engaged to Wylie. After Wylie married Patty, Alice married a man named Dwight Cooper. Ergo. Alice Cooper."

"Gotcha'."

"Old-timers still talk about how Dwight helped lead our high school football team to its only national championship. We all hero-worshipped Dwight. Patty could have captured him, but her boyfriend, Stewie, looked like John, Paul, and George put together; the quintessential Beatle. Alice had a crush on Dwight, yet she remained loyal to Wylie. I never really forgave him for dumping her."

"Did Alice ever forgive him?" This time Cee-Cee fingered a sharp-toothed Taz.

"I can see you digesting my dump Alice comment along with your omelet, and you could be right. Maybe Alice does carry a grudge. But, to be perfectly honest, she... well, she's such a mouse. She's not the least bit impulsive or threatening. I can't imagine Alice bopping Wylie over the head just because he broke off their engagement twenty-something years ago."

I finally took a bite out of my bagel. "Every high school has an Alice in its ranks. She organized pep rallies and homecoming dances, dominated decorating committees. Alice was into themes. For instance, she chose our senior prom motif. 'Red Roses for a Blue Lady.'"

"Was that a tribute to you?"

"Me?"

"You said you were a rose."

"Oh. No. Alice simply wanted to use the colors red, white, and blue. She originally proposed a patriotic theme. Stars and stripes. Flags. Uncle Sam pointing his finger, demanding human fodder. When my small group of dissenters heard about it, they threatened to demonstrate."

"Why would your group care? Why would they even consider attending the senior prom?"

"Most didn't. But some of us wanted to dress up, dance, play kids for a night. And my mom almost had a heart attack when I said I might shun what she called 'the most important event in a young girl's life.' Anyway, Alice recommended the roses-lady theme, which was kind of ballsy, not to mention steadfast. After she and her crew finished decorating, the gym pulsated with red, white, and blue banners. Dracula would have loved our senior prom, Ceese. Red crepe streamers billowed from basketball hoops, suggesting the flow of blood. Tissue roses, sprayed with cheap cologne, smelled like funeral wreaths. Most girls had hickeys rather than tooth marks on their necks, but the rented tuxedos could have belonged to vampires."

I sipped my orange juice. "It was the merry month of June. U.S. troop strength in Vietnam would be increased by 18,000, bringing total troop strength to 285,000. The whole country was bloodthirsty."

"How can you remember the exact numbers?"

"I wrote them into one of my lesser-known songs. It was called 'New Math.'"

"New math," Cee-Cee repeated. "Wow."

"In any case, we quenched our thirst that night with a mixture of nonalcoholic beverages. Alice's recipe—-lime Jell-O ice cubes, un-sweetened lemonade and ginger ale—-made the punch look like urine. It tasted like piss, too, until Wylie spiked it with vodka. We couldn't afford Wayne Newton, so Alice bagged a local deejay who had this thing for Clint Eastwood. Have you ever tried dancing to 'The Good, the Bad, and the Ugly'?"

"Not that I can recall."

"Alice hired a local photographer and we lined up to have our pictures taken. Ben and me, the couple most likely to succeed; Stewie and Patty, the couple most likely to conceive; Wylie and

Alice, the couple least likely to achieve consummation. Alice had virgin written all over her."

The waitress gave me a strange look as she refilled our coffee mugs.

"Please go on, Ingrid," said Cee-Cee.

"Following our photo session, we danced to the theme from 'Rawhide.' Then, outside in the parking lot, Wylie challenged Dwight to a drinking contest. After chugalugging eight Coors, Dwight gave up, so we all piled into his convertible. Ben and me. Stewie and Patty. Wylie and Alice. Dwight and a popular cheerleader, I don't remember her name. I don't remember the car crash either, because Ben was ingesting the lace on my strapless bra, while, at the same time, he ingested nipple. When we crashed, I was semi-conscious, filled with passionate ecstasy.

"Nobody was hurt very badly," I continued, picturing the accordian-crumpled car and the scabbed tree trunk. "Except Dwight. He woke up in the hospital, paralyzed from his waist down. Which killed his football scholarship, and his dreams. Dwight always wanted to play for the Denver Broncos."

"You poor, poor lamb. Proms should be filled with good memories."

Looking down at the gold CU buffalo on my black sweatshirt, I bit my lower lip. "Everything happens for a reason, Ceese. The car crash made me re-evaluate my goals. I figured my life should have some meaning. Maybe I thought that by writing songs and protesting, I could keep others from getting hurt."

"You're a mighty strange armadillo, my friend."

"What? Oh. Hey, we're talking the late sixties. Hippies didn't wear chain mail. We didn't even send chain letters." I nodded toward my coffee mug. "Please excuse me, rest room. Coffee stimulates my bladder. Like nicotine. I finally stopped smoking when I learned that nicotine was used as an insecticide."

Standing, I hitched up my jeans and walked toward a door that displayed the kindergarten-ish outline of a full-skirted woman. Who, I thought with a tight grin, had been painted with my mother in mind.

Shortly thereafter, I rubbed my hands beneath the slo-mo blow dryer, and despite my vow not to accumulate any more face wrinkles, I felt my forehead knit. Because recent events had brought back memories I'd tried so hard to suppress. With the reunion in mind, I had joined a diet club and lost twelve pounds. Revamped, I could wear my old high school clothes, but I couldn't fit into my old high school skin. Cee-Cee was right about that. The armadillo's armor came much later.

Returning to the table, I murmured, "Where were we?"

"Alice Cooper."

"Right. Alice Cooper, nee Shaw, wanted to be a Clover, but Wylie wouldn't let her."

"Why not?"

"She couldn't carry a note, much less a tune. After graduation, Alice sent out monthly newsletters, touting marriages, progeny, divorces, recipes. Alice thought up the reunion; she was so excited. At first Wylie said he couldn't make it, but he capitulated... obviously. Wylie was a workaholic. He flew his paints and canvasses from New York, and borrowed a friend's house. That's where he was killed."

"Who would have a motive?"

"Me," I blurted.

"Why you?"

"It's a long story."

"I'm a good listener."

"Maybe later," I said uncomfortably. "Okay?"

"Okay." She waited until the waitress had re-filled our coffee mugs, watched me shake a packet of Equal into the steam, then asked, "Did you kill him, Ingrid?"

"No."

"Anybody else with a motive?"

"Patty, I guess. Isn't the wife always suspect?"

"Is there a big life insurance policy?"

"Patty doesn't need money. At the reunion dance she wore a white number that must have cost a couple thousand. Her bracelet was twenty-four K, her perfume potent, and her ring was almost ostentatious. Wylie was very successful."

"Maybe he kept her on a short leash, limited but expensive wardrobe. The gems and perfume could be birthday presents."

"Patty doesn't have birthdays."

"She has them," Cee-Cee said dryly, fingering Sylvester. "She just doesn't celebrate them. Don't forget, Ingrid. Wylie's paintings will increase in value now that he's dead."

"I've known Patty since elementary school, Ceese. She has her faults, who doesn't? But she couldn't murder in cold blood. Patty won't even watch a horror flick. She once apologized over the phone because I had scored a chainsaw massacre movie and she didn't have the guts to watch it. Besides, Wylie worshipped Patty. You can't buy that kind of pedestal with filthy lucre."

"Sure you can, or else the word gigolo would have vanished from our vocabulary. Look, money can't buy happiness, but it sure helps you to be unhappy in comfort."

"That's a Wylie philosophy. Don't tell me you like elephant jokes."

"Love 'em." Cee-Cee winked. "Why do elephants have teeth?"

"To chew their toenails."

"Why do elephants have toenails?"

"So they can have something to chew?"

"Very good." She pulled a stray thread from one of Tweety Bird's guileless eyes. "Okay, let's chew. Who else was... shall we say motivated?"

"Alice. Not because of the broken engagement, but because she was pissed. Wylie ruined her lovely reunion dance."

"Really! How?"

"He acted crazy. Hypercritical. Rotten, like a shiny red apple that's wormy inside. To paraphrase the young girl who found Wylie's body, Alice didn't faint or scream, yet you could practically see the steam rising from her ears. And she pursed her lips. When Alice becomes agitated, she compresses her lips until she looks like she's blotting lipstick on a tissue."

"You said Alice was a mouse."

"She is. I think we're on the wrong track."

"Okay," said Cee-Cee, gesturing toward the waitress with her empty mug. "Who else had a motive?"

"Dwight Cooper, Alice's husband. He's always blamed Wylie for the car crash. By the way, that's the reason Ben and I split. He was the only male sober enough to drive, and Dwight wouldn't let a girl touch his new convertible. I think we all felt guilty, but I blamed Ben. We argued. Ben wasn't into politics. I called him lazy and braindead. He called me an idealistic bitch, and worse. I told him I never wanted to see him again. God, I was stupid."

"You were young. Why did Dwight blame Wylie? I mean, why didn't he blame Ben?"

"Because Wylie always made fun of jocks. He drew cartoons for the school paper, especially athletes with enormous bodies and tiny heads. And there was never the slightest bulge between their thighs. You know how guys feel about that, Ceese. In my opinion, wars are started by large egos and small dicks."

She grinned, then turned serious again. "So Dwight's our prime suspect?"

"I suppose."

"You sound uncertain."

"Dwight's confined to a wheelchair. Even if he managed to silently maneuver his chair through the house, how could he clunk Wylie over the head?"

"Brute strength. Dwight's arms might be powerful."

"They are. But I'll bet my next royalty check that Wylie wasn't seated."

"Seated?" Cee-Cee mopped up the last of her eggs with the last of her bagel. "Oh, I see. If Wylie was busy painting, he'd be standing up."

"Wylie was fidgety. He'd never paint from a stool."

"Is that it?"

"Suspects? I guess. At the reunion dance, Wylie pissed off this ex cheerleader. She told him to eat shit and die, but that's a tad farfetched, don't you think? Then there's this ex football jock, Junior Hartsel. Wylie put him down, made fun of him physically, but Junior hasn't got the stomach for murder. I mean, he's all whine and no bite."

What happens when an elephant steps on a grape? The grape gives a little whine.

Could the whiner give a little grapple?

"What about your note, Ingrid?"

Still picturing Junior, passed out on the drum, I glanced down at the piece of paper, anchored by the salt shaker. "Do you think

Wylie had a premonition, Ceese? He didn't say anything during the dance, at least he didn't pin-point murder. He never mentioned the painting, either."

"Who's on the painting?"

"I don't know. When I questioned the homicide detective, he said that the subject was a famous blonde."

"Marilyn Monroe?"

I shrugged. "Maybe I'm a suspect, and the detective thought I'd let something slip. 'I wonder why Wylie painted Marilyn Monroe. Oops.' In any case, my taciturn cop would only admit that the subject was blonde and famous."

"Well, that certainly narrows it down."

"I plan to visit Patty after breakfast. But Wylie couldn't have depicted his killer, Ceese, or the police——"

"I'll call Bill," she interrupted eagerly.

"I thought Bill was retired."

"Cops never retire, Ingrid. Bill says the worst thing about retirement is having to drink coffee on your own time. I suspect he knows all about yesterday's murder, every sordid detail, so I'll give him a quick ring. Okay?"

"Okay. But first I'll confess *my* motive. You're probably curious."

"No, I'm not. Well, maybe a little."

I sipped my coffee, then said, "You've got to promise you'll keep it a secret."

"Why? Do you honestly believe you could be charged with Wylie's murder?"

"Nope. I have an alibi. The Bronco-Cowboy game. Of course I could have driven to Mile High Stadium during the first half, and my middle-finger gesture could have meant 'screw you, Wylie Jamestone!'"

"Ingrid, you're losing me."

"To make a long story short, last year, when I visited New York, Wylie came to my hotel suite and he... well, he wanted me to sleep with him."

"How did you respond?"

"Wylie was persuasive and I was tempted, but I couldn't do that to Patty, so I refused. Wylie was very nice. Wink-wink, only kidding, maybe another time. Then he raped me."

"He raped you? Ohmigod!"

"Did I say rape? I meant seduced. You see, he plied me with vodka until I was weepy, defenseless and——"

"Did he force you?"

"At first he was sympathetic. I was a leaky water faucet, dribbling tears and——"

"Did he force you, Ingrid?"

"Yes. He listened, urged me to gulp down the booze, then made his move. I kicked, scratched, bit... finally capitulated. That's the worst part. I submitted, even climaxed. Afterwards I said I'd have him arrested, but he just laughed. He knew I wouldn't. I had climaxed, for Christ's sake. Then there was Patty. I figured he'd have one hell of a time explaining his scratches, so I merely screamed something about bashing his head to pieces if he ever touched me again."

"Did that sorry bastard ever touch you again?"

"I never saw him again, not until the reunion."

My impulse was to calm Cee-Cee down. Picasso was wrong. I wasn't a goddess. I wasn't a doormat, either. Yet doormats got stepped on and still spelled out WELCOME. Damn! I'd have to remember that line for a song, try something Bonnie Raitt. I could ring up Bonnie and ask her to record my doormat song, maybe even shoot a video.

While I was visualizing Bonnie and videos, Cee-Cee calmed down on her own. "You poor baby," she said. "Did you tell anyone?"

"No."

"Not even your parents?"

"God, no. My father's deceased. Mom thawed somewhat after I abandoned my life as Rose Stewart, but she'd insist that it was my fault, and she'd be right."

"Wrong!"

"Listen, Ceese, technically it wasn't rape. I shouldn't have said that. It was seduction, plain and simple."

"Simple? Ingrid, you need professional counseling. I know a psychologist who——"

"Please! I've learned to deal with this. I even forgave Wylie."

"When?"

"At the reunion dance. No big deal."

"No big deal? Rape is a violent crime."

"Seduction. Wylie didn't hurt me, at least not physically. I think I wanted it to happen, 'else why get drunk and weepy? I wanted someone to love me."

"Rape isn't love."

"*Seduction,* damn it!"

"*Semantics,* damn it! You said Wylie worshipped Patty. If that's true, why did he make his move on you?"

"I don't know. Who could I ask? Patty?"

"Okay," Cee-Cee said thoughtfully, "you couldn't discuss this with anyone. But why confess now? To me? If you didn't report the rape, you'd never be one of Wylie's murder suspects."

"Well, I goofed and told Ben. We were getting ready for bed and he caressed me. It was the first time I had been touched by a man since New York, so I flinched. I didn't use the word rape, but Ben was furious. He threatened to destroy a different part of Wylie's anatomy, south of his head."

"Wait a minute! After high school you and Ben split up."

"Three nights ago, during the reunion's introductory cocktail party, Ben pinned my nametag above my left breast. I stumbled backwards. Ben caught me, but not before I fell. In love. For good."

"Good for you."

Cee-Cee patted my wrist and I felt an overwhelming urge to weep against her shoulder. But I had kept my emotions in check for such a long time, I couldn't self-destruct now.

"Ingrid," she said, fingering Daffy Duck's plumage. "Do you think Ben killed Wylie?"

"Ben heals sick animals. He's a *doctor.*"

"Doctor's kill, especially on those tabloid news shows."

"You watch that junk?"

"I surf through the channels." Her cheeks turned one shade lighter than her scarlet lipstick. "Okay, I watch. It's a substitute for junk food."

"Junk food. How I used to love those miniature blueberry pies. Then I joined Weight Winners, Ellie Bernstein's diet club. Good-bye pie."

"You look great, hon. You even looked great on TV, and that's supposed to add ten pounds."

Compliments again; I felt my face flush. "Could you call Bill now?"

"Sure. But only if you promise to call a rape counselor."

"I promise to think about it."

While Cee-Cee headed toward a pay phone, I dismissed the counselor bit. Once again, I thought about Saturday night's reunion dance. Wylie and Patty had made quite an entrance. Pretty Patty. Her face looked so much like an Impressionist painting that you had to smile at the irony of Wylie's phenomenal success.

He created colorful canvasses with cartoon heads and bubbled blurbs. *Taylor-Made* was Wylie's most photographed piece. To the right of Elizabeth Taylor's beauty mark, inside a bubble, was her famous quote: I'VE ONLY SLEPT WITH THE MEN I'VE BEEN MARRIED TO. HOW MANY WOMEN CAN MAKE THAT CLAIM?

Squeezing my eyes shut, I pictured a very young Wylie, his lips pressed against a microphone.

Pre-senting The Four Leaf Clovers.

Sunshine. Ben wanted to save sick animals.

Rain. Stewie wanted to kill sick animals and save the world. He believed that Vietnam was John Wayne's Alamo. Which, in a sense, it was.

Roses. Where did all the flowers go? Ingrid the Idealist wanted to defeat death by writing protest songs that made the whole world cringe.

Somebody I Adore. Adorable Patty wanted to be Audrey Hepburn, Debbie Reynolds, Doris Day- —innocent, seductive, larger than life. And although Patty never graced a movie screen, she achieved star status as Mrs. Wylie Jamestone.

Patty was a butterfly trapped inside a rainbow. When she walked into a room, all the harsh colors turned pastel. If you could market her mystique, you'd earn a fortune.

Suddenly, I visualized J.C. Penney's cosmetics aisle.

Before the reunion, shopping for my sweater, I had lingered in front of Penney's perfume counter. Among the sample spray bottles was a potent scent called Poison, much too expensive for my limited budget.

I conjured up another image. Patty at the reunion dance.

Behind her perfect ears, between her perfect breasts, Patty had dabbed Poison.

Chapter Four

"Small world," said Cee-Cee.

Her presence brought me back to the present. "What do you mean small?"

"Your homicide detective, Lieutenant Peter Miller, just happens to be Bill's good friend and protege."

"So Bill knew all about the murder?"

"He did. In fact, the case has been solved, the perpetrator arrested. Motive, robbery. The perp was an ex employee, aware that Wylie's friend would be wintering in Arizona. Patty had the rental car and the house looked deserted, only it wasn't, so the sneak thief bopped Wylie over the head."

"How did the cops find him? Her. It."

"Him. Through fingerprints. Bill says the perp was really stupid. He wiped the murder weapon clean but left prints on the refrigerator and milk carton."

"Milk carton?"

"Uh-huh. For some ungodly reason, he decided to feed the cat some milk."

"Sinead O'Connor. That's the cat's name," I explained. "It was on the news. Sinead's owner found Wylie's body. Didn't the thief wear gloves?"

"He did. But it was a new milk carton, and he had trouble opening that vee-shaped, push up here part—-"

"Where the wax usually sticks. I think they over-wax it on purpose, Ceese. Whoever invented that milk carton has a grudge against humanity. Everybody lately has a grudge against humanity, although I've been trying very hard to un-grudge. Sorry. Please go on."

"The perp took off his gloves to get a better grip. Then he

placed the carton back inside the refrigerator. What a dope!"

"The elephant," I murmured, "left footprints in the butter."

"What?"

"Just a riddle Wylie mentioned Saturday night. Speaking of which, how did Bill explain Wylie's painting and message?"

"Bill thinks Wylie was playing a practical joke. Patty told Miller that Wylie liked jokes and treasure hunts."

"True." I pushed my cold plate of cold eggs toward the edge of the table, where the waitress, who had probably finished her shift by now, could pick it up. "Did the thief confess?"

"Not really."

"Define 'not really.'"

"He was wasted, couldn't even spell his own name. Before he exited the murder scene, he pocketed enough loose cash to buy drugs." Cee-Cee's cheekbones turned the same shade as our neglected strawberry jam. "I'll probably find out more tonight," she said, "when I wheedle."

"You plan to visit Bill tonight?"

"I do."

"You wheedle with sex?"

"Sometimes. A marinated roast, dry red wine, plus an obvious lack of undies——"

"Cee-Cee! Shame on you!"

"Bill's a big boy. He can always cop a plea. " She winked one turquoise eye.

"Ouch! What an awful pun."

"How about this? After I wheedle, Bill lets it all hang out. Oh good, I've made you smile."

"I shouldn't be smiling. Despite what happened in New York, Wylie was my friend. Once upon a time we were both so idealistic; me with my protest poetry, Wylie with his smart-alecky cartoons. I think he truly believed he had sold out, or at least turned Republican. Then, at the reunion dance, I pushed some kind of button, and Wylie exploded. He jumped up onto the bandstand, grabbed the mike, and started sermonizing. He insulted everyone, especially Junior Hartsel."

"The ex jock?"

Face grim, I nodded. "Everyone booed, but the cheerleader really got upset and—-rats! I just thought of something."

"What?"

"The cheerleader. She was Dwight Cooper's date at our senior prom. She could hold a grudge against Wylie."

"Why?"

"Wylie spiked the punch, then challenged Dwight to that stupid drinking contest, which led to the car crash. Dwight was a big shot, and she had snagged him good. After the crash, she dropped him like a hot potato, the bitch. I don't remember her name, but Alice would know."

"Ingrid, they caught Wylie's killer."

"Yeah. Right. Still, I plan to follow Wylie's treasure hunt to its conclusion. I owe him that much."

"You don't owe him anything," Cee-Cee said indignantly."

"Patty, then."

"Why do you owe Patty?"

"New York. I can blame what happened on my failed marriage, the booze, even Wylie's forceful strength, but I can't deny my capitulation. Don't you understand? I screwed the husband of my best friend."

"No, Ingrid, you were screwed by the husband of—"

"Maybe Patty found out. Maybe she blamed Wylie. If she did, and if she killed him, Wylie's death is all my fault."

Patty's street was filled with cars and vans so I parked in the Broadmoor Hotel's lot then walked eight blocks. But first I searched through my jeep's debris and retrieved my black turtleneck sweater, impulsively purchased when the Broncos lost Superbowl XXII. Unlike the Broncos, my sweater smelled musty. But it was large, loose, cable-knit, and comfy; perfect for an afternoon that wasn't freeze-your-ass-off-cold. However, the weather was chilly enough to melt the sun, which looked like a scoop of lemon sorbet.

The musty sweater smell diminished when I caught the scent of greasy burgers, fried chicken, and Styrofoam coffee. Damn! They were holding an alphabet convention. ABC, CNN, NBC and CBS had all come to broadcast Wylie's death, witness Patty's grief, and hopefully catch a glimpse of the Rich and Famous.

Why hadn't Patty moved to the Broadmoor? Why remain at the murder scene? Why ask why? My immediate problem was how to avoid those wagtail newshounds. I wasn't rich, but I was infamously famous, and Ingrid Beaumont, a.k.a. Rose Stewart, wanted to avoid publicity.

Once upon a time I had craved publicity. Once upon a time I had chained myself to recruitment center gates, then asked my short-lived rock group to belt out *Clowns*, because I had promised never to sing until Stewie came marching home again, hurrah, hurrah. Once upon a time I had created a top-ten song through hostile hype. But once upon a time ended when government officials insisted that marijuana killed brain cells and the FBI swore that anti-war demonstrators smoked dope.

Therefore, rebellious Rose Stewart had defied Darwin and evolved backwards, finally regressing into Ingrid Beaumont, who scored buddy-cop movies and horror flicks.

I glanced toward the media crowd, milling about like wasps without a hive. Was I flattering myself? After all, the years had swiftly flown, I had aged, and I didn't spend mega-bucks on Wylie's face creams or plastic surgeons. Well, maybe the face creams, not to mention Ellie Bernstein's diet club.

Hell! Why all the internal fuss? I could probably stroll through that alphabet convention, flash a few brainless smiles, and never be recognized.

On the other hand, why take foolhardy chances?

Skirting the next door neighbor's front lawn, I climbed their back fence, cut across their yard, and heard the sound of thundering bass; a deep growl that momentarily left me standing stock still. Then I saw it, and my sneakered feet, on their own accord, began to skim grass, decorative rocks, and cultivated flower beds. I hurdled an ornate doghouse that boasted the letters T-O-N-T-O. I heard the Lone Ranger's theme and recalled Wylie's wrinkled-toothless comment. Although Tonto was wrinkled, he definitely wasn't toothless. A combination Shar-pei and Loch Ness monster, he nearly bayoneted the seat of my jeans.

Desperate, I turned and shouted, "Tonto, *sit*, Tonto, *stay*, Tonto, *friend*, Tonto, *kemosabe!*"

It worked. The damn monster actually flopped to the dirt,

drooled saliva, and glared at me from above his corrugated snout.

After climbing the fence, I swung my shaky legs over the top, loosened my hold, and landed in Patty's backyard. My ankles protested, but no bones snapped. Then I listened for the sound of Tonto's body whooshing over the fence, or his paws digging, but all I heard was a disappointed growl-whimper. Plus the muted music of the buzzing media.

How the bloody hell would I return to my car?

I could try the Tonto stay, Tonto friend bit again, but I had a feeling the huge mongrel's small brain was already regretting his capitulation. Next time he'd savor the fleshy cheeks inside my jeans.

Patty's backyard was serene, almost pastoral. A manicured lawn, with birdhouse rather than doghouse, was protected by a periphery of blue-barked willows, gray poplars, white birch trees, and dark green firs. No wonder the cat, Sinead, had chosen this safe haven over Tonto's intimidating turf.

And yet a dark pall of despair curtained the sorbet sun, not to mention the birds who chirped their do-waps above the feeder.

Or was I imagining things?

One can't see the forest for the trees, I thought, walking toward Patty's back door.

She was standing there, watching me, an enigmatic smile on her face. As she ushered me into the kitchen, I had a momentary memory flash. Jacqueline Kennedy. Patty reminded me of Jackie, after the assassination. Brave. Self-possessed. Even Patty's tapered pants and cowl neck blouse had assumed a pleated (royal blue) dignity. In high school she had worn her hair loose, a charcoal cloud. Now she tended to pull it away from her oval face. Today she'd clasped the shiny strands inside a jeweled barrette, emphasizing the two diamond teardrops that pierced her perfect earlobes. However, not one salty teardrop betrayed Patty's cool-as-a-cucumber demeanor.

"Your sweater smells moldy," she said by way of greeting, crinkling her cute nose.

"Hey, kiddo," I responded softly. "This is me, Ingrid. You don't have to keep your true feelings hidden."

Her velvet-brown eyes suggested... annoyance?

Strolling over to a window, she straightened the frilly curtains, pulled a dead leaf from a window plant, then turned toward me again.

"What do you mean by hidden?" she asked.

"Cry, Patty. Boo-hoo, keen, wail..."

I paused as I recalled her reaction upon learning about Stewie. Everybody else had gotten rip-roaring drunk. We had listened to Jimi's fire-breathing anarchy, especially his controversial *Star Spangled Banner*. Then, while Marianne Faithful crooned *Sister Morphine*, Ben swiftly propelled me into the bathroom and held my head over the toilet bowl. Afterwards, gargling Listerine, I vowed never to drink again. Naturally, I broke that vow. Because booze dulled the anguish. Because booze brought a nebulous state that allowed my body to experience guilt-free orgasm, to explode internally, even though I couldn't erase the image of Stewie's body exploding externally.

Ben and I had already parted. In fact, he had flown back from Ithaca, then attended our improvised wake with a brassy-haired, sloe-eyed creature, who sprawled, naked and comatose, across Wylie's un-stuffed armchair. However, through impotent rage, not to mention wretched heartache, Ben and I had come together, as if our imperative screwing would have to last us a lifetime, which it almost did.

When we emerged from the bedroom, I heard a very drunk Wylie chanting, "This is your lucky day, this is your lucky day, this is your luck——"

"Make him shut up!" I screamed, then wept against Ben's chest until he guided me back into the bedroom, lowered me to the mattress, and calmed my hysteria with more sex.

Sometime during the night, Alice Shaw consumed an hallucinogen and threatened to jump from Wylie's first story window. We let her jump.

Subsequently, Alice denied the drug, the bad trip, and the "suicide leap." We let her deny.

In any case, Patty accepted the tragic news stoically. She attended Stewie's wake, but she didn't indulge, even though Wylie urged her to drink, snort, smoke, swallow the ample supply of amphetamine candy. Instead, she drifted through the room like a wraith, changing records, covering Ben's drugged-out date with a blanket, emptying ashtrays. And nobody—not even I—tried to turn Patty inside out, expose the hurt, allow it to heal.

"Earth to Ingrid."

I rubbed my eyes like a swimmer who had just emerged from a chlorinated pool. "Sorry, Patty, daydreaming. I do that a lot. Old age."

"We're the same age," she replied indignantly, "and I don't consider myself old."

"Neither would anyone else," I soothed.

It was true. Patty and I had been born three months apart, yet she looked ten years younger. An almost invisible web of fine lines, radiating from the corners of her sad eyes, were the only evidence that she had tiptoed past the big four-oh and was gracefully heading toward decade five. Maybe there was a senescent portrait inside the Jamestone attic.

As if she had read my mind, Patty said, "Do you want to see Wylie's painting? It's considered part of his estate, but he wanted you to have it, and I shall honor his request."

"I'd rather talk about Wyl—"

"I don't want to talk about Wylie."

"Hey, Patty, we've been best friends since the third grade. We've shared everything from our first period to our first set of high heels. We cried over Fess Parker's death at the Alamo, and practically destroyed our friendship when we both chose the same Beatle to marry."

"Paul."

"No. We wanted to marry George."

"You're wrong, Ing. It was Paul. We wanted to sleep with George and marry Paul."

"We wanted to sleep with John."

"Alice wanted to sleep with Wylie."

"What?"

"It's true, Ingrid. Alice once told me that if she couldn't fuck Wylie, she'd die a virgin."

"Alice doesn't use the F-word, Patty. Do you think that's why she married Dwight? So she'd stay a virgin?"

"I don't know. Probably."

Subtle me changed the subject, hoping to elicit tears. "Are you planning to bury Wylie in New York?"

"I don't plan to bury him at all."

Aha, I thought. *That's why she won't talk about Wylie. Because she can't admit he's really gone. Maybe that's the reason she acted so dispassionate following Stewie's death.*

"My husband had some very definite ideas about his funeral," Patty continued. "He insisted that we wait for a windy day, stand on that rise above Cripple Creek, then scatter his cremated ashes."

"We?"

"The Clovers. He wanted us to sing that old song Ray Charles recorded with Betty Carter."

"Baby, it's cold outside?"

"Correct."

"God, that's so Wylie-ish. Why Cripple Creek?"

"The gambling. He said life was one humongous gamble. At first he suggested we toss his ashes over Monaco and sing 'True Love,' you know, that Bing Crosby-Grace Kelly ditty? He said the first person he wanted to greet on the other side was Princess Grace. But I said Monaco was a tad far away, not to mention expens—-"

"Wait a sec! Did Wylie know he was going to die? Did he have some fatal disease, Patty?"

"Yes. It's called screwing around. Although he carried condoms like other men might carry handkerchiefs, Wylie was scared of AIDS."

Well, that explained Patty's sad eyes, and opened Pandora's box. How many rejected women waited patiently for the chance to bash Wylie's head in? Was Alice one of them? Did Dwight know about Alice's secret desire? And let's not forget the masochistic cheerleader, the one who spurned Dwight and was spurred on by rowdy Clint. Could Wylie have rejected her?

"I'd really love to sit here and chat," said Patty, "but I have a million things to do. Wylie's parents are deceased, but his sister lives in Houston. Remember Diane?"

"Of course. We called her Woody."

Patty opened a floral box, pulled out a single rose, then extended it toward me. "I've received flowers and telegrams from a bunch of celebs who collect Wylie Jamestone portraits," she bragged. "Paul and Joanne, Bruce and Demi, Ted and Jane, even Bill."

"Bill?"

"Clinton. Hilary sent a lovely letter."

I stroked velvety rose petals. "Are you planning to hold a memorial service, Patty?"

"Yes."

"Would you like me to sing?"

"Dylan's already volunteered."

"Bob Dylan?"

"No, Dylan Thomas. Of course, Bob Dylan. Remember the portrait Wylie did of him?"

"How could I forget? It was one of my favorites."

The bubble above Dylan's head had stated: NO ONE'S FREE, EVEN THE BIRDS ARE CHAINED TO THE SKY.

"Speaking of portraits," said Patty.

"Okay. Yes." Suddenly I was anxious. Let the treasure hunt begin.

Patty led me through an archway into a studio roughly the size of a large utility room. Sunlight slashed the glass of several small square windows, set just below the ceiling. The furnishings were sparse—a stool, an easel, a nondescript table, an army cot. Sinead was trespassing again. Asleep on the cot, she looked like a calico wreath. I smelled lingering traces of linseed oil and turpentine. Stacked against one wall were a few canvasses, covered by a white sheet.

Patty sneezed, glared at the cat, then gestured toward the window wall.

I don't know what I expected, but it wasn't Doris Day.

Wylie's painting was approximately four feet by three. Doris Day's freckled face grinned impishly. Her head reclined against colorful pillows and her bubble stated: THE REALLY FRIGHTENING THING ABOUT MIDDLE AGE IS THE KNOWLEDGE THAT YOU'LL OUTGROW IT.

My eyebrow instinctively assumed a curvature. "What does that mean? Could Wylie," I said, thinking out loud, "have decided he didn't want to grow old and killed himself?"

"Hardly. He was hit on the back of the head. How could he kill himself? It would be like trying to clean the wax from your ears with your toes."

My eyebrow continued rising until it merged with my bangs. "Dammit, Patty, how can you make jokes?"

"If I died, Wylie would crack wise."

"That's different. Goofy schticks were Wylie's defense mechanisms. Remember Dwight? And Stewie?" I took a deep breath. "Did you love Wylie, Patty?"

"Define love, Ing."

I looked down at my rose. "Duke Ellington said that love is supreme and unconditional."

"Yeah, but Jimi Hendrix said that the story of love is hello and good-bye."

"Were you planning to say good-bye?"

"If you mean divorce, no."

"Was Wylie planning to say good-bye to you?"

Her lips curled. "That's a stupid question."

"Here's another stupid question. Don't you wonder who really killed your husband?"

"They caught his murderer."

"Right." My eyes touched upon the painting, and I wondered why Lieutenant Miller hadn't asked my opinion. Hell! If I knew cops, and I did, Miller was scouring Colorado Springs, searching for a silver-blond, statue-hefting Doris Day. "Did Wylie have an affair with a woman named Doris, Patty?"

"I don't know. Probably. I'm surprised at you, Ing. Wylie never made his treasure hunts that easy."

"True. I remember when we all invaded the Chief theatre. Wylie's clue was buried inside a box of popcorn."

"No. Crackerjacks. The Chief's feature film was 'Breakfast at Tiffany's.' Shit! I think I'm gonna' cry."

"Good. Tears hurt, but they also heal. It's like pouring peroxide over an open wound. At first it stings something awful, but——"

"Such a beautiful moo-moovie," she sobbed. "Remember how it was raining and Audrey Hepburn hugged her wet pussy?"

I had a fleeting image of Wylie cleaning wax from his ears with

his toes before it dissolved into the image of Audrey Hepburn trying to hug her own pussy.

"Then George Peppard kissed Audrey," Patty continued, "while
the puss played peek-a-boo from the lapels of her trench coat. It
was so romantic. That scene always makes me cry."

"Gosh, I remember your supreme, unconditional feelings for
'Moon River,'" I said sarcastically.

"Moon...oh God...River. After Dylan does his thing, would you
sing 'Moon River' at Wylie's memorial service? Please, Ingrid,
please?"

"I'd rather sing Janis Joplin's 'Piece of my Heart.'"

Unexpectedly, I felt the nape of my neck prickle. Because I heard
a distant echo. The words could have come from Doris Day's
painted lips.

Are you dying, Wylie?

And the reply might have come from Joplin, chained to the sky.

We all die by bits and pieces.

But the third refrain sounded just like Wylie. Maybe he was
chained to Janis.

How do you make a statue of an elephant?

Chapter Five

"She was hugging her wet pussy?"

Ben's voice sounded amused, and even though I had conjured up the same mental image, I said, "Wet cat, honey."

Hitchcock growled. His knowledge of human speak wasn't very extensive, maybe eight words—sit, stay, friend, biscuit, baddog, gooddog, getdownoffthecouchyousonofabitch, and cat. When I wanted him to leave the family room, I'd verbally bribe him with: "Look, Hitchcock, there's a cat, chase the cat." It worked every time.

"In retrospect," I said, "this afternoon's Breakfast-at-Tiffany's-crying-jag was Patty's way of expressing genuine sorrow. When JFK was assassinated, everybody else wept buckets. But Patty was dry-eyed, until we watched 'The Miracle Worker,' shortly thereafter. Patty Duke said wah-wah for water and our Patty burst into tears. 'Oh God,' she sobbed. 'Why can't miracles happen in Dallas, too? Why couldn't he be crippled or blinded? Why did he have to die?' She said virtually the same thing when Stewie died, but only after Warren Beatty, as Clyde Barrow, was riddled by bullets."

"Enough, Ingrid." Ben knelt on the family room's carpet and tousled Hitchcock's shaggy, maple-leaf ears. "We don't have to obsess over Wylie's demise or Patty's grief."

"You sound so unemotional. I thought you and Wylie made up during Sunday morning's phone call. Before I left for the game, you even said something about kidnapping Wylie and buying him dinner. Did you do it?"

"Did I do what? Kill Wylie?"

"No, dopey, buy him dinner."

"Ingrid, he died."

"Dinner doesn't necessarily mean night fare, especially on a Sunday. Dinner means the principal meal of the day."

"Are you asking if I saw Wylie before he was killed?"

"Yes."

I recalled Cee-Cee's wheedle with sex remark—-roast beef, booze, and a lack of undies. But I hadn't worn panties, even provocative panties, since 1970. Also, I couldn't cook worth a damn, and it was supper time, so I sat on the edge of my lime couch, scrutinizing several Chinese take-out containers. The food was real Chinese, seasoned to perfection, ordered from a hole-in-the-wall restaurant that Wylie had recommended. Nana Ana would have eaten there since the place looked, smelled, even sounded authentic. In fact, when the man at the counter handed me our to-go package, the only word I could decipher was "cookie." I thought he appeared disgruntled, as if fortune cookies were too... American.

Ben bit into a fried wonton, chewed, swallowed, then said, "I went to Wylie's house around eleven, but I never saw him."

"He wasn't there?"

"He was busy painting. Patty offered me a Bloody Mary."

"Before noon?"

"Alcohol doesn't necessarily mean night fare," Ben mimicked, "especially on a Sunday. Anyway, Patty had already downed a few."

"What? Patty never drinks, not since our senior prom."

"She was upset."

I finally made my selection; hot and spicy bean curds. I felt hot and spicy, so I unbuttoned my blouse down to where my bra would have been, had I been wearing a bra. "Why was she upset, Ben? The reunion dance?"

"Of course. Wylie ruined it for her."

"Wylie ruined it for everybody. Damn! I wonder if that was Patty's tusk."

"What do you mean?"

"Patty was supposed to be crowned Queen of the Elephants."

Rising, Ben walked across the room. Hitchcock followed. Ben stoked the fire. Hitchcock stroked Ben's denim crotch with his tongue, then rolled over on his back and waved his paws.

"You're right, Ingrid, that's exactly why she was so upset." Hunkering down, Ben scratched Hitchcock's belly. "I wanted to sober her up, so I suggested we take a stroll outside. There's a wooded area behind the house."

"Yes, I know. That's how I made my escape. From Tonto, the saw-toothed dog next door. The foliage grows wild for three full blocks, and Patty's house isn't fenced. Well, the neighbors have fenced it in on one side, but there's a clear path to the trees and..."

I hesitated, aware that I was babbling. The bean curds suddenly looked unpalatable, so I grabbed a sweet and sour shrimp with my chopsticks, rose to my feet, walked across the room, then glared down at Ben until he stood, facing me. Hitchcock felt my vibes, sensed a silent baddog, and slunk toward the fireplace tiles. "Patty seduced you, right?"

"Wrong!"

"You seduced her?"

"No. I don't take advantage of drunk——"

"Baloney! You took advantage of my nebulous state during Stewie's wake."

"That's different."

"Why?"

"Because I love you!"

Those four words momentarily halted my verbal onslaught. Then, still seething, I asked, "What happened between you and Patty?"

"Nothing happened."

"Patty just stood there contemplating her navel? Or maybe she was contemplating yours."

"My navel was hidden by my shirt, belt and jeans."

"Aha! What about Patty's navel?"

"Okay. She took her clothes off. But nothing happened."

"She stripped in the middle of a deserted forest and you just watched?" I orchestrated my rage with the chopsticks, and the damn prawn soared through the air like a dead, slimy, wingless moth, until it landed inside my blouse. "Women seem to do that a lot when they're around you, Ben. I remember your comatose date at Stewie's wake. She was naked as a jaybird."

"Dammit, Beaumont, you're fixated on Stewie's wake."

Ben's anger was beginning to match mine, but I ignored his dark, blazing eyes. "I can't believe you screwed Patty."

"I can't believe you screwed Wylie."

"He screwed *me!*"

"That's not what *he* said."

"I thought you didn't see him. I thought he was busy painting."

"On the phone, Ingrid. Wylie insisted that you got drunk, weepy, very... shall we say aggressive?"

"Say anything you like. It's a lie."

"Okay. Sorry."

"No, you're not. Was Patty as good as she looks? Does a butterfly achieve more than one orgasm, Ben?"

"Nothing happened," he said for the third time. "I gave her my jacket."

"Oh, sure. You covered her beautiful body with your jacket then led her back inside." Suddenly, I realized that Ben's sheepskin jacket had been missing since yesterday. It wasn't in the bedroom, nor the kitchen, nor the front hall closet. "Where is your jacket, Ben?"

"At Patty's house. She insisted on having it cleaned."

"Why? Did you roll around in the dirt?"

"No. She threw up. I held her head. Then I did lead her back inside, and brewed some coffee."

"That's the truth?"

"I swear."

"Where was Wylie all this time?"

"Working."

"He didn't emerge once? Out of curiosity? I mean, we're talking about a puking wife. Or had she finished?"

"She finished at the kitchen sink. Christ, she'd downed five or six Bloody Marys. When I refused her, uh, generosity, she screamed bloody murder. It must have primed the pump. In the middle of a rather profane double-whammy, she erupted like a volcano."

"Lava mixed with Tabasco sauce. No wonder she insisted on having your jacket dry-cleaned."

"I thought she had finished, but when we reached the kitchen she started all over again. She was very edgy, and it wasn't me, or even the dance. I think she suspected that Wylie might continue his abuse from the night before."

"Abuse? What abuse? He exposed our hypocrisy, that's all. Okay, here's the scenario," I said slowly. "Patty nude beneath your jacket, puking into the kitchen sink. You were holding her head again. I assume there was no background music."

"Yes, there was. The music came from Wylie's studio. Very loud. That's probably why he didn't hear Patty."

"Ray Charles, right?"

"No. Henry Mancini."

"Wylie was playing Mancini? Moon River Mancini? Never mind. What happened next?"

"Patty showered and got dressed while I drank coffee. Then I drove her to the Dew Drop Inn."

"And all the time Patty washed and primped, you never said boo to Wylie?"

"I guess I felt guilty."

"But you've just sworn that Patty instigated the seduction. Nothing happened, you said."

"I felt a certain guilt, regardless."

Lifting the chopsticks to my lips, I realized that the shrimp rested between my cleavage and my waistline. Something smelled sour, and it wasn't my saucy breasts.

"Ben, are you absolutely certain that Wylie was working inside his studio?"

"Well, I never actually saw him. Why do you ask?"

"The music and—-wait a sec! Why did you drive Patty to the Dew Drop? Where was her car?"

"In the garage. I drove because I wanted to watch the football game, I knew the reunion crowd was planning to meet there, and Patty still looked slightly green around the gills. What's your point?"

"A thief thought the house was vacant because Patty had the rental car."

"She didn't, Ingrid. I drove us. But if the car was in the garage, a thief might still believe it was gone."

I tried focusing on a thought that wouldn't stay put. "Did Patty say good-bye to Wylie?"

"Of course. I heard her. She even kissed him."

"How do you know?"

"Her lipstick was smeared."

With a shrug, I returned to the couch. "C'mere, Hitchcock, good dog."

My ganglionic mutt wagged his tail, and every other portion of his body, as he bounded across the room, skidded to a halt, then snuffled my sweet and sour blouse.

"Sit, Hitchcock," said Ben, joining us. "Stay! Leave Ingrid alone. You're trespassing on my property."

"I'm not your property, Cassidy. My breasts are not your property, either."

"Who paid for the Chinese take-out, Beaumont?"

"You did."

"Then I have proprietary rights, exclusive and absolute. For instance, that shrimp belongs to me."

Sitting, Ben pulled my body across his lap, unbuttoned the rest of my blouse, and captured the prawn with his teeth. Then, extracting the prawn with one hand, he tossed it toward Hitchcock...the prawn, not his hand.

Hitchcock didn't catch the shrimp, of course. Hitchcock couldn't catch a rubber ball unless you wedged it between his jaw and muzzle. After sniffing the floor, he gulped it down in one swallow...the prawn, not the floor.

Ben swallowed slowly, leisurely licking sauce until his tongue reached my left nipple.

I pressed my breasts together so that Ben could suck both nipples at the same time. That left his hands free to unzip my jeans and roll them down. "Your crotch is soaked," I gasped, as my bare butt encountered denim.

"Hitchcock has a very large, very wet tongue." Ben shifted my body to couch cushions and took off his own jeans. Kneeling, he spread my legs, lowered his face between my thighs, and began to caress.

"So do you, Cassidy." I spasmed six or seven times. "Oh, God, I'm sorry."

I felt his grin spread across my belly-button. "Don't ever apologize for multiple orgasms," he said.

"But I came without you."

"Not quite. I was definitely involved. It's very satisfying, almost narcissistic for a man to evoke that kind of response. In fact, my ego's swollen with pride."

But, in fact, it wasn't only his ego that was swollen.

Afterwards, he said, "You talk tough, Beaumont, but you're soft, smart, talented, forgiving, independent, and consumed with guilt. My daughter would say you have the 'smart guilties.' In other words, you have a conscience."

"Except for politicians and serial killers, everybody is born with a sense of right and wrong. Don't you agree?"

"Nope."

"You believe in that bad seed shit?"

"No, not really. But I do believe that brains..." Pausing, he raised his eyes to the ceiling. "Okay, brains are like a ruffled tuxedo shirt, and sometimes God forgets to iron one flounce."

"Name somebody who lacks a moral sense."

"That's easy. Hitler, Manson, Bundy——"

"Somebody we know personally."

"Alice Shaw Cooper."

"Alice doesn't have anything to be guilty about."

Rising to his feet, Ben stepped into his jeans. "I once had a patient," he said, zipping his fly, "a Cocker Spaniel named Suzy. Her owners wanted to breed her. But every time a male Cocker Spaniel approached, Suzy snarled and sat on her rump. Then one day this brute of a Rottweiler leaped into Suzy's yard. The only thing they had in common was a stubby tail. Suzy's owners finally separated the two dogs with cold, gushing water from a garden hose."

"And?"

"After Suzy's litter arrived, they had her spayed."

"I don't understand. Are you suggesting that Alice would fool around with a Rottweiler?"

"No. But she does assume this virtuous facade."

"Alice can't possibly have a wrinkled ruffle, Ben. If she did, she'd send her brain out to be pressed. Or," I added thoughtfully, "she'd be the prime suspect in Wylie's murder."

"The police caught Wylie's killer. It was on the news. So were you, honey. They showed highlights of the Bronco game, and there you were, hefting your sign. Thanks for the salutation."

"Didn't you see it yesterday?"

"Sure."

"No, you didn't."

"Okay, I missed it. I heard all about it, though. Patty told me."

I had a vision of Patty draping her lithe body across Ben's broad shoulders and whispering: "Ing printed our names together, darling. How appropriate."

Since the vision really bothered me, I blurted the very next thing that popped into my head. "Ben, how do you make a statue of an elephant?"

"Well, I guess you'd buy some clay and sculpt an elephant. If you really wanted to be creative, you'd add ivory tusks, although people with a conscience shun ivory."

"Tusks. I wonder if Wylie's riddle involved tusks." Rising from the couch, donning Ben's shirt, I rushed toward my bookcase. "Where's the dictionary? Here it is. Tsetse fly... turnover... turtleneck... tusk." I scanned Webster's definition. "Basically, it's a long protruding tooth. Do we know anyone with prominent canines?"

"Yup. Me."

"Teeth, not dogs."

"Okay. Theodora Mallard."

"Who?"

"She was better known as Tad. Dwight's——"

"Cheerleader! Of course! At the reunion dance she criticized Wylie's Lone Ranger remark." My mind conjured up a picture of Theodora Mallard. "She doesn't have elongated teeth."

"She did. Wylie nicknamed her 'The Vampire.' Inside the locker room, we joked that she could pierce a prick with her teeth, like you'd pierce ears. We thought we were so funny. We didn't know that one day kids would hang hoop earrings from their groins. By the way, Tad now wears braces."

"I didn't notice braces."

"That's because you didn't dance with her."

"When did you dance with her?"

"After Wylie and Patty left, while you were calming Alice down."

"Was Tad freaked out?"

"Define 'freaked out.'"

"God, I sound like Alice. Disconcerted. Traumatized. You know, because of Wylie's sermon. Everyone was upset, but Tad and Junior were really pissed, and Alice said that Dwight was brooding. No. Sulking. Which, I suppose, is the same thing."

"Dwight wasn't sulking. He was thoughtful, nostalgic. And Tad wasn't traumatized. She was... tipsy."

"Don't be such a gentleman, Ben. If she was drunk, say drunk."

"Okay. Drunk. She danced like a pretzel, looping her body around mine. I had to dig my fingers into her shoulders to keep her at a discreet distance."

"I'll bet she enjoyed that."

"Why?"

"She's a tad masochistic."

"Tad bragged about her braces because she got them through Workman's Comp. She's a waitress at the Olive Garden restaurant, and another server smacked her in the mouth with a tray. She was injured on the job, you see, so the orthodontist didn't cost her a cent."

"What a bitch. She was always a bitch."

"True, Ingrid, but she's a bitch with sharp canines. Hey, that's not a bad pun. I sound like Wylie."

"I wish you thought like Wylie. I wish I thought like Wylie. I wish I could figure out the answer to his damn riddle."

Soaking in my antique tub, with Ben's butt between my legs and his thick wet hair resting against my breasts, I said, "Maybe the riddle has nothing to do with anything. Maybe I should focus on the painting."

"Focus on my back, babe."

Ben squirmed to a sitting position, spreading my legs wider, and I felt shivery all the way down to my toes. Was there a lyric that rhymed with orgasm? Yup. Spasm. How about hump? Easy. Pump, bump, *plump.*

Swishing the washcloth across Ben's bronzed shoulders, I

thought: Plump. *Plump cushions. No. Plump pillows. Doris Day's head reclined on pillows. Hadn't Wylie once...*

"Ingrid, you're scarring my spinal column with your fingernails."

"I just thought of something, Ben."

"Me, too. It's been at least fifteen years since I had the urge to come twice. Well, maybe the urge, but not the stamina. Or, if I had staying power, my wife lacked enthusiasm."

"Always? Even in the beginning?"

"In the beginning I thought she lacked experience. Toward the end I realized that she just wanted to get the dirty act over with. Sperm was so sticky. My wife would have loved a Teflon penis."

"Then she would have loved my husband," I murmured under my breath.

Later, toweling Ben's body, I said, "Cassidy, you make me feel as if I've stared at the sun too long."

"That's because I'm sunshine. At first I resented Wylie for giving me that tag. I thought it was a dumb designation for a guy, until I read about Ra and Sol and Helios."

"Ra was the Egyptian sun-god and chief deity. Crossword puzzles," I added diffidently.

"The sun-gods were very macho. Sol was the Roman sun-god, Helios Greek."

"That makes you Egyptian, Roman, Greek, Irish, and Cherokee, while I'm just a plain old rose."

"A rose is a flower, Ingrid. Do you know what the word flower means?"

"I left my dictionary in the family room."

"A flower means the best of anything. For example, the flower of our youth."

"Please, Ben, I'm not used to compliments. Anyway, if I'm a flower, you're the sunshine that causes me to bloom."

"You may not be used to compliments, Ingrid, but you sure know how to give them. Thank you."

"Welcome." I murmured, embarrassed, because I wasn't used to giving compliments either. My world was tough, male-oriented, and I had to fight to get every good film I scored. I had to accept rejection with gruff grace and assume responsibility when things went askew. I had once overheard somebody describe me as

"Mickey... Spillane, not Mouse" and at the time I thought it was the highest accolade I'd ever receive.

Until Ben uttered his flower remark.

So I kissed him. Then, panting for breath, I said, "Would you... care to... try for... three?"

"Three what?"

I felt an unfamiliar blush spread across my face. "Three... uh... you know."

"Three you-knows in a row?"

"Naturally."

"That's not natural, honey, not at my age. Still, I'd be willing to give it a shot if I could have some sustenance first."

"I'm afraid our dinner is cold and... ohmigod, Hitchcock!"

Together, we raced toward the family room.

It smelled like soy sauce, and looked like the Chinese Air Force had made a surprise attack on Colorado Springs, bombing the inside of my house with snow peas, cashews, and water chestnuts.

Hitchcock knew that a baddog was inevitable, but he had weighed the consequences and opted for instant gratification. Lo main noodles dangled from his snout like Christmas tree tinsel, pork fried rice dotted his paws, and he was joyously lapping from a container that contained the last of our egg drop soup.

"Bad dog," I said mournfully. "Oh, such a bad, bad dog."

Repentant, Hitchcock carefully jawed a container filled with broccoli in garlic sauce, toted it across the room, then offered it to Ben.

Hitchcock's expression seemed to suggest that Ben counter with at least one gooddog. But Ben was too busy laughing.

"It's not funny," I wailed. "That food cost a fortune."

"Have a fortune, Ingrid." On his knees, Ben dug beneath the coffee table until he found then tossed me a cookie.

Curious, I pulled out the tiny strip of paper. Once upon a time, fortune cookies had real fortunes. Now they usually had dumb sayings. Only this one wasn't dumb.

"No individual raindrop is responsible for the flood," I read out loud. "No individual soldier is responsible for the mud. Those are the words from 'Clowns,' my song. How many cookies came with our order, Ben?"

"Four packages, four cookies."

"Is there another cookie, or did Hitchcock get to it?"

"He got to the cookie, but spit out the paper. See?"

"What does it say?"

Ben glanced down at the soggy strip. "'The biggest farce of man's history has been the argument that wars are fought to save civilization.'"

"I wonder who bakes the cookies."

"Chinese elves," said Ben, "who live in hollow trees."

"I'm serious. Isn't there usually an address on the cellophane wrapper?"

"Maybe, but there's no cellophane. Hitchcock ate it."

"He spit out the paper but ate the cellophane? Bad dog!"

"Why do you want the address, honey?"

"I don't know. A hunch? Woman's intuition? Wylie recommended the restaurant and... look, there's another cookie!"

"I suppose you want me to read the fortune. Okay, here goes. 'Wise man say that intuition is something women have in place of common sense.'"

"Rats! Wait a sec! You just made that up, didn't you? The grin on your face is a dead giveaway. Bad Ben!"

Hitchcock's ears, which had drooped at the word bad, practically levitated at the word Ben.

"C'mon, Cassidy," I urged. "What does it really say?"

"'Peace is a thing you can't achieve by throwing rocks at a hornet's nest.'"

"Chinese elves didn't create those fortunes, Ben. They were written by an anti-war advocate."

"Or an aging hippie."

"What makes you think it's an aging hippie?"

"Your song, honey. I'll bet there's another strip of paper that says something about answers blowin' in the wind."

As if on cue, a gust of wind blew rain and nature's debris through my open window. I ran behind the couch and tugged at my stubborn window pane. Unfortunately, the answer to Wylie's death didn't mingle amid the swirling leaves and water.

Staring down at the floor, I tried to determine which raindrop was responsible for the murder.

Patty?

Dwight?

Alice?

The nympho cheerleader, Theodora Mallard?

Poor, pathetic, disgruntled Junior Hartsel?

Or maybe it was merely a pissed off "lost boy" in that cellulose, cellular Never Never Land of petered, panached reunionites. Which meant that I had at least seventy-five suspects.

Me. Ingrid Anastasia Beaumont. Who had never solved a mystery in her life. Who always guessed wrong while reading books or watching TV. Who, at this very moment, felt like Audrey Hepburn's wet, confused pussy.

What was the name of Audrey's cat?

Oh yeah, Cat.

As in curiosity killed the.

Chapter Six

On our knees, we searched for the fourth cookie.

Hitchcock decided this was a fun game. He duplicated the position of our rumps, and let loose with doggie gas that sounded like human burps and smelled like moo goo gai pan.

Rising, I extended my first finger. "Look, Hitchcock, there's a *cat*. Chase the *cat*."

My gullible mutt bounded toward the kitchen while I closed the connecting door. Then I retrieved Ben's jeans and shirt from the bathroom, handed him the jeans, and donned the shirt.

"Ingrid," he said, "what happened to my shorts?"

"You weren't wearing shorts. Maybe," I said sarcastically, "you left them at Patty's house to be dry-cleaned."

"Maybe I left them inside your dryer. Look, if this Patty thing's going to become an issue, I'll reclaim my hotel room. I didn't really check out, you know."

"God, Ben, I'm sorry. I sounded just like my ex."

"He was jealous?"

"Yes. Also, scared. Afraid I'd leave him. We fought all the time, but the biggie was my prom picture. He insisted that I destroy Wylie. Remember the photo with all of us together?"

Stupid question. I'd seen it while scanning Ben's wallet. But I couldn't admit that, so I waited for his nod, then said, "My ex thought Wylie Jamestone was the love of my life."

"Why didn't you set him straight?"

"Because he would have wanted me to destroy you. I threatened divorce if he didn't seek help. Instead, he stole the photo, disappeared, and I haven't seen or heard from him since."

"When did he sign the divorce papers?"

"He didn't."

"You're still married?"

"Yes. I use my maiden name and call him my ex, but I'm still married." I felt stupid tears drench my lashes. "Do you want to go back to the hotel?"

"Come here, Ingrid." Ben extended his arms, and I hid my face against his warm shoulder. "Poor sweet baby," he crooned.

"Don't, Ben. It's harder for me to accept sympathy than compliments."

"You'll have to deal with both. I love you, babe, and I have no intention of leaving."

"Your practice—"

"Is being handled by my assistant. I haven't had a vacation in years." He tilted my chin. "I plan to make up for lost time."

"Speaking of lost," I said, walking toward the fireplace. "Did you find the fourth fortune?"

"Nope. Just three pennies and one of those subscription postcards that always fall out of magazines."

My eyes encompassed the room. "Maybe if we clean up Hitchcock's mess first."

"I'll clean while you make us a broccoli omelet. That seems to be the only container that wasn't punctured by your canine's canines."

"Ben, I can't cook."

"We're talking eggs, Beaumont."

"We're talking burnt, Cassidy."

"Okay. You clean while I cook."

On his way out, Ben halted to thumb away the tears that still stained my lashes.

"I love you," he repeated softly.

"I love you, too."

After stoking fireplace logs, I entered the den, planning to confiscate its wastepaper basket. Originally a dining room, my comfy lair was furnished with a desk, a chair, a sofabed, a large metal cabinet, a stereo, woofer, tweeter, baby grand, and Wylie's painting.

It had been a bitch, carrying that painting back to my car. But Doris Day seemed to enjoy the ride. Reclining against her pillows, she had smiled passively. She was probably smiling at my elbows——my funny bones——thunking multiple tree trunks. Or maybe she smiled at the Oz-like branches that attacked my hair. Or the birds who tried to blitz me with poop grenades.

Arriving home, I had immediately pigeonholed Doris inside my cabinet. Which hadn't bothered her, I noted, opening the cabinet door. She still smiled brainlessly, and I had the insane notion that Doris Day had once smoked lots of dope.

Gazing at her freckled face and silver-blond hair, I finally focused on the vague concept that had caused my fingernails to pockmark Ben's back.

Patty was right! Doris wasn't the clue, per se!

I raced toward my desk, opened its deep middle drawer, retrieved an old shoe box, and pulled out a letter. Wylie had sent the letter after I'd scored a buddy-cop movie whose white hero looked like Rock Hudson. In fact, the lead actor's name was Rock Huttson. Originally titled *Death Is Psychosomatic*, the sleazy film was released sparingly. Years later it appeared in video stores under its new title, *Killer Shrink!*

But Wylie had caught the real Mccoy at a Manhattan theater, God knows why. Maybe, in retrospect, he was humping some Rock Huttson fan. Anyway, Wylie subsequently dispatched an acknowledgment suggesting that the recurrent pattern of my simplistic, albeit haunting, melody would make a supreme song for Diana Ross. On a second sheet of paper he had depicted the genuine Hudson, who, along with Doris Day, crouched atop a huge pillow. Behind Rock and Doris stood Oscar Levant, the piano player who always dangled a cigarette from his lower lip. Oscar's hands were raised as though giving benediction, and his bubble stated: I KNEW HER BEFORE SHE WAS A VIRGIN.

"What the hell does it mean?" Ben asked for the second time.

Standing by my antique half-moon spinet, he chomped a stalk of broccoli. Two plates of garlic- flavored eggs decorated the family room's Hepplewhite coffee table. So did Wylie's drawing.

"You'll never be President," I grumbled. For some dumb reason, the blues had set in. Maybe it was because the original wind and rain have given way to a thunderstorm. Maybe it was because broccoli gave me heartburn, yet I ate the damn stuff to prevent clotting arteries. Maybe it was the almost overwhelming scent of garlic. Vampires wouldn't be caught dead outside Ingrid Beaumont's front door. Or even Hitchcock's doggie door.

Ben's craggy brow furrowed. "Why can't I be President? I'll confess up front that I smoked grass, lusted after women, and bought useless real estate."

"I was talking about your broccoli fetish, your extravagant irrational devotion to functional florets."

"You've lost me, babe."

"Remember President Bush and broccoli?"

"Of course."

"Remember 'Pillow Talk'?" I gestured toward Wylie's caricatures. "Rock Hudson pretend to be this shy Texan—"

"Ingrid, Our Gang saw that movie together. Alice thought it was 'cute.' Patty said it was 'romantic.' Stewie fell asleep. Wylie hated it. Correction. He loved Rock's redecorated apartment, which was supposed to be grotesque."

"Did we love it or hate it?"

"We argued. You said it poked fun at gays, and I said you shouldn't take everything so seriously."

"What a memory! Okay, Mr. Total Recall, who did we know before she was a virgin?"

"You."

"Who else?"

"Patty."

"Who else?"

"The whole senior class," Ben said, his voice filled with amusement.

"Except Alice. According to Patty, Alice is still a virgin. Unless..."

"Unless what?"

"Unless Wylie deflowered her."

"What? You're nuts."

"Wylie could have been Alice's Rotweiller. She, in turn, could have bopped him over the head. Rodin's The Thinker split his skull. Isn't that an Alice weapon? And she'd mentally erase the dirty deed, just like she did after her first-floor suicide leap. You even pinpointed her as a person without a conscience."

"Why are we debating this, honey? Wylie's clues are moot. The cops already traced his murderer."

The phone rang, effectively silencing my denial. I raced toward a small gate-legged table and fumbled for the receiver.

"Hi, Ingrid, sorry to call so late," said Cee-Cee.

"That's okay. Ben and I were debating."

"For what it's worth, I wheedled more information out of Bill. The perp finally admitted that he planned to rob the house, with an accomplice no less, but he swears the blood was already pooling beneath Wylie's bald head."

"Aha!"

"The police don't believe him. Both Bill and Miller think he's trying to avoid a murder rap."

"Who's the accomplice? Maybe its someone who knew Wylie and used the robbery as a cover- up."

"The perp wouldn't say. He seemed scared of reprisals. Then his lawyer arrived, and he promptly shut up."

"Did the cops question the neighbors? Maybe they saw something."

"Yup. Football. Every neighbor was glued to his or her TV set, watching the Broncos."

"What about Kim O'Connor? She looks more the MTV type."

"Miller told Bill that Kim wasn't talking, that she had guilt written all over her face. Miller thinks she was sneaking boys into the empty house next door, before the Jamestones showed up. That would explain why the cat was so familiar—-"

"Kim's thirteen, fourteen, fifteen tops!"

"Have you seen the stats on teenage pregnancies?"

"Yeah. Right. Do you think I should question her?"

"You can try, but you might not get much information. Bill says Kim's grounded. Her parents were furious because she talked to reporters. The O'Connors shun publicity, unless it's a posh society event."

"Do you know them?"

"I've met Mary. She did some volunteer work for Canine Companions, then decided the organization wasn't prestigious enough. Dogs don't genuflect. They use their tails and tongues to express appreciation."

I glanced over at Ben, petting Hitchcock.

"Mary's gems weigh almost as much as she does," Cee-Cee continued, "and she's paranoid about being robbed."

"Tonto."

"What?"

"She has a Loch Ness monster dog named Tonto. If the perp tried to rob her house, he wouldn't get very far."

"Mary's also paranoid when it comes to kidnappers. Kimberly attends private school, and is chauffeured every day, so it might be difficult to question her, especially alone. Good luck."

"Thanks."

"By the way, who's on the painting? I forgot to ask Bill."

"Doris Day."

"Good grief. Miller would call her a famous blond. He's a tad anachronistic."

"Speaking of Tad, that's the nickname for Dwight's cheerleader, the one I told you about. I plan to question her, too, just for grins. She doesn't seem the killer type."

"Please be careful, Ingrid. Sleuthing can be dangerous. I'd help, but I have to deliver a dog to Aspen, then train its new owner."

"Who's watching Sydney?" I blurted.

Sydney is Cee-Cee's Australian Shepherd, and a real bitch. She could never be a Canine Companion. She's too independent, too growly, and definitely a one-woman dog. Last year Cee-Cee left Sydney with a couple of servants. Sydney pooped the parlor and chewed up everything within reach. The servants quit two days before Cee-Cee's return, so I played dog-sitter. "It's awfully hard to find good servants," Ceese had sighed, tossing Sydney a biscuit. A perfect little lady, the dog's one blue eye and one brown eye had gazed adoringly at her mistress.

"Sydney will stay with Bill," Cee-Cee replied. "She, uh, tolerates him. I'm leaving tomorrow, Ingrid, so I'll give you my Aspen phone number. Don't hesitate to call. Promise?"

"Yup. Hold on." I retrieved my electric bill from the mail stacked atop the table, found a pen, turned over the envelope, and jotted down the number. "Please don't worry, hon. I've already outwitted Tonto, Kim's no threat, and Tad says things like 'eat shit and die.' If she bopped Wylie over the head, she'd probably claim

Workman's Comp for a broken fingernail."

"Did you decipher Wylie's painting?"

"Maybe." I told Cee-Cee about the virgin bit. "I feel as though I've been taken advantage of. If Wylie had a premonition, why didn't he simply say so-and-so wants me dead? I prefer a treasure hunt that leads to some treasure. I mean, the prize at the end of this one is a killer, not money, or a vacation, or even tickets to a Bronco play-off game."

"Oops. Bill's awake, raiding the refrigerator. Sex gives him the munchies. Gotta' go. Good luck, sweetie."

Hanging up the receiver, I felt stern eyes, and my reaction was not unlike Hitchcock's when he sensed a baddog coming.

"What the hell was that all about?" Ben's body language suggested that I might consider slinking toward fireplace tiles with my tail between my legs.

"The thief swears Wylie was already dead."

"The thief's name is Cee-Cee?"

"Of course not. It's really quite simple. My good friend, Cee-Cee Sinclair, has an ex husband named Bill Lewis. Bill's retired, but he was once a big-shot homicide detective. His protege is Lieutenant Peter Miller, the cop who's investigating Wylie's murder. I met Cee-Cee for breakfast this morning, and she said she'd query Bill."

"I don't call that simple, Ingrid. I call it amateurish snooping, chitchatting over toast."

"Bagels, you bastard!"

"Why are you so angry?"

"You must be kidding! Chitchatting?" I counted to ten, reached eight, then said, "Why don't you want me to find Wylie's killer?"

"It's not your job. That's why God invented cops."

"I suppose God invented the Dallas police department?"

"What?"

"Police sometimes screw up."

"Are you comparing Wylie's murder to Kennedy's assassination and Oswald's——"

"I'm comparing police bureaucracy to riddles."

"Ingrid, I'm trying to follow your logic, and I apologize for the chitchat remark, but——"

"Do you honestly believe our Colorado Springs homicide division has the time or even the inclination to decipher elephant jokes? Wylie used to spout them at the drop of a hat. How does an elephant charge or how do you make an elephant float or—pillows! Maybe the painting has nothing to do with Rock and Doris. How do you get down off an elephant, Ben?"

"A ladder? Parachute?"

"I never realized you were so literal."

His craggy jaw jutted. "I'm not good at riddles."

"You don't get down off an elephant, you get down off a goose."

"Right. Now everything's perfectly clear. A goose killed Wylie."

"You said Wylie dubbed Tad Mallard 'The Vampire.'"

"Okay, vampires killed Wylie."

"Dammit, Ben, shut up and listen! Wylie used to call Alice 'Mother Goose.'"

"You weren't inside our locker room, Ingrid. He called her 'Motherfriggin' Goose.'"

"Why?"

"He said that Mother Goose, the old lady not the bonnet-clad waterfowl, looked like she needed to get laid."

"Well, of course she did. The nursery rhymes were composed during Puritan times." I scowled at my coagulating eggs. "I wonder why Wylie got engaged to Alice."

"He didn't. She got engaged to him."

"What does that mean?"

"Wylie had to scratch for a living, and Alice had plenty of scratch. She bought Wylie, or at least she bought his food and art supplies. He absolutely refused to leave that roach-infested rat trap he called an apartment, even thought Alice would have paid for a nicer place." Ben strolled over to the coffee table and stared down at my plate. "You haven't eaten a thing."

"I'm not hungry. Why don't you nibble my share?"

"I'd rather nibble your—"

The phone rang again, this time cutting off Ben's appetizing innuendo.

"Let your machine get it," he suggested, but I had already lifted the receiver.

"There's someone prowling around outside," said Patty, "and I'm scared. Could you come over, Ing? Spend the night? Is Ben there? He is, isn't he?"

"Yes. Calm down. It's probably a reporter who——"

"No. They went away."

"Maybe it's Kim O'Connor's cat."

"A cat doesn't shine a flashlight."

"Rats! Call the cops!"

"I don't want cops. I want you and Ben and Hitchcock."

"Okay, but it might take some time. We have to change clothes then hustle Hitchcock into the car, which is like trying to lasso a stampeding buffalo with a choke-collar. Meanwhile, call one of your neighbors."

"I haven't met them. I don't have their telephone numbers."

"Run next door. The O'Connors have security up the gill. A dog named Tonto and——"

"No!"

Holding my hand across the mouthpiece, I said, "Ben, talk some sense into her. Patty says there's a lurking prowler but she won't contact the police."

He took the receiver from my outstretched hand. "Hi, beautiful," he said calmly, as though stroking a schizy Afgan Hound. Then, of course, I could only hear his side of the conversation.

"Yes, Ingrid told me... okay, lock the doors and don't go outside... yes, we'll come as fast as we can, but you've got to promise to call the police... look, if the reporters show up, I'll bet your prowler hotfoots... no, that's stupid."

"What's stupid?" I reached for the receiver.

Ben waved me away. "Leave the gun where it is, honey. Promise? And you'll call the police? That's my good girl. You're welcome. Yes, we'll hurry. 'Bye."

I felt my eyes widen. "She has a gun?"

"Apparently Wylie's absent friend keeps one handy. Let's get dressed."

There was a crescendo of thunder, followed by lightning, or maybe it was the other way around. The whole house vibrated as I scurried into the bedroom, opened my bureau drawer, reached for a pair of jeans, then said, "What's the rush? The cops——"

"Patty won't call them. She promised she would, but she won't. She's afraid the reporters'll hone in on the police radios and today's circus will start all over again."

"Better a circus than another funeral!"

"Ingrid, you don't have to convince me!"

Without warning, I felt hysteria build. Gun! Prowler! Patty all alone! Scared!

"You call the cops, Ben," I said, tugging my lucky orange sweatshirt on inside-out and backwards so that the washing instructions tag rested beneath my chin.

"Right." He reached for the bedroom extension, listened, then replaced the receiver. "It's dead."

"But it can't be. We just talked to Patty."

"The lightning must have hit——"

"Where's my other knee-sock? Rats, my sneakers are missing! Who kicked them under the bed?"

"Take it easy, babe."

Ben's voice had regained that calm the schizy Afgan quality. Except, considering the physical discrepancy between Patty and me, it was probably more like calm the schizy Yorkshire Terrier.

"Ingrid?" Ben buttoned his plaid flannel shirt.

"*Rats!* My shoelace just snapped."

"Ingrid?"

"*What?*"

"Everybody knows an elephant charges with a credit card, but how do you make an elephant float?"

I psyched out what he was doing; a valiant attempt to calm my rising hysteria with a verbal nudge rather than a face slap. Yet, I resisted his efforts. Racing toward my bureau again, I dug through my underwear drawer until I found an extra pair of shoelaces. Then I sat on the edge of the bed and played a game called miss-all-the-tiny-fraying-Reebok-holes.

"Answer me, Ingrid, or I'll stroke Ace Promazine down your throat." Ben grabbed my sneaker and began to cobweb the laces like an efficient spider. "How do you make an elephant float?"

"Add two scoops of ice cream and one elephant to a quart of root beer. What on earth is Ace Promazine?"

"A pet tranquilizer more potent than Valium. I have some in

my emergency doctor's pouch."

"Some Valium?"

"No, you nut. Ace Promazine."

"Good. That's good. Where's your doctor's bag?"

"Inside the trunk of my car. Why?"

"Hitchcock. Wait until he gets a whiff of Tonto."

Chapter Seven

Tonto's welcome volley didn't bother Hitchcock. Sinead's pussy perfume, however, agitated the hell out of him. Hitchcock roved through Patty's borrowed house like a bloodhound, nose to the floor, paw and tail angled, a shaggy semaphore. Once I even thought I could decipher his frantic signal: E-X-I-T. When I pointed this out to Ben, he laughed and asked, "Where did you learn semaphoring, Ingrid?"

"Girl Scouts."

Hitchcock didn't really know the difference between a cat and a caterpillar, but he could smell eau de feline, and he could growl, whimper, bark—-lord, could he bark!

"Ace Promazine!" I shouted. "Hurry, Ben!"

"Ingrid, we don't want to sedate our watchdog, do we? Hitchcock, sit! Hitchcock, stay!"

My mutt gave one last quivery sniff, then flopped to the kitchen floor. His expression seemed to suggest that he had done his job, warned the stupid humans who, for some reason, were totally unaware of strong, distinctive, odoriferous scents. In other words, a morally offensive, carnivorous mammal lurked.

Not the prowler. He or she had vanished into thin, rain-slashed air.

"Ingrid," said Patty, "your shirt's on backwards."

"Yes. I panicked needlessly, too."

"There was somebody outside," she insisted. "I'm not crazy. He shined his flashlight. I could see it shimmer."

"Maybe it was the police," Ben soothed.

"Police don't skulk."

"Ingrid says they do."

"Wrong! I said they screw up. Skulk and screw are not the

same th..." I swallowed the rest of my words, thinking about how Wylie had, first skulked, then screwed me inside my hotel room. As usual, I stashed the image, like storing snagged panty-hose at the bottom of my bureau drawer.

"I'm such a baby." Patty gave a tremulous smile. "That kid in 'Home Alone' could cope better than I."

"That kid," said Ben, "had a script."

"Well, I can't thank you enough. Ingrid, too."

"Don't forget Hitchcock," I mumbled, feeling grumpy again. And hungry. After all, I had abandoned my ethnic feast for sexual gratification.

As if she had read my mind, Patty said, "I know it's late, but I have food, already prepared. Lots of friends stopped by this evening. Alice and Dwight Cooper, Tad Mallard and Junior Hartsel, just to name a few. They all left donations. Tuna casserole, roast beef, soup-salad-and-breadsticks from Tad. She said it like it was one word. I think it's restaurant fare. There's also a blueberry pie, Ingrid, your favorite."

"It used to be my favorite, before I joined Weight Winners." Gazing enviously at Patty's size six cranberry slacks and black cotton turtleneck, I tried to justify the consumption of pie. "Too bad you don't have any ice cream."

"But I do. Haagen Dazs. Honey—-"

"Vanilla. Wylie's favorite. Okay. It's an emergency, so I'll break my perpetual diet with berry pie a'la mode."

Seated at the kitchen table, I savored every bite. "This is delicious, Patty. Very sweet. Who baked the pie?"

"I don't remember. There had to be at least a dozen visitors, and everybody handed me food along with their platitudes. Tad was the worst. She kept blubbering about how she had told Wylie to eat shit and die, but she didn't really mean it. Another piece, Ingrid?"

"I really shouldn't. Well, maybe a sliver."

After filling a bowl with minestrone soup, Patty sat next to me, then glanced toward Ben, who was scratching Hitchcock's belly. "Don't you want something to eat, Ben? The soup's tasty, and Ingrid says her pie—-"

"I don't care for desserts, honey, thanks anyway. Maybe later I'll fix myself a roast beef sandwich."

"In your dreams," I said. "We need to get some sleep. What's wrong, Patty? Your face is all scrunched up."

"I thought we might watch TV, just to make sure the prowler doesn't return. I have creme de menthe and fresh-brewed coffee. There's a VCR and hundreds of tapes; we could watch Alfred Hitchcock movies." Restless, almost twitchy, she scrubbed our bowls, spoons, my fork, then stuck everything in the dishwater and turned it on. Her gaze swept the kitchen. "Would you take the leftover pie home, Ing? Please? I hate blueberries. They stain your teeth."

Self-consciously, I ran my tongue across my teeth. "Dump that forbidden fruit down the garbage disposal, Patty, or I'll be tempted to sneak a piece for breakfast."

The disposal noisily consumed calories. It sounded as if it was grinding its teeth and smacking its lips at the same time. It sounded like my ex husband who isn't really my ex.

"You don't have to bribe me with movies," I said. "I'm always in the mood for Hitchcock."

My mutt wagged his tail at the sound of his name, but he didn't bark, thank God.

We shifted our bodies to an overstuffed family room. Ben perused the tape collection while I sank onto an overstuffed couch. Reaching out, I could stroke the fronds of a potted palm. Dark- paneled walls were filled with scenic prints, plus one Wylie Jamestone painting. The Beatles. Above George Harrison's head, his bubble stated: IS IT TRUE JOHN DENVER IS SPLITTING UP?

I turned to Patty. "Do you know the kid next door?"

"The one who found Wylie's body?"

"Yes."

"I've seen her. Why do you ask?"

"Do you think she might have used this house for assignations? Screwing around?"

Patty looked startled. "How did you know?"

"A friend of mine suggested it."

"Well, your friend is right. There's a finished basement with a sofa and a wet bar. We discovered junk everywhere... soda cans, a Jack Daniels bottle, condoms, even a bra."

"Wasn't the house locked? How could she get inside?"

"The same way her damn cat sneaks inside. There's a doggie door off the utility room, a big one. Wylie's friends adopted a mongrel named Truman Capote. He came from the same litter as the dog next door."

"Wait a sec! This house has no fence."

"Truman Capote has been trained to stay in the yard. He's very territorial, just like me." Patty shrugged her slender shoulders. "I could have moved to a hotel after Wylie was killed, but it's so much easier to coordinate the memorial service from here. Now your face is all scrunched up, hon."

"It's hard to believe another Shar-pei monster exists. What happened to Truman Capote? Where is he?"

Patty gave me a strange look. "With his owners, of course. They don't like to board him at a kennel. They said they did it once and he came home with fleas."

"What's the difference between an elephant and a flea?"

"One's huge, one's tiny," Ben relied. "Patty, when I give you the signal, please dim the lights."

"An elephant," I said, "can have fleas. But a flea cannot have elephants."

"Aha! Here it is. 'Psycho.' It was wedged between 'Halloween' and 'Killer Shrink!.'" Ben grinned. "Okay, kids, are you ready for a good safe scare?"

I waited for Patty to voice an objection. After all, she preferred romantic movies like *Breakfast at Tiffany's*. Wasn't Breakfast scripted from a story by Truman Capote? Sure it was. Hadn't Wylie once painted a portrait of Capote? Sure he had. Truman's bubble had stated: ALL LITERATURE IS GOSSIP.

I pictured Tonto and Truman Capote gossiping through the fence. Lord, I was feeling fuzzy. It had been a long day and I was tired. But it would be rude to renege now, leaving Patty and Ben all alone, watching *Psycho*.

Psycho. Jeeze! Maybe Patty had changed. People changed all the time. Me. Wylie. No. We hadn't changed. We'd sold out. Maybe Wylie's death had changed Patty. But only a short while ago she'd been frightened by a prowler. Why on earth would she want to watch a scary movie? Maybe it was okay to watch a scary movie because reality was so bloody frightening. Did that make any sense? Guess so, because my own senses were muddled. I felt scatterbrained, out of focus, as if I had borrowed someone else's glasses. Wait a sec! I didn't wear glasses. My vision was twenty- twenty. So how come I couldn't see the forest for the trees, huh?

"I'm ready," said Patty, cuddling up in a stuffed armchair, clutching a stuffed toss pillow against her perfect breasts. "After we watch the movie, we can all take showers, one at a time. Ben can play Tony Perkins, Ingrid Janet Leigh, and I can pretend I'm what's her face... the heroine."

"Vera Miles. Ben has already bathed. In fact, we took a bath together. Spasm rhymes with orgasm." Absurdly, I felt an orgasm build. I wanted nothing more than to push Ben down onto the floor, shed my jeans, straddle his hips, and ride him like you'd ride a merry-go-round horse. Up and down, up and—-

"Easy, Ingrid." While Patty trotted off to the bathroom, Ben joined me on the couch, and I saw a crease of annoyance crimp his craggy brow. "Too much liqueur packs one hell of a wallop."

"I haven't had any creme yet, Cashidy," I slurred, placing his hand between my thighs. "Not even one teentsy-weentsy drop."

His hand lingered, his first two fingers pressing gently, intimately, urgently. My nipples peaked. I had always read that in books—-her nipples peaked—-but I had dismissed it as rhetoric. Now, I believed every word. Leaning back against the couch cushion, I raised my sweatshirt, anchored it beneath my chin, and rubbed my breasts suggestively.

Ben gave a small groan.

I leaned sideways and reached for his fly. Patty returned. Ben jerked his hand away. "Ing's already got a buzz on," he said, as if that explained my bared breasts.

"No, no," I protested.

Smiling indulgently, he nodded toward my snifter.

It was empty.

Okay. Who the hell had gulped down my creme de menthe? I had turned my back on the snifter while talking to Patty, so that eliminated Patty because I would have seen her drink. Well, not really. As I contemplated changing personality traits, Patty had left my line of vision to fiddle with the light dimmer. But why would Patty drink from my snifter? She had her own.

Ben had been hunched over the tape shelf, except when he joined Patty to help her adjust the lights. But, once again, Ben had his own full snifter. Why drink from mine?

That left Hitchcock. The snifter had been placed on a low coffee table. Could my klutzy mutt neatly lap up creme de menthe and leave the glass intact?

Curious, I adjusted my sweatshirt, filled the snifter, and took a few sips, letting my tongue do most of the work. Yes. It was possible, if Hitchcock was very careful and very sneaky.

Ben turned off the VCR when I expressed an urgent desire to visit the powder room. Staggering back to the couch, I saw that my snifter was empty. Ben stood by the VCR, waiting to push the button. Patty sat, clutching her pillow. I glanced toward Hitchcock. He looked guilty.

But then Hitchcock always looks guilty.

I don't remember the movie, not even the part where Janet Leigh gets stabbed. Because I felt woozy. Drunk. Dead drunk. And the funny thing was... the really funny thing was... I forgot what the funny thing was. It had something to do with my vanishing creme.

"Hey, you guys, I lost my creme. We're little lost creme who have gone astray," I sang. "Bah, bah, bah."

"She's finished the whole bottle," said Patty. "You'd better help her to bed, Ben. There's a guest room on the second floor, third door on your left. I've already turned down the spread."

"How do you get down off a goose?" I asked slyly.

"Hush, baby," said Ben. "Let's go beddy-bye, okay?"

"What has twelve legs, is pink, and goes bah, bah, bah?"

"Six pink sheep?"

"God, Benji, you're so liberal. It's three pink elephants, singin' the Whiffenpoof song."

"You're three sheets to the wind, Ingrid."

"Am not!"

"Yes, you are. The word is literal and you haven't called me

Benji in thirty years."

"I can't see the forest for the... something. Oh, yeah. Trees. Can't walk. Legs don't work."

Scooping me into his arms, Ben carried me upstairs.

It was like that scene from *Gone With the Wind*, the one that fuels every rapist's ultimate fantasy. For some dumb reason, when Rhett scoops Scarlett into his arms, ignoring her emphatic struggles, women see romance, while men see the truth—-control. Spousal rape!

I wasn't feeling very romantic any more. In fact, I felt seasick. Everything mellowed, yet at the same time everything rocked. The stairs. Clark Gable's arms.

Ben kissed me, then laughed. "Your breath tastes like mint, Beaumont."

I wanted to tell him I didn't remember finishing the creme bottle. I wanted to explain that I had lapped creme with my tongue, testing my Hitchcock theory. I wanted to suggest that he examine Hitchcock's tongue, which was probably green.

But I couldn't. Because I was gone with the wind, three sheets to the wind. In other words, by the time we reached the guest bedroom, I had passed out cold.

Hot. There was a burning sensation in my stomach. I felt sick to my stomach, throwing-up sick. Could I make it to the bathroom without waking Ben?

He had removed my Reeboks and jeans. Good. It would save time. Because I knew that throwing-up sick wasn't the whole story here. Diarrhea was a definite subplot.

"Ohhhh." Despite my best intentions, not to mention my clenched teeth, the sound emerged.

Ben stirred, but didn't wake.

I struggled to a sitting position and felt worse, as if I stood on the deck of a storm-ridden ship. God, I felt dizzy, just like Ingrid Bergman in *Notorious*, just like Ingrid Bergman when she'd been...

"Poisoned! Ohmigod! I've been poisoned!"

"Ingrid? What's wrong, honey?"

"Food poisoning," I gasped. "Sick."

"Are you sure it's not the flu?"

"She didn't have the flu?"

"Who?"

"Ingrid Bergman. 'Notorious.'" I flopped back against my pillows. "I'm dying, Ben."

"Don't be silly," he said tenderly. "Everyone feels like they're dying when they have a bad case of the flu. Let me help you to the bathroom."

"Too late. Can't throw up. Can't stand up. Sorry."

I heard him fumble for the lamp, and the sudden bright light hurt my eyes.

"Jesus, Ingrid, you're not kidding." He grabbed my wrist. "Your pulse is racing."

"Why would I kid about poison? Ingrid Bergman did, but that's because she thought Cary Grant didn't love her."

"Hush, baby. No, don't hush. Keep talking."

"Tired. Sorry."

"You've got to stay awake, Ingrid. Patty!" he shouted. "Patty, get in here!"

"Don't bother." My voice sounded as if it ricocheted off walls. "Patty would sleep through Mick's 'Street Fighting Man.' God, Ben, I'm sorry."

I couldn't understand why I kept apologizing. I guess it's because food poisoning is so damn inconsiderate.

"Sit up." Ben cradled my head against his chest. "If you feel like whoopsing, don't try to hold it in. Okay?"

"You're not wearing jammies, Ben."

Thrusting all four pillows behind my back, he stepped into his jeans. "The bathroom's down the hall, not very far. We're going to walk. You're going to walk."

"Can't."

"Yes, you can."

"I don't have slippers."

"What?"

"'Notorious.' Ingrid Bergman wore slippers."

"What else? Tell me exactly what she wore, exactly what she said and did, every detail."

"She... she... that was the end of the movie."

"Start from the beginning."

"She was a spy for Cary Grant."

As Ben supported me down the hall, he suddenly interrupted my synopsis by calling for Hitchcock. "What will make him bark, Ingrid?"

"Why do you want him to bark?"

"Patty. She might sleep through Jagger, but she can't ignore Hitchcock."

"Try 'biscuit.' When you don't give him one, he might get pissed."

"Biscuit, Hitchcock," said Ben.

My dumb mutt immediately sat. At the same time, he wagged his tail. Dust motes danced like fleas, intensified by the nightlight's glow.

"*Biscuit, you sonofabitch!*" yelled Ben.

Hitchcock looked puzzled, but his tail still swept the floor. Ben was friend, and friends didn't tease.

"Catch the *biscuit*." With his free hand, Ben pitched an imaginary baseball.

Hitchcock looked around for his treat, then glanced toward me. "Bad Ben," I said.

That did the trick. Hitchcock let loose with an indignant series of barks that probably woke up Tonto, Sinead, the entire O'Connor family, and everybody inside the Broadmoor Hotel, eight blocks away.

It also woke up Patty. Rubbing her eyes, she emerged from her bedroom. "What the hell's going on?"

"Ingrid has food poisoning. Call an ambulance. Then mix milk with egg whites and bring it to the bathroom. Hurry!"

Patty sprinted toward the stairs while Ben said, "Where were we? Ingrid Bergman marries a Nazi big shot and they hold this party. Okay, what happens next?"

"When Cary Grant arrives, she shows him the wine cellar."

"Go on."

"I can't. Please, Ben, my stomach's burning."

"Milk will help douse the flames. Hang on, baby, we've reached the bathroom." He lowered me to the icy tiles. "Stick your finger down your throat."

My arm felt heavy, my hand titanic, but I managed to lift then insert my middle finger. I gagged. That's all.

"Try again," said Ben.

His voice had assumed its calm-the-Yorkie quality, yet I detected a hint of panic.

"First time worked. Oh, God." Hugging the toilet's rim, I finally began to retch.

"Good girl," said Ben, but it sounded like baddog. Because retching wasn't vomiting, not by a long shot. Retching was making the effort to vomit.

By now I was so weak I couldn't raise my head, much less my hand, so I could only hear Patty's footsteps as she entered the bathroom, and I decided that she didn't walk on invisible clouds after all.

"There's no milk," she said. "The damn cat from next door drank it."

"Where the hell are the egg whites?"

Ben's voice sounded angry, impatient, and I took a brief moment to savor the fact that Patty had provoked Ben's irascibility. Or, for that matter, any male's irascibility.

"Do you want eggs without milk?"

"Just the whites, Patty. Raw. Hurry, dammit!"

Ben was on his knees now, holding my waist with one hand, my forehead with his other, because my limbs had lost all resiliency and I had begun to plunge forward. Wouldn't it be funny if I lived through the poison but drowned in the toilet bowl? I could see newspaper headlines: POTTY KILLS INGRID BEAUMONT, A.K.A. ROSE STEWART.

I laughed, retched, heard sirens. So did Hitchcock. And Tonto. And every other dog in the neighborhood. It was a musical score from hell; a collaboration between Antonin Dvorack, Walt Disney, and Frank Zappa.

"Hang in there, baby," said Ben, as Patty led paramedics toward the bathroom. "You're not going to die."

"Then why do I see Stewie? He's raining."

Rain pelted ambulance windows. I couldn't see any droplets, of course, but I could hear windshield wipers. The driver had goofed earlier by sounding his sirens, cueing the dogs. However, once we'd left posh neighborhoods behind, the loud wail began again and the swish of wipers decreased.

I am the *viper*, I thought, the *vindshield viper*. And heard the echo of Wylie's laughter.

I wanted to laugh at my dumb joke too, but I couldn't. Because the viper was probably Death, cruising the streets of Colorado Springs, looking for a tasty morsel to appease his appetite.

Glancing up toward the ambulance roof, I saw an extraordinary pyrotechnic display of blue objects; circular, with irregular edges. Pain shot through my temples.

"Ingrid," said Ben, squeezing my hand, "are you allergic to any kind of medication?"

Meditation? I was confused. Why would I be meditation to allergic? Wait a sec! Medication. Medicine.

Since an oxygen mask covered my mouth, I shook my head, and the blue spots changed to dancing sparks of fire.

Ben checked my IV, then said something that sounded like "lactated ringers."

He was acting very doctor-ish.

I felt my body quiver, just a little at first, but soon I was shaking my booties, attempting the Charleston, Can-Can, and Twist, all from a prone position.

"She's having convulsions," said Ben.

Convulsions, hell! I was dying, jitterbugging my way up to heaven.

They call it gastric lavage, which is a polite way of saying "she had her stomach pumped." People say "enema" rather than "she took an imperative shit." Same principle.

The doctor solemnly stated that I'd had a near miss with death. Wrong! I'd had a near *hit*.

I pity the poor chemist who had to sift through the contents of my stomach. Fortunately, I hadn't eaten much. Egg rolls, creme de menthe, Haagan Dazs, and blueberry pie.

It was the pie. Or, to be more exact, *baneberry* pie.

Baneberry, it seems, is also called necklaceweed, doll's eyes, and snakeberry. The shiny berries can be found in wooded areas, especially during summer and autumn.

It was autumn.

"Baneberries," said Ben, towering above me, "are often confused with blueberries."

I sat up in bed and adjusted my hospital gown's Velcro. "Are you saying that I wasn't poisoned on purpose, Cassidy?"

"Jesus, Beaumont, who'd want to poison you?"

"The FBI, my ex, and whomever killed Wylie."

"What?"

"The FBI, my ex—-"

"I heard what you said, Ingrid, but I don't understand why Wylie's killer would want you dead."

"Is baneberry poisoning contagious, Ben? I know for a fact that the mind becomes confused, and there's a total disability to remember anything distinctly, or even arrange ideas with any coherency." I heaved a deep sigh. "I'm on a treasure hunt, and the prize isn't hidden inside some damn Crackerjacks box. When I decipher Wylie's clues—-"

"When the police decipher Wylie's clues!"

"The police arrested some klutz who didn't have the smarts to keep his gloves on. Oh, God!"

"What's the matter? Do you feel whoopsy again?"

"I feel fine."

"Then you're the first person in history to go through gastric lavage and feel fine."

"Okay, so I'm not exactly up to snuff. But my mind's clear. Clearer. Patty said there was no milk because the cat drank it. Cee-Cee said the thief left his fingerprints on the milk carton, then put the carton back in the refrigerator."

"So?"

"Wait a sec! Let me finish! The thief took off his gloves because it was a brand new carton and that stupid vee part stuck together. How much milk can a cat drink in one day, Ben? A whole damn carton's worth?"

"Are you suggesting that Patty lied?"

"I'm not suggesting. It fits." I gave Ben a tight-lipped smile. "Just like a pair of OJ Simpson gloves."

"OJ's gloves *didn't* fit. Neither does your theory. If you're saying Patty poisoned you, that's ridiculous. How could she possibly know you'd eat the pie?"

"Blueberry pie is my all-time favorite dessert. And the evidence went down the garbage disposal."

"That was your idea."

"She made up some bogus story about a prowler so that we'd drive over and spend the night. She refused to call the police or one neighbor. She bribed me with Hitchcock movies, even though she prefers romance flicks."

"Hold your horses, babe. How could Patty know I wouldn't eat the damn pie?"

"You hate desserts. You've always hated desserts."

"Okay. She serves poisoned pie. Then you get sick, puke, and the whole thing's for naught."

"Wrong! She gulps down my creme, or gives it to Hitchcock, or even pours it into the potted palm."

"Why?"

"So that when I start to feel the effects from the poison you'll think I'm drunk."

"Forgive me, Ingrid, but you *were* drunk."

"I was woozy. My mind had already started to rot."

"You sang bah, bah, bah."

"The poison."

"You couldn't even walk."

"The poison."

"You passed out."

"Right. What's the first thing I do when I get drunk, Ben?"

"Ingrid, it's been thirty years."

"I get horny. I lose all inhibitions. Okay. What happens when I continue drinking?"

"You get maudlin," said Ben, almost reluctantly.

"Correct."

"The Whiffenpoof song is mawkish, honey."

"Only when you sing about lost lambs, not lost creme. And what would happen if I drank practically one whole bottle of booze? C'mon, Ben, you know the answer. It's not some goddamn riddle."

"You puke," he murmured.

"Remember holding my head while Marianne Faithful sang 'Sister Morphine'?"

"Yes."

"And the prom?"

"You were... uninhibited."

"And?" I prompted.

"You drank Alice's spiked punch, glass after glass. I could have tried to stop you, but I wanted you uninhibited. You're very uninhibited when you're uninhibited, very un-Doris Day. Remember tonight, during your creme consumption?"

"I didn't consume any creme, dammit!"

"Ingrid, you tasted like mint."

"My tongue tasted like mint!" I lay back on the pillow, emotionally and physically drained. "Okay, Ben, what happened at the prom, immediately following my glass after glass?"

"We found an abandoned classroom and... er, did it... on the teacher's desk. Then you drank some more. We danced to Clint Eastwood. You stopped, pressed your hands across your mouth and pleaded with your eyes, so I hustled you down the hall until we reached the coach's office. It was locked, but there was a huge mail slot. You spewed through the slot, cried, and swore you wouldn't drink any more that night. But you did."

"I had reached the uninhibited stage again when we all piled into Dwight's convertible. Ben, I never, ever pass out."

"Sorry. I just don't buy it." His craggy jaw jutted. "You've been acting squirrelly since Wylie's death, imagining all kinds of things. You even made a big deal out of those stupid fortune cookies."

"Squirrelly? As in nuts? Don't be such a gentleman, Cassidy. We didn't 'do it' on the teacher's desk. We screwed our brains out. And if I'm acting like a basket case, say it!"

"Okay. You've been acting like a basket case. I'll accept the premise that you didn't pass out from drinking, but you were burned out."

"My stomach was burning, not me!" I recalled the pyrotechnic display inside the ambulance and let loose with a volley of shudders.

"Ingrid, you're shaking like a leaf. And you're so pale. Let's talk about this some other time."

"Go home," I said wearily.

"To Tulsa?"

"No, dopey, my house. Rats! You have to pick up Hitchcock. Ben, please don't tell Patty, I mean, don't mention my suspicions or say anything about—-"

"Calm down. May I ask her who brought the pie?"

"She said she didn't remember."

"That was before. She might now, when it's important. If you want my opinion, it was simply a case of mistaking baneberries for blueberries." Ben took a deep breath. "Try and get some sleep, babe. I'll pick you up tomorrow."

He stroked my brow, kissed me, then waved good-bye.

I felt awful, sick to my stomach, even though there was nothing inside my stomach, except frustration. So I rang for the nurse. Maybe she possessed some medicine that would dissolve my angry frustration.

In other words, I wanted to sleep my suspicions away.

My sleep was restless. I dreamed that Hitchcock licked me with a tongue the size of a skateboard. I dreamed that a downy goose pecked away at Wylie's eyes. I dreamed that Tonto and Truman Capote stood beneath a pulsating shower head. Not the dogs. The human Tonto and Truman. I joined them. We were naked. I swigged from a jelly jar filled with creme de menthe.

The jar refilled itself after each swig.

I felt sexy, uninhibited, but Ben wasn't there, so I started to cry. The others didn't notice my tears, probably because shower water pebbled my face.

We all sang baby, baby, where did our love go.

I sang Benji, Benji, where did our love go?

Tonto nuzzled my neck. His braids brushed my breasts and his wet feather tickled my nose. I sneezed. "Tonto sit!" I shouted. "Tonto stay! Tonto kemosabe!"

This time Tonto didn't obey. I writhed, scratched and bit. Then, like a bad movie, I heard the tap-tap of footsteps. Somehow, I managed to wrench myself free from Tonto's grip.

On the other side of the shower curtain stood Doris Day.

Her eyes blazed. She wielded a sharp knife. Was she planning to slash Truman, Tonto, or me?

It was such a stupid question, I woke up screaming.

Chapter Eight

"Home, home on the range..."

I couldn't wait to get home, change clothes, and hit the road again. Screw the gastric lavage! I had a score to settle with Miss Poison Perfume. Despite my sore throat, I finished my song. "And the skies are not cloudy all day."

"Too bad we don't live on a range, darlin'," Ben drawled. His sunglasses forked the car's visor because the sky was all clouds, a choppy, cresting sea of clouds. On this particular afternoon, cartographers might have dubbed Colorado's vista the Heavenific Ocean.

Ben drove. It wasn't a great distance, but we got held up by several red lights, allowing me time to explore my Patty-murdered-Wylie-and-poisoned-me theory. Although, to be perfectly honest, a four-way stop sign would have done it.

"Patty didn't do it," said Ben.

"Do what? Poison me?"

"Kill Wylie."

"How can you be so sure?"

"She said so."

"Dammit, Ben, I told you not to mention my suspicions."

"Patty's not stupid," he stated, halting at the next corner. We drove down a street called Uintah, where the lights were staggered in such a way that you'd miss at least two. Unless somebody made a left-hand turn, in which case you'd miss them all. "When I questioned her about the pie, creme, and milk——"

"Who donated the pie?"

"Junior Hartsel."

"Our ex jock? Don't tell me he's into baking."

"Nope. He bought the pie at a church bake sale. So you see,

the baker simply mistook baneberries for blueberries."

"How——"

"Patty called him, woke him up. She said Junior was very upset, very apologetic."

"Where did Patty get his number?"

"From her purse. She has a purse-size phone book."

"Did you talk to him?"

"Who? Junior? Why would I talk to him?"

"Maybe Patty called any old number. Time, for instance."

"Ingrid, please!"

"What about the creme de menthe? How come the bottle was empty?"

"Patty said she kept re-filling your glass."

"But I didn't drink it, Ben, I swear."

"Easy, honey. I believe you."

"Then how did Patty explain the creme, or the lack thereof?"

"Hitchcock. Last night, after we left, Patty checked out the family room. It was a mess. Talk about your hangdog countenance. Hitchcock was contrite. He was also pie-eyed, if you'll excuse the expression, considering that pies aren't exactly your favorite dessert anymore. Hitchcock chewed up video tapes, un-stuffed the pillows, knocked over the potted palm, and pooped in the dirt."

"Maybe his poop was green. Ben, you're a vet. You can examine Hitchcock's poop for creme de menthe, right?"

"Wrong. Patty cleaned everything up." Hitting the brakes, Ben shifted into first gear. "Did you really expect her to keep dog shit around for analytical dissection?"

"Yes! Dammit, Ben, Hitchcock wasn't goofy from the liqueur. He was upset because he sensed I was dying. After the ambulance drove away, he vented his feelings on the tapes and pillows and plant." I took a deep breath. "What about the milk?"

"Simple explanation, just like I told you."

"Define 'simple.'"

"Patty adds a few drops of milk to her morning coffee. Wylie drank his black. So Patty bought a small carton the night before Wylie was killed. They stopped at a convenience store on their way home from the reunion dance."

"How convenient," I said between clenched teeth. "Wait a sec!

The carton was waxed shut when the thief fed the cat."

"So what?"

"Wylie was killed Sunday afternoon. Why didn't Patty add 'a few drops' Sunday morning?"

"She was drinking vodka and tomato juice. Remember?"

"You said you brewed coffee while she got dressed."

"I did, but she didn't drink any. She was anxious to join the gang at the Dew Drop Inn."

"You take your coffee with sugar, no cream, right?"

"Yup. Why?"

"I'm just trying to tie up loose ends. Why didn't Patty put milk in her coffee yesterday morning?"

Ben shrugged. "I didn't ask. She was sedated the night before. God, babe, she wept until she had no tears left. Then I left. Dwight said he'd stay a while, watch over her, give her more pills if she woke up." Ben downshifted. "Maybe she slept late. Maybe she didn't drink coffee. Maybe she drank it black."

We waited for a clear lane, then turned left, causing other cars to miss the rest of the lights.

"Who's standing on my porch, Ben?"

"I don't know."

"Why isn't Hitchcock barking?"

"He has a hangover," said Ben, pulling up to the curb. "Would you bark with a hangover?"

Obviously attempting a joke, Ben's voice lacked conviction. Which meant that Hitchcock had spent the morning barking up a storm.

Ben helped me from the car, then supported me down the path and up five porch steps. Now I knew why my faithful watchdog wasn't raising the roof. Leaning against the front door was *friend*. I had said it. He had said it. And Hitchcock, not the brightest mutt in town, had actually believed it.

"Good afternoon, Lieutenant Miller."

"Ms. Beaumont. And Dr. Cassidy, I presume."

"Guilty." Ben chuckled.

"For Christ's sake, Lieutenant, please don't call me Ms. Did you come about the poison?"

"Poison?"

For the first time in our brief but apparently lasting relationship, Peter Miller lost his cool. I could sense the wheels in his head spinning. Arsenic? Hemlock? Poison gas? Poison ivy? Rat poison? Baneberries?

"Ingrid just survived an almost fatal case of food poisoning," Ben said gravely, hugging me closer, "and she went through gastric lavage. Now she suspects that somebody tried to 'do her in.'"

"Not somebody," I murmured. "Patty Jamestone."

"It's a long story," said Ben.

"Which you can describe, in detail, on our way to the precinct. I need you to make a statement, Dr. Cassidy, answer a few simple questions."

I felt Ben's fingers dig into my shoulders. "Do you have a warrant?" he asked.

"Do I need one?"

"Why can't you question me here?"

Miller studied my pale face and raccoon-smudged eyes. "Can Ms. Beau... Ingrid be left alone?"

"Yes," I said.

"No," said Ben. "Can't you see she's neurasthenic?"

"I'm neuras-what?"

"Weak as a kitten. In fact, Lieutenant, I believe she's about to faint. Let's go inside. Please?"

Before Miller could reply, a woman strolled down the sidewalk, then turned and walked up my path. In her hands, she carried a thermos, probably filled with coffee from the 7-11 a few blocks away. I could hear Hitchcock. He was outside, behind the back yard fence. I wondered if the fence would survive.

"Ingrid Beaumont, Dr. Cassidy," said Miller, "this is my partner, Shannon LeJeune."

Unlocking the front door, Ben propelled me inside. I heard the sound of a huge body hurl itself through the doggie door. Bounding into the room, Hitchcock headed straight for LeJeune.

"Hitchcock, *friend*," I said quickly. "Sit! Stay!"

Accepting friend but ignoring sit and stay, my ganglionic mutt galloped toward me. Hitchcock has no sense of time. If I walk to the corner mailbox, he'll greet my return with an accusatory what took you so long and why did you abandon me? I'll get the same response if I grocery shop or fly to California. Issuing forth a joyous whimper, Hitchcock kneaded my breasts with his paws and washed my face with his tongue.

My joy matched his. Convulsing inside the ambulance, I had thought I'd never see my beloved mutt again. "Down," I said. But my actions belied my words as I hugged his shaggy body and kissed his cold nose.

"Down, Hitchcock," Ben said firmly, then led me toward the couch. It still smelled of soy sauce, even though Ben had Pledged and scrubbed the family room.

"Do you have to use the bathroom, honey?" he asked. "You look a tad green around the gills."

"Maybe later," I replied sarcastically, then changed my tune. Furious at Ben's ploy, I was curious about Miller's unexpected visit. "Would you fetch me a carbonated drink, Benji darling? The bubbles might settle my stomach."

"Of course."

"I'll go with you," said Miller.

"That's not necessary."

"Yes," said Miller, "it is."

Three words. Three little words. Yes it is. My throat constricted, my stomach knotted, and my heartbeat accelerated. Because I now suspected that Miller wanted Ben for more than a few simple questions.

Why? Had the police finally accepted the thief's story? Had Cee-Cee told Bill about Wylie's rape-seduction and Ben's subsequent reaction? Had Bill told Miller? My mouth felt dry, my palms felt wet, and my pulse rate soared. Hitchcock sensed my distress and tried to wriggle into my lap.

"Getdownoffthecouchyousonofabitch," Ben ordered. "Your mistress is a bit under the weather."

That was putting it mildly. Fear had replaced weakness, and fear felt like gastric lavage.

As if on cue, the sky outside my family room window turned dark, and God began to spew rain mixed with sleet.

"Forget the carbonated drink," I said. "Sit down. All of you. Lieutenant, ask your damn questions."

LeJeune placed the thermos on my coffee table, then leaned

against the front door. Miller appropriated the spinet's stool. After flicking the light switch, Ben joined me on the couch.

"Dr. Cassidy," said Miller, "first I must warn you that everything you say——"

"Yes, okay, I'm aware of my rights, and I don't need an attorney present. I didn't kill Wylie Jamestone, which, I assume, is what this is all about."

"Didn't the thief murder Wylie?" I asked, even though I had denied the thief's participation ad nauseam.

"He's still a suspect," said Miller, but I could see by his expression that the thief wasn't a suspect at all. "Dr. Cassidy, do you own a sheepskin jacket?"

"He does," I replied. "Dr. Cassidy left the jacket at Patty Jamestone's house. She wanted to have it dry——"

"Please, Ingrid, I can speak for myself."

"There was blood on your jacket," Miller stated.

"It wasn't blood," I said indignantly. "It was vomit. Sorry, Ben, I'm doing it again."

"Ingrid's right, Lieutenant. What might have looked like blood was really tomato juice. Patty upchucked some Bloody Marys. I held her head. That's why she offered to dry-clean——"

"It was blood."

"Wylie's blood?" Ben shook his head. "That's impossible. I never saw Wylie. He was locked inside his studio, painting."

"Where did you leave your jacket, sir?"

"What room?"

"Yes."

"The kitchen. But I didn't exactly leave it. Patty did. She wore it because... well, she was cold, you see, and——"

"Don't be such a gentleman!" I shifted my gaze toward Miller. "Patty made an attempt to seduce Ben. She took off all her clothes. They were outside and it was chilly. Ben used his jacket to cover her body. She insisted on cleaning the jacket. End of story."

"Not quite," said Miller. "Ms. Jamestone never mentioned one word about wearing Dr. Cassidy's jacket."

"Well, it's obvious, Lieutenant. Patty killed Wylie, framed Ben, and poisoned me."

"Why would she poison you?"

"Because she knew I'd follow Wylie's treasure hunt until I pinpointed her as the killer."

"That makes no sense, Ingrid," said Ben. "Anybody could follow Wylie's clues."

"Oh, really?" I glanced toward the blurry, storm-streaked window. "What do you call a parrot in a raincoat?"

Both men just sat there, looking as if their brains had been vacuumed by an Electrolux.

"Shannon?" Miller focused on his partner. "What do you call a parrot in a raincoat?

LeJeune's pretty face looked perplexed. She shrugged.

"Polyunsaturated," I said triumphantly. "That was one of Wylie's favorites. By the way, Lieutenant, how do you make a statue of an elephant?"

"I give up. How?"

"I don't know, but I think it's an important clue."

"Speaking of clues, why did Jamestone leave you his Debbie Reynolds painting?"

"Doris Day, not Debbie Reynolds."

"Right. Doris Day. Sorry."

"I think the painting has something to do with virgins."

"Sacrificial virgins?"

"No. Promiscuous virgins. Given time, I'll solve Wylie's puzzle."

"Speaking of time," said Miller, reaching into his pocket for a spiral notebook and a ball-point pen. "Where were you at the time of the murder, Dr. Cassidy?"

"What time was the murder?"

"You don't know?"

"How could I, Lieutenant, unless I'm the murderer?"

Miller looked thoughtful, as if he didn't want to reveal any details, like maybe the time of the murder and whether Wylie was really dead, or vegging someplace with Elvis. Finally Miller said, "We estimate that Jamestone's death occurred between the football game's second and fourth quarters."

"That clears Dr. Cassidy," I said smugly. "He was watching the game at the Dew Drop Inn."

"The Dew Drop isn't far from the murder scene, Lieutenant," said Ben, "and the Dew Drop was packed. Anybody could have left, then returned very quickly, very quietly."

"Right," I said. "Patty could have slipped away—"

"She didn't have a car," Ben interrupted. "We used mine."

"Why are you defending her? She lied about your jacket and..." I swallowed my next words. Because Ben had sworn that nothing happened Sunday morning. Because Ben had said he'd never laid eyes on Wylie. But what if Ben had laid Patty? What if they had plotted Wylie's murder together, and now he was protecting her?

Unacceptable! How could Ben sleep with both Patty and me? Could he be that nefarious? And would Patty allow her Romeo to bang another Juliet?

By her own admission, Patty was proprietary. She was also possessive, and boffing two reunionites exhibited a definite lack of etiquette. Which, come to think of it, might be another reason why she wanted me out of the picture.

I couldn't believe that Ben had instigated the poison plot. No way! And yet he didn't believe I was poisoned.

"Where did you find Ben's jacket, Lieutenant?" I asked.

"The jacket was stuffed inside a green plastic bag," Shannon offered eagerly, "waiting for Monday's trash pick-up."

Miller grimaced and LeJeune's face flushed.

My mind raced. Why didn't Patty burn the jacket? Because she wanted to frame Ben. Which erased the romantic liaison theory and took me back to step one.

I only knew that, despite my recent suspicions, I had to protect my significant lover. "Spilt milk," I said.

"What?" Miller looked totally bemused.

"Sunday night's TV broadcast. They said the only witness was a calico cat, and Kim O'Connor found her pet standing next to a bowl of spilled milk. The thief swore he arrived after Wylie was killed. Wylie was bashed on the head, which meant he bled a lot. Maybe the thief sloshed milk on the floor, then tried to clean it up with Ben's jacket."

I realized my theory was ridiculous and the cops would never buy it, but I had to say something.

Miller's eyes bore a hole through the bridge of my nose. "What makes you believe the thief arrived after Jamestone was killed? Sunday night's broadcast didn't mention it, Neither did Monday's. In fact, we kept it a secret."

"Patty mentioned it."

"How did *she* know?"

"Ask her," I shot back.

Cee-Cee had mentioned it, of course, but two could play the same game. I'd throw suspicion at Patty, where it belonged.

"Maybe," I said, "Patty was so drunk she didn't remember wearing Ben's jacket. Or maybe she was afraid she'd be blamed for Wylie's murder and took measures to frame Ben, just in case the thief didn't work out." *Better*, I thought.

Miller wasn't impressed. "Dr. Cassidy," he said, "would you please come downtown and sign a statement? Ingrid, do you have a friend you can call?"

Sure, I thought, my best friend. Patty Jamestone. She can bop me over the head, then stuff me inside a Glad bag.

"I don't need anybody," I said. "I'm feeling a little weak, but I'm not incapacitated. My brain is functioning very well. Over the last few days I've been neglecting my music, and I have a score to settle... compose."

Nobody caught my slip of the tongue. Shannon LeJeune was busy retrieving the thermos. Peter Miller was glancing toward the window, anticipating saturation. Ben was tying his shoelace.

"I'll dictate and sign your damn statement, Lieutenant." Rising, Ben gave Hitchcock a hearty chin scratch. If my mutt had been the lion he resembled, he would have purred. "Ingrid, keep the home fires burning," Ben added for good measure.

I didn't burn any fires, but I did bathe.

Then I pulled my last clean pair of jeans from my bureau drawer. Bleached a murky combination of white and light blue, the jeans had butt-patches and were air-conditioned at the knees. I'd have to do laundry soon, or buy some new used jeans at one of the consignment shops I frequented.

My sweatshirt drawer was thinning rapidly, too. In fact, only one sweatshirt remained; an old gray cotton jersey with a hand-painted peace symbol.

Maybe I should wear a more conservative top. Kim O'Connor was on my agenda, and if she was anything like her mother, she might regard my shirt with suspicion. Or she might consider rebellion an asset, which would be to my advantage.

Compromising, I donned a black velvet vest.

My lips curled as I realized that my what-to-wear dilemma was unnecessary. The shirt and vest would be covered by my camel's hair jacket. Camel's hair jackets had been popular in the late fifties and early sixties, but were making a comeback.

Just like Rose Stewart, I thought, anticipating mental, possibly even physical battles.

Finally, I tugged on cowboy boots, re-soled countless times. The old boots were as comfortable as... well, an old pair of shoes. The boots gave me confidence, and I needed confidence, because my battle plan included a confrontation with Patty.

One thing bothered me. Wylie's Doris Day clue. I knew her before she was a virgin. That wasn't Patty. Patty had never pretended to be virginal.

With that last thought, I added Alice Shaw Cooper to my agenda.

Rainy sleet had washed away the scent of hamburgers and fried chicken. God had stopped spewing, and the air was refreshingly fresh, as wet and cold as Hitchcock's nose. No new fowl smells wafted or enticed because the media was missing. Which meant, of course, that Patty was missing.

I didn't care. Boldly stomping up the path, I rang the doorbell and shouted, "Hello, Patty, it's Ingrid! Open the door, you traitor! Liar! Slut!"

The fury of my brush with death was in those last few words, and yet I sounded as if we were still in high school. All I needed to add was: "Long time, no see." Instead, I absurdly added, "Please, Patty, if you're home and hiding, open the door."

Granted, my lungs and larynx had not been primed by the hospital's stomach pump. But I was loud enough for Tonto to hear. He barked.

A young-ish voice yelled, "Shut up, numb-nuts!"

Kimberly O'Connor?

Yup. I heard the bang of a screen door, then watched her walk toward me. Kim wore an oversized Denver Bronco jacket, unzipped. It was the only thing oversized about her.

"The merry widow ain't home," she said.

"Why do you call her that?"

"She's a widow, ain't she?"

Kim O'Connor was too well-bred for ain't. Verbal rebellion?

"She's a widow," I said. "But she's not very merry."

"That's what you think."

"What makes *you* think she's merry?"

"That's for me to know, and for you to find out," Kim chanted, sounding very first-grader-ish.

"Why did you call Tonto numb-nuts?"

"Because he's been fixed. That's the word Mom uses. My boyfriend says Tonto's balls were *nixed*. Hey, how do you know his name's Tonto?"

"It's painted on his doghouse."

"You were trespassing," Kim said smugly.

"True. But I have a good excuse. You see, I wanted to avoid reporters."

"Why?"

"If I appeared on TV, there'd probably be recriminations. Punishment, so to speak."

"Who'd punish *you?*"

"My mom," I answered truthfully.

Kim's face changed instantly, just like the weather. Her scowl became a smile, revealing a previously hidden Shirley Temple dimple. Her blue eyes opened wide. Even her permed brown hair seemed to spring into life, as if a sharp knife had slashed through a tightly coiled mattress.

"Boy oh boy," she said, "sometimes a person doesn't mean to be bad, but she gets chewed out just the same. My mom gives demerits. Can you believe that shit? I get one demerit if my room's messy, even though we have a maid. Three demerits if I'm late for dinner. Ten demerits if I flunk an exam. Last week my math teacher gave a surprise quiz, but I turned the F into an A."

"How many demerits did you get for talking to reporters?"

"None. Mom grounded me. I can't even use the phone. It was disconnected."

"Your mother disconnected the phone? How can she make calls?"

Kim stared at me as if I had suddenly sprouted wings. "Mom turned off my phone," she said. "It looks like Snoopy. Do you want to see it?"

I wondered how anyone could sound so old and young at the same time. The bumps beneath Kim's blue Cashmere sweater and the curved rump beneath her tight white jeans suggested fourteen, fifteen, maybe even sixteen, but her do-you-want-to-see-it was pure preadolescent.

"Is your mother home?"

"Nah," said Kim. "She's at the thrift shop. It's her pet project. She and her friends sell junk for charity."

"I'd love to see Snoopy, honey."

Kim led me toward her front door. "I left it unlocked," she said, grinning impishly. "Five demerits."

My cowboy boots echoed along the vestibule's genuine marble floor, and I'd barely had time to glance toward a prominently displayed, ornately framed Wylie Jamestone painting before Kim eagerly guided me up a staircase. We turned right and walked down a hallway. Hanging a left, we entered her bedroom.

A man sprawled atop Kim's patchwork quilt, amid a virtual plethora of stuffed animals and dolls. Raggedy Ann lay across his groin, face down. But even Ann couldn't hide the fact that he wore his birthday suit.

In other words, he was as naked as the day he was born, which was probably twenty-plus years ago.

Chapter Nine

While I had fantasized a brief but lasting relationship with Blood Sweat and Tears, the man on Kim's bed had been conceived. While I was protesting Lyndon B. Johnson's Vietnam policy, the naked man on Kim's bed had been born. While I was bonding with Kim O'Connor, he had sneaked through the unlocked front door, entered her room, and removed his clothing, every stitch.

Instinctively shielding Kim with my own body, I shouted, "Run, honey! Call the police!"

"Don't be silly," she said, stepping around me. "Hi, Dex."

"Hi, kid. Who's your friend?"

She swiveled. "What's your name?"

"Ingrid Beaumont," I replied, totally nonplused.

Kim made an about-face. "Her name's Ingrid something, but I call her Grid for short."

That was a new one. I had been called Rose, occasionally Ing, but never Grid. It was too rich, too Kennedyesque, too touch-football.

"You picked a crummy time to invade my bedroom, Dexter," Kim said critically. "Grid was next door," she added, apropos of nothing.

Dex sat up. Raggedy Ann still hid the family jewels, but only temporarily. Without embarrassment, he tossed the doll toward a mirrored dresser, found the carpet with his feet, walked over to a pink-tufted chair, and donned underpants, black slacks, and a white shirt.

Kim had apparently witnessed this performance before. She didn't blink or hide her eyes. Neither did I.

Dex noted my lack of feminine squeals. "Mary... Mrs. O'Connor is doing her charity thing. I'm supposed to pick her up at five, but I think charity begins at home." He nodded toward the bed. "Let's get it on."

Kim's dimple vanished. "Shut up, numb-nuts."

"Hey, kid, I ain't fixed."

"One word to Daddy and he'll use your balls to play golf."

Dex merely grinned. His strangely colored, silver-brown eyes found mine. "Kim's daddy can use my dick as a golf club."

Considering that I had already viewed the cocky young man's equipment, I ignored his brag. And although it wasn't on purpose, I yawned.

His blond crew cut seemed to bristle. "You some goddamn reporter, lady?" he asked, his voice belligerent.

I was tempted to answer yes. But most reporters were on my hate list, below cops.

Before I could respond, Kim said, "You look familiar, Grid. Oh! Ohmigosh! You're Rose Stewart!"

I must admit that I was flattered.

"You look just like the picture on your album, only much older."

My ego balloon deflated. I heard the whispered whoosh, then realized it was simply my sigh of resignation. "Where on earth did you find Rose Stewart's album, Kim? Stores haven't stocked it for years."

"Daddy bought you a long time ago. Mom wanted to donate 'Clowns' to the thrift shop, but Daddy gave you to me instead."

"Big deal," said Dex, still bruised by my yawn. "She ain't nobody no more."

The mystery of Kim's ain't was solved, even if Wylie's murder wasn't. Not yet. However, when I finished with Patty Jamestone, Kim's daddy could use her balls to play golf.

"Get out of here, Dex," Kim said, "and don't forget your smelly socks and shoes."

He slammed his chauffeur's cap atop his bristles. "Next time, kid," he sneered, "you can come to me."

"Don't hold your breath!"

Scooping up his sock-filled shoes, he exited.

The chauffeur! What a cliche! My mind immediately began composing background music. Something rags to riches, something Richard Gere, something Rolls-Royce.

"He'll be back," Kim said smugly. "Don't mind Dex, Grid. He's a has-been."

"Has he ever been a has?"

"Dex used to sing with a heavy metal group called Hitler's Youth. But he never made it to Denver, much less the Coast."

"I can understand that. Hitler's Youth! Good grief!"

"Oh, it wasn't the name. Dex got into fights all the time. He'd hit on some girl, and her friends would lay into his group. Soon clubs refused to book him, and Youth kicked him out. By the way, Dex hit on the merry widow."

"But she's only been here... what?... five days?"

"It takes Dex five minutes. It took less than that to hit on you."

"Me?"

"Who do you think he was talking about when he said let's hit the bed?"

"You."

"Us."

"Christ! Kim, how old are you?"

"Fif... sixteen."

I let it pass. "And how old is Dex?"

"Twenty-five. No, Grid, he'd not old enough to be my father. That was last year. My history teacher."

I sank onto the quilt, next to a stuffed Pooh. "Kim sweetie, why do you..." I hesitated, trying to think of a tactful way to put it.

"Sleep around? Well, I thought I was in love with my history teacher, I really did."

"And Dex?"

"I figured he might be worth enough demerits for a one-way ticket out of here."

"Why would you want to get out of here?"

Eyes downcast, Kim worried the lush plum carpeting with the toe of her expensive sneaker.

I glanced around her perfect bedroom. Too perfect. The dolls and stuffed animals looked brand new, never touched. Where were the posters? Where were the photos? Where was the noise? No TV, CD, stereo, not even a radio.

Despite my mother's lack of imagination, she had allowed me

to defiantly thumbtack Tony Curtis and Sidney Portier above my bed's headboard. Dozens of snapshots had almost obliterated my mirror, and my record player's needle had grooved the Beatles' *Love Me Do* ad nauseam.

Kim's few nose-freckles merged. "Grid, have you ever been locked inside a cage?"

"I've been locked inside a jail cell."

"For what?"

"Protesting. Vietnam," I added, just in case her history teacher had skipped that chapter.

"Then you know how I feel."

"Forgive me, honey, but it's not the same. You have a yard, trees, good food to eat." I glanced toward Snoopy. "You have a phone..." I paused, aware that her line to the outside world had been disconnected.

"I also had an older sister who committed suicide. She couldn't stand cages either, so she killed herself. I found her body in the bathtub. It was... unpleasant."

That had to be her mother's word. Now I understood Kim's reaction to Wylie. If her sister's suicide had been unpleasant, Wylie's bloody head must have been untidy. Poor baby.

"Daddy tries to forget by keeping busy," Kim continued. "Mom tried to hush it up. She tells everybody that my sister's at some college back east. I guess sis'll start graduate school soon."

I felt as though I'd swallowed rocks. "I'm sorry, honey."

"Yeah. Thanks." Kim sank onto the carpet, next to Raggedy Ann, who had missed the dresser yet apparently survived her fall. Retrieving the doll, Kim said, "Raggedy gives good head. So does the merry widow."

"How do you know that?" I asked, trying to keep my tone conversational.

"Once I snuck through Truman Capote's doggie door and watched."

"Watched who?"

"Dex. But there were others."

"Others," I repeated, dazed.

"Sure. There was this guy in a wheelchair. He looked like Elvis."

Dwight Cooper!

"He drove a van with a handicap sticker. Then there was this balding nerd who wore an old high school jock jacket."

Junior Hartsel!

"And there was this really gorgeous guy, Grid. He looked like an Indian."

Ben!

I swallowed rocks again. "Kim, did the other men... the Indian, for instance... did they sleep with the merry widow?"

"I never saw that happen, Grid, but they all looked as if they wanted to."

"Did any of the men stop by last Sunday?"

"Yeah. The Indian."

"Before lunch or after lunch?"

"Before lunch."

"But that's okay," I said, thinking out loud. "He planned to visit Wylie."

"No, he didn't."

"Yes, he did."

"No, he didn't," she insisted, "because Mr. Jamestone wasn't home."

I felt my mouth gape, dentist-wide, hippopotamic. Kim could probably count my teeth. "What did you say?" I managed.

"He wasn't home, Grid. Every Sunday morning Daddy plays golf and Mom sleeps late, so I usually sneak downstairs to watch HBO. I'm not allowed to watch cable, except the Disney channel, so I have to keep the sound low, just in case. Last Sunday I heard a car, ran to the front window, and watched Mr. Jamestone pull away from his driveway. He saw me and waved. Then I heard another car, and I saw the Indian park at the curb. He raced up the path and rang the merry widow's doorbell."

"What time did the Indian and merry widow leave? Did they leave together?"

"I don't know. I went upstairs to finish my homework so I could watch the Bronco game with Daddy. I can watch football with Daddy if my homework's all done."

Rising from the bed, I walked over to the bedroom window. The view encompassed Kim's back yard, Patty's back yard, and the distant trees. Tonto gnawed a rawhide bone, roughly the size of a dinosaur's squatty hind leg.

Kim joined me, then dusted the sill with Raggedy Ann's pinafore. "The maid," she said, "doesn't do windows."

My mother would have a fit. We never had a maid, but sills weren't windows, not by a long shot. "I don't suppose you saw the Indian and the merry widow enter the woods."

"How do you know they went into the woods?"

"A little bird told me," I said dryly, gazing toward the bird feeder. "How do you know?"

"Tonto howled. I ran to the window and yelled 'Chill out.' Then I saw them."

"What did you see?"

"Not much," Kim admitted. "They were hidden by trees. When they walked back to the house, the merry widow's legs were bare, just shoes, and she wore the Indian's jacket. It really grossed me out, so I didn't watch any more."

"What grossed you out, honey?"

"Blood. The Indian's jacket was covered with blood."

"Tomato juice and Tabasco sauce," I corrected. "Why did you think it was blood?"

"Well, I kinda' figured they had performed some sort of religious ritual, sacrificed a bird or small animal. I had just seen 'Carrie' on cable..." She paused, her freckles merging again. "You won't tattle, Grid, will you? It's worth ten demerits, but Mom won't let me watch TV anymore."

"I won't tattle, I promise."

I remembered *Carrie* very well, since it had a decent soundtrack. Plus a talented cast, including one of my favorite actors, John Travolta. Blood had gushed from the gym rafters during Amy Irving's senior prom, so Kim's mother probably believed the scene "unpleasant."

My Carrie was *Psycho*. Kids were excluded, barred from the theater, unless they were accompanied by an adult. However, even at age thirteen, Patty had charmed the ticket seller with her seductive mystique. I had screamed and screamed, then wouldn't take anything except bubble baths for a full month. Patty hadn't screamed. "Grow up, Ing," she'd said. "It's pretend." But she never, repeat never, watched another horror flick.

Until The Night of The Poisoned Pie.

I brought my attention back to Kim. "Do you know what time Mr. Jamestone returned home, honey? Did you hear the garage door open?"

"Nope."

"Did you see the thief arrive?"

"What thief?"

"Somebody tried to rob—-wait a sec! A friend of mine said there was an accomplice. Did you see a strange car parked at the curb next door?"

"Nah. I was watching football with Daddy and Tonto. Tonto barks when the Broncos score."

"So do I. What about your mother, Kim? Maybe she saw something, heard something."

"Nah. Mom hates football. She and her friends always drive to the Woodmor Country Club for brunch. Mom says the champagne's cheap and the food tastes awful, but afterwards 'the girls' play bridge." Kim's dimple flickered. "Just before the fourth quarter, I remembered Sinead, my cat. That's a clever name, isn't it Grid? I mean, with my last name and all?"

"Yes, very clever. I call my dog Hitchcock because I was named for Ingrid Bergman."

Kim's freckles merged again; she didn't get it. "Anyway," she said, "I had forgotten to feed Sinead, so I went next door to look for her."

"And found Mr. Jamestone."

"Yeah. I almost tripped over his body because I was staring so hard at the painting on his easel."

"Doris Day?"

"Not even close."

"Kim, do you know who Doris Day is?"

"Sure. Pillow Talk. Dumb movie."

"Who was on the painting?" I asked, trying to hide my excitement.

"Charles Manson."

"Manson? Wylie pained Manson? Wait a sec! How do you know what Manson looks like?"

"Charlie's talked to Geraldo. And he has this Nazi thing on his forehead."

"Swastika. Were there any words on the painting, Kim?"

"Yeah. Two. Death is."

"Death is psychosomatic?"

"No. Just death is. Charlie wore a soldier's uniform and a green hat. No, not hat. What's it called?"

"Beret?"

"Yeah. Beret."

Green beret! John Wayne! All at once, the most bizarre thoughts occurred, so off the wall that I didn't want to think about them. But that was like listening to 1973's *Sing* on the radio. How could one refrain from humming the tune? Singing the simple lyrics? In other words, sing sing a song. Sing it loud. Sing it strong.

What if Stewie didn't die over there? They had never shipped his body home. Just suppose, for argument's sake, that he had been sent home alive, but he was an amnesiac or something.

Stupid, Grid! Soldiers wore dog tags, even macho marines.

But what if Stewie was scarred? That would "gross Patty out." After all, her tattoo was perfection.

I had once surfed TV channels and discovered this wonderful old film. Briefly, the hero and his brother were in love with the same girl. They shipped out for World War One. The night before leaving, Our Hero slept with Girl; in those days they didn't use the F-word. Brother was jealous. He sent Hero on a difficult mission. Hero died. Brother was consumed with guilt. So was Girl. But Our Hero hadn't really been blown away. He was blind, you see, and didn't want to ruin Girl's life. The war ended happily ever after. So did the film.

Okay. Suppose over the last few years Stewie had undergone re-constructive surgery. Doctors had learned so many new techniques in that field.

Then what? Stewie murders Wylie. The perfect crime, masterminded by perfect Patty, committed by a dead person.

I was letting my imagination run amuck. But the Charles Manson Green Beret painting fit. Death is. Death is what? Psychosomatic? Psychosomatics dealt with the interrelationship between the emotions and the body. That fit. So did the swastika. Facial scarring.

Think. Think loud. Think strong. If my ridiculous theory had even the slightest hint of validity, why hadn't Wylie left the Manson painting to me? Why Doris Day?

Maybe I should examine Doris again, look beyond the pillows and the quote above her head.

Look for what?

I didn't know, but I suddenly itched to find out.

Bidding a fond farewell to Kim, I promised she could accompany me during my next trip to Hollywood, if she stopped accumulating demerits. Kim was a spunky kid, and I felt warm inside, very maternal, very un-Ingrid, very... I don't know... Grid? According to my crossword puzzles, a grid was a network of conductors for the distribution of electric power.

I thought about the movie *Carrie.* Carrie's conductor was in her head. She could move objects with her mind while my mind couldn't even conjure up the answer to a simple riddle.

How do you make a statue of an elephant?

As I drove home, my stomach growled. I would have to eat some food soon. Craving chicken fajitas with globs of guacamole, I parked in my driveway, navigated my porch, entered through my front door, then retrieved Doris Day's portrait from the cabinet.

Lugging her into the family room, I placed her against the marbled fireplace.

Hitchcock whined joyously.

Doris smiled brainlessly.

Eyeballing the painting with a vengeance, I saw the musical instruments.

Chapter Ten

I had contemplated the pillows, Doris Day's face, and the quote above her head, ignoring background images. Blending into the background, wallpapering the canvas, were miniature musical instruments—piano, drums, violins, sax, clarinet. Even if I had focused on the instruments, I probably would have dismissed them, because Doris had been one hell of a singer before she'd hit it big as a film star.

After last night, however, my senses were synchronized.

Alice Shaw Cooper played the clarinet, at least she did. She had marched during our high school football games, and she was always out of step. For example, the band members would be playing *Tie a Yellow Ribbon 'Round the Old Oak Tree,* their left feet stomping forward on yellow while Alice's left sneaker heel-toed the turf on ribbon.

I thought maybe Doris Day's clarinet was larger than the other instruments. Was that a clue?

What about Manson? Another clue? Or had Wylie portrayed Manson as a soldier because Wylie believed that war and Charlie were equally evil? Murder was murder, even if it was politically, therefore morally sanctioned. Once upon a time I had believed that, and I guess I still did.

Forget Manson! Forget Stewie! Sing sing a song.

I couldn't forget Stewie. But I could hide him inside my snagged pantyhose drawer, along with Wylie's rape-seduction.

Hitchcock sat by the answering machine, his maple-leaf ears on a par with its blinking red button. I gave Hitchcock's shaggy black head a pat, then hit MEMO.

"Ing, it's me. Bet you thought I was dead, huh? Well, I'm not. Surprised? Look, we have to talk. There's this restaurant across from the shopping mall, called the... um ... what the fuck is it called? The Fig Garden? No, the Olive Garden. Meet me there between five... no, five-thirty and six. Come alone. You like crossword puzzles so much. What's a seven letter word that means a state of distress?"

That was it. The whole message. I turned off my answering machine and stared at the phone. My condition was one of distress. Hitchcock bounded toward the kitchen and his doggie door. When he returned, he carried a dirt-encrusted bone in his mouth. Placing the bone at my feet, he wagged his tail. Then he flopped down in front of the coffee table.

"Thank you," I said. "What a good, sweet dog." But my voice seemed to come from far away... another planet, maybe.

I've never fainted in my life, not even when Dwight's car crashed and he lay there with his shattered body and shattered dreams, not even when the dreadful, deadful news about Stewie squeezed itself through multiple telephone lines. I'm simply not a better-go-fetch-the-smelling-salts- again kind of gal.

With that last thought, I plunged into darkness.

I blinked open my eyes to find Hitchcock licking my face. His tongue felt warm, then cold. So did I.

Blame my brief fainting spell on recent events. Blame it on the poisoned pie. Blame it on the gastric lavage. Or place the blame where it really belongs, on my ex husband who isn't my ex.

Bingo!

Barry Isaac Nicholas Gregory Oates had been born to a rather indecisive woman with several rich relatives to honor. For three days and two nights she'd called him Barry. Then, arriving home from the hospital, he had immediately been christened Bingo.

And Bingo was his name-oh.

His voice sounded the same, yet different. The genetic indecision lingered, but a brand new abrasiveness had been cultivated. And the crossword puzzle bit was a subtle reminder that he knew me well.

For instance, he knew that I would meet him at the restaurant. He knew that I had been searching for word of his whereabouts. And he probably suspected that I had given him up for dead.

I hadn't. Not really. I'd given him up for gone.

Bingo and I first bumped into each other on November 14, 1969, during the second Vietnam Moratorium Day. We were in Washington D.C. We marched single file, Bingo behind me. His body bumped mine, and for balance his hands circled my unfettered breasts. Bingo smelled clean and looked like Moondoggie—- Gidget's boyfriend—only blonde. We were both from Colorado, a good excuse to spend the night together. After all, we didn't want to sleep with strangers.

The next day 249,998 protesters joined us, and we lost each other in the crowd. Bingo's last words to me were: "Hell, no, we won't go. Ingrid, where the hell did you go?"

We met again on April 30, 1973, at a sleazy bar that served the best baby ribs in Denver. Richard Nixon gazed down at us from an overhead TV as he denied any involvement with the Watergate break-in, or any subsequent cover-up.

Bingo still looked like Sandra Dee's Moondoggie. "Ingrid," he said, "where the hell did you go?"

Exactly two months later, while John Dean testified that Nixon had discussed the use of executive privilege as a means of avoiding involvement in Watergate, Bingo and I flew to Vegas.

We didn't consummate our marriage the first night because Bingo was too busy gambling. I drank free shots of vodka, which made me uninhibited. "Bingo," I pleaded, "let's hit the sheets." But he wouldn't leave the dice table, so I retired to our hotel room alone. During our flight home, Bingo accused me of picking up the lounge piano player and consummating with him. That was the beginning.

Bingo was born in 1945, the Year of the Cock. Cocks are selfish and eccentric. Cocks are shrewd. Cocks are dreamers. My cocky husband had two obsessions. One was jealousy. The other was his plan to accumulate a portion of the family fortune.

While I composed movie scores, Bingo spent hours composing long letters to Barry, Isaac, Gregory and Nicholas, mapping out intricate investment opportunities. The only relative who responded was Isaac. NOT INTERESTED he printed across a postcard. The postcard made Bingo impotent.

That didn't stop him. He had in his possession a Hallmark card that read: CONGRATULATIONS ON YOUR NEW BABY BOY. Inside the card, Nicholas Oates had penned: "Thanks for the name, Cousin. I'll leave the little nipper something in my will, ha-ha."

Bingo took it personally. And literally. After Nicholas, a successful Chicago real estate developer, passed away, Bingo found an attorney, then proceeded to hound Mrs. Nicholas Oates and her kids, Herbert, Beatrice, and Stanley.

I listened and sympathized because it was easier than arguing, but I defied my husband on two occasions. First, I refused to destroy my prom picture. Second, I insisted on using my maiden name. I needed my own identity, I told Bingo, although, truthfully, I didn't want my movie credits to read Ingrid Oates. To me, it sounded like a breakfast cereal.

Anyway, I begged my jealous, impotent, obsessed husband to seek help. Instead, he stole my prom picture and disappeared.

Did I mention that Bingo left me thousands of dollars in debt? "I hate to say I told you so," said Mom. Insolvency was one reason for my sparse wardrobe.

Speaking of clothes, I couldn't wear my old sweatshirt and air-conditioned jeans to the Olive Garden. Oh, the hostess wouldn't kick me out; I had eaten at fine dining establishments where the clientele sported I'M WITH STUPID tees. However, I had just conjured up an image of my mother, who tended to shudder when my purse didn't match my shoes.

"I know what you'd say if you could talk," I told Hitchcock, who was busy gnawing his dirt- encrusted bone. "You'd say that my mother has no control over me anymore. It's simply not true. You see, there's this invisible umbilical cord."

Hitchcock whined and snuffled. He was one hell of a sympathetic listener.

"Bingo's seven-letter word probably means divorce, wouldn't you agree?"

This time Hitchcock didn't reply, so I re-ran the answering machine tape, listened to Bingo again, then heard a second message.

"Ingrid, it's three-forty-five, and I hope you're napping. Please call an attorney and tell him to get down to the precinct

ASAP. Remember that I love..."

The rest of Ben's message was smothered by atmospheric disturbances. In other words, his you was lost in static.

"Ben wants me to get in touch with an attorney," I told Hitchcock. "Should I ring up Bingo's lawyer? No. He's a sleaze. Besides, I still owe him money."

Desperate, I found the cable bill envelope and called Cee-Cee, long distance. She said she knew a good attorney. Perceptive as always, calming me down, she promised to contact the woman immediately.

Immediately took twenty minutes. Cee-Cee called back and said the matter had been taken care of.

Thank God for a little help from your friends.

Six-fifteen. Six-thirty. I lounged inside the Olive Garden's frugal lounge. It was no larger than an oversized carport, and all the miniature round tables were occupied. Next to me stood a middle-aged man. His T-shirt read: LIFE'S HARD THEN YOU DIE. He wasn't Bingo.

I had forgotten my cocky husband's third obsessive quality. He was always late. Like Marilyn Monroe, he wouldn't arrive until he was prepared to give a good performance. Unlike Marilyn, Bingo's performances usually lacked sensitivity, not to mention self-assurance. Indecisiveness isn't really genetic, but it is environmental.

My current environment was congested; wall to wall people. Lounging next to Life's Hard Then You Die were three giggly middle-aged women sipping margaritas. The heaviest kept saying, "It's my birthday, gonna get a free dessert, they give free desserts here." Several kids with colorful balloons played hide and seek. One little girl tried to crouch behind my beige leather boots. Her sticky hand clutched at my green, belted shirtwaist, circa 1965, just before she fell on her rump, bursting her balloon, then bursting into tears.

Thank God my old dress survived. Fortunately, an expensive pair of boots can make any outfit stylish.

Unfortunately, the same could not be said for Bingo.

He wore brand new lizard-skin boots, ancient Levi's, and a red plaid shirt that had seen better days. The frayed collar and cuffs looked sad and weary. So did Bingo's frayed silver-blond hair and faded blue eyes.

"I asked for smoking," was his opening line.

"Okay, Bingo, but I gave it up."

"Sure you did," he said enigmatically, then bicked a Pall Mall and lapsed into silence.

I couldn't help comparing him to Ben. They were the same height, tall. They had once possessed the same muscular bodies, only Bingo had let his body go slack. He wasn't fat, but I could see that a paunch was beginning to form. Lines grooved his face like an old Smokey Robinson record, and his once obstinate chin sagged then tightened slightly with each deep draw on his cigarette. Tobacco flecked Bingo's chapped lips while Ben's lips practically invited tongue-teasing.

"You look okay, Ing," said Bingo. "Different."

"After you disappeared, I lost weight. Speaking of disappeared, Bingo——"

"Do you want something to drink?" His thumb tiddly-winked the snaps on his shirt.

"No. I want you to tell me where the hell you've been."

Truthfully, I wanted to scream, pound his chest with my fists, stomp on his reptilian boots, bash his head with a bar stool. But I couldn't. Because we had to act civilized. Which was probably why he had chosen this crowded restaurant for our secret rendezvous.

"Bingo, where have you been? Answer me!"

Before he could reply, a young voice boomed "Johnson, party of three" over the lobby's microphone. Whereupon the three giggly women grabbed Life's Hard Then You Die by the arms and guided him toward the lobby. He had obviously been invited to their party, lucky stiff.

Glowering at Bingo again, I had a premonition that my own party wouldn't be so giggly.

The mike voice boomed, "Barry, party of two. Barry party," she repeated impatiently.

"That's us, Ing," said Bingo.

"Why Barry? Why not Oates?"

"I have my reasons."

"Barry party, last call."

"Let's go." Carefully snuffing out his cigarette, Bingo pocketed the unfiltered butt.

As luck would have it, our table was situated between the three giggly women and their guest, and five, count 'em *five* bouncy balloon kids. It was also non-smoking.

I started to rise, but Bingo said, "Sit down, Ing. Let's just order our drinks and talk, okay?"

"Talk first, drink later. Look around, Bingo. Wall to wall people, just like the lounge. Our server's probably a tad busy."

As if on cue, a cranberry-colored apron blocked my vision and somebody said, "Ingrid Beaumont! What the hell are *you* doing here?"

I gazed up at jutting breasts, a white blouse stained with tomato sauce, a gaudy Daffy Duck tie, a platinum ponytail, and braces. "Hi, Tad. What luck! I was hoping——"

"We'd like to order drinks," Bingo interrupted. "I'd also like an ashtray, please."

His please sounded like bitch.

"You're seated in non-smoking, sir," said Tad. "That means you can't smoke. Sorry."

Her sorry sounded like screw you.

I heaved a deep sigh. From experience, I knew that if you pissed off a waitress your service was apt to be slow or sloppy or both. Glancing at the drink menu, I selected one at random. "Would you bring me a Roman Colada, please Tad? And my friend here will have... do you still drink Stoli neat?"

"Double," he replied. "Forget the olives."

"Would you care for a lemon twist, sir?" asked Tad.

"No, dammit!"

"Thank you, sir, I'll be right back." Tad approached the balloon table. "Refills?" she asked sweetly, eyeing several Coke glasses. Then she ambled over to the three ladies and their guest. "Ain't it the truth!" she exclaimed, ogling Life's shirt. "I understand we're celebrating a birthday tonight. Twenty-one?" The heavy lady shrieked and giggled. "May I suggest a bottle of wine? There's the wine list, right there, printed on the menu. And let's select an appetizer, shall we?"

"Shit!" Bingo stood and stomped through the room. When he returned, he carried one glass.

"Where's mine?"

"I couldn't remember what you ordered."

"Pina Colada."

"No. It was some stupid Italian drink."

Bingo's voice sounded funny, not funny ha-ha, funny strange. His silvered hair was drenched with perspiration, and his face was so pale his eyes took on a brighter shade of blue.

"What's wrong, Bingo?"

"Nothing." He glanced around the crowded room as if searching for a hidden nest of rattlesnakes.

Unwrapping my napkin, I fiddled with one knife, one spoon, and two forks. "Where have you been, Bingo? And why did you want to meet me here tonight?"

"I'm in trouble, Ing."

Trouble. The seven-letter word for distress was trouble.

"What kind of trouble, Bingo?"

Before he could answer, Tad placed our drinks and a plastic bread basket on the table. "Are you ready to order?" she asked. "Our special tonight is Shrimp Alfredo. It cost—-"

"Fine," said Bingo.

"You're allergic to shrimp," I said. "Bring him spaghetti, Tad."

"Do you want spaghetti, sir?"

"Fine," said Bingo.

"Meatballs, sir? Sausage? Meat sauce?"

"Yes," said Bingo. After polishing off his first drink, he reached for the second glass.

"Which one, sir? Meatballs?"

"Tad," I said, "my friend isn't feeling very well. Just bring him spaghetti. I'll have the same."

"That's stupid, Ingrid. You can eat spaghetti at home."

"You choose, Tad. No shrimp, no veal, okay?"

"Soup or salad?"

"Tad, leave us alone, I'm not kidding. Salad's fine, and don't you dare ask what kind of dressing." I glanced toward the Roman Colada. "When you have time, please bring me a real drink. Vodka, splash of tonic."

"Stoli?"

"It doesn't matter."

"You're right, it doesn't matter." Abruptly, she turned and walked toward the giggly women.

"What kind of trouble, Bingo?"

"Well, I... shit! Doesn't she ever leave the room to get food or something?" Bingo gestured toward Tad, who was within earshot, making a play for Life's Hard Then You Die.

"Hey, he's mine," screeched the birthday girl. "I found him first. Bring us some more stick things or I'll find a manager."

"Yes, ma'am, right away."

I noticed we had stick things too, and extended the bread basket toward Bingo. "Here, eat. Soak up some of that vodka, kiddo." My ex-ex really did look sick, generating my kiddo. "What kind of trouble, Bingo?"

Ignoring the basket, he lit a Pall Mall.

"It's non-smoking," I reminded him.

"Fuck you! Fuck everybody!"

"You're not s'posed to say fuck," said a balloon boy. He stood by my elbow, right next to one of his little sisters. "And you're not s'posed to smoke."

"True," I said. "But kids are *supposed* to behave and stay with their parents."

"You're gonna' kill yourself, Mister. You're gonna' get cancer and die. You'd better put that out."

While I watched Tad balance an overloaded tray, Bingo extended his cigarette and burst the kid's balloon. It made one hell of a noise.

The birthday girl reacted by dropping her wine glass and spilling red wine all over her white sweater.

Life's Hard stood up and tried to catch the wine glass, but caught Birthday Girl's breast instead. Birthday Girl instinctively lashed out with one pointy-toed foot, kicking Life's Hard between his thighs. He clutched his crotch, sang "Ohsitohshitohshit," and sank back onto his chair.

Balloon Boy said, "You're not s'posed to say shit." His little sister chanted, "Pop my bloon, too, Mister, pop my bloon, too, Mister, pop..."

Bingo complied, probably to shut her up.

This time the unexpected bang caused Tad to jump. Her tray jack fell, and her tray seemed to jump out of her hand. Pasta, salad, bread sticks, and my vodka splash landed everywhere. Tad landed on the floor. "Oh, God," she wailed, "I think I broke my foot or sprained my ankle, something hurts."

"Son of a bitch!" shouted Balloon Boy's father. Lasagna covered his head like a cheesy toupee.

"Don't cuss, dear," said his wife. Removing lettuce leaves and black olives from her prominent bust, she turned toward Bingo. "You tried to burn my children with a lit cigarette, you bastard. I'm gonna' call the cops."

Bingo bolted.

"Wait!" I yelled, rising. "Bingo, wait!"

I fumbled inside my purse, extracted a ten dollar bill, and tossed it toward the Roman Colada. Stepping over Tad's prone body, I heard her say, "Ingrid, it does matter. I've got to talk to you."

Ignoring Tad, weaving my way through five balloon kids, two bus boys, and one apoplectic manager, I sprinted toward the lobby. Bingo wasn't there. I checked the lounge, the parking lot, and ultimately the mens' room. No Bingo.

"Did you see a tall man wearing boots, jeans, and a red plaid shirt?" I asked the hostess.

She stared at me as if I had lost my mind. The restaurant was filled with men wearing boots, jeans, and red plaid shirts. In fact, somebody could have staged a production number for a new musical called *Colorado*.

"He looks a little like Moondoggie," I said desperately. "Only older."

"Moon who?"

"Doggie. Never mind. My friend has white-blond hair, and he was in one hell of a hurry."

She glanced down at her pad of crossed-out names. "Mr. Barry?"

"No. Yes."

"He's gone, ma'am."

"Shit!"

"That's what he said."

I backtracked toward the dining room, searching for Tad. And found her, standing in a small alcove near the kitchen—the servers' station. Surrounded by beverage apparatus, holding an ice-filled napkin against her ankle, she looked like a genetically-altered flamingo.

"Talk now, talk fast," I said.

"I saw Wylie the night before he was killed, Ingrid. I was supposed to go home with Junior Hartsel, but he left after I danced with Ben. I guess he was jealous. Anyway, I drank too much champagne. I'm ashamed to say it, but I was standing in the corner, singing round 'em up, herd 'em out, rawhide, and showing off my butt. I'm so embarr—-"

"Hurry!"

"Dwight wouldn't let me drive. I felt sick, so he and Alice took me to their house. Dwight went straight to bed. Alice brewed coffee. Somebody knocked. Alice opened the door. Wylie walked in. Alice was so mad, she forgot I was there. Wylie didn't see me. I was on the couch, curled into a ball, wishing I could throw up and get it over with."

"Tad!"

"Wylie said he was sorry. Alice began to cry. Then Alice said something that sounded like tomorrow. I'm pretty sure she said tomorrow, Ingrid, even though she was sobbing. Wylie told one of his riddles, some dumb joke about mulligan stew."

"How do you make an *elephant* stew?"

"That's it. Wylie said he couldn't wait. I passed out. Later I woke up and went looking for a bathroom. There was a lamp inside this guest bedroom, across from the bathroom. Its bulb wasn't very bright, but I could see them. I guess they were in such a big hurry they didn't lock the door. They didn't even close the door. I guess they figured Dwight couldn't walk in on them and I was out cold. At first I couldn't see Wylie's dick, just his butt. But he must have sensed that someone was watching. He rolled away from Alice, and he was under the light, and he was still... um... aroused, and I could see that he wasn't wearing a condom. Isn't that stupid, Ingrid?"

Not really, I thought, because Alice had been a virgin. She had never been... shall we say tainted?... by other men, not even her husband.

How do you make an elephant stew? Keep him waiting.

Obviously, Wylie couldn't wait to get it on with Alice. But Alice had waited thirty years.

Dear God! After boffing Mother F. Goose, did Wylie refuse to divorce Patty? Could an angry, rejected, no-conscience Alice kill in cold blood?

Maybe.

A definite maybe.

Chapter Eleven

My first impulse was to visit Alice and verify Tad's story, but Alice could wait. Other, more pressing matters made me splash through parking lot puddles, fumble for my jeep keys, almost strip my transmission shifting gears, then run three yellow lights that were more red than yellow.

Would Bingo leave another message on my machine?

Was Ben home from the precinct?

Parking in my driveway, I saw Ben's rental car, which meant nothing, since Ben had been towed away, so to speak, by Miller.

It occurred to me that Ben's car looked impersonal, almost alien. Jeep was my friend. I had driven Jeep up and down the mountains, seeking inspiration. Once upon a time, I had caught a TV special about Paul Simon, who composed his music inside a house by the ocean. Jeep was my house, Pikes Peak my ocean.

Why was I contemplating jeeps versus rental cars? Why was I suddenly scared to confront Ben? Or was I just scared? I had this funny feeling in the pit of my stomach. Intuition? Hunger? Or did Wylie's killer lurk? No way! Hitchcock would be barking his head off. Unless it was Bingo. We had adopted Hitchcock nine months before Bingo hit the road, and while my ex-ex tended to verbally abuse wives, waitresses, and balloon kids, he had this thing for animals.

"I'm in trouble," he had said. What kind of trouble? And why did he contact me after the reunion, immediately following Wylie's murder? Newspapers had touted the reunion, touted Wylie. Bingo, obsessively jealous, possessed Wylie's picture. But Bingo was a pacifist. He couldn't kill.

Yeah. Right. People changed. I had changed. Patty had changed. And Alice, married, moral to the max, had slept with the late great Wylie Jamestone.

Why would Wylie sleep with Alice? He had fame and fortune, thus could score with any number of young, nubile nymphs. Except I wasn't young or nubile. Why "score" with me?

Was it because I had mentioned Bingo's impotence and my subsequent chastity?

In other words, Wylie didn't have to worry about dropping dead after sleeping with me, and he definitely didn't have to worry about Alice. She hadn't even slept with Dwight, who had slept with Tad, who had probably banged the whole football team.

Alice and I had once rented *Sleepless in Seattle*. Alice said she loved that movie because there weren't any scenes where Tom Hanks and Meg Ryan buffed each other. Alice meant boffed, of course. After one glass of diluted sherry, she had drunkenly confessed that she had never buffed Dwight.

Bottom line: Alice was clean as a whistle, unbuffed. Wylie was scared of AIDS. In a weird sense, it all made perfect sense.

A muted glow emanated from my family room's window. I didn't remember flicking the wall switch off, so I could have left it on. *Stop procrastinating, Beaumont! Open the damn door!*

Hitchcock greeted me joyously.

Doris Day smiled brainlessly.

Ben's eyes were icy.

"Good-bye, Ingrid," he said. "I thought you'd be here waiting, but you obviously consider Wylie's treasure hunt more important..." He paused, breathing hard. "I wish I could say it's been fun and games, but all it's been are games."

Staring down at my boots, contemplating toenail polish, I noticed four distinct objects—Ben's Nikes and a set of matching luggage. Since I was bothered, to put it mildly, I blurted the first thing that popped into my head. "Would you cook me one last meal?"

"I'm the condemned prisoner, Ingrid."

"Please, Ben, I'm hungry."

"Where the hell have you been?"

"At the Olive Garden restaurant."

"That's probably why you're hungry."

"I didn't eat, dammit!"

"You went to a restaurant, but didn't eat? I suppose you've smoked pot, but never inhaled. What did you do at your damn restaurant? Visit their rest room?"

"No! I met Bingo and—"

"You played bingo?"

"Not played, met."

Alice's newsletter had publicized the blissful union between Ingrid Anastasia Beaumont and Barry Isaac Nicholas Gregory Oates. During a calmer moment, Ben might have been able to decipher an obvious acronym. But he wasn't calm. He wasn't even listening.

"I've tried to understand why you want to jeopardize our relationship," he said. "Maybe your so-called ex was right. Maybe he sensed your deranged devotion to Wylie and that's why he took off with your prom picture."

"God, Ben, that's so unfair."

"You have the nerve to talk about unfair after your Patty accusation?" His craggy jaw jutted. "Patty's vulnerable. For Christ's sake, she just lost her husband."

"Her *husband* entrusted me with a mission. If I got killed and left you a clue, wouldn't you follow up on it?"

"That's a ridiculous hypothesis."

"Patty wants to sleep with you, Ben. If I'm dead, it will make it so much easier."

"I'm shoving off, Ingrid. I just waited around to wish you a happy life."

"You could have left me a note. Everybody leaves me notes," I said, trying to sound tough, failing miserably.

"A note would have been inappropriate, all things considered."

"Define 'all things considered.' My multiple orgasms? My near hit with death?"

"Good-bye, Ingrid."

"Hold it! Are you going back to Tulsa?"

"No. Wylie's memorial service is Sunday. Besides, the cops told me to stick aroun—"

"Sunday? Why would Patty wait so long?"

"Celebs have to adjust their schedules."

"Oh. Of course. And Wylie's sister—"

"Isn't coming."

"Why not?"

"I don't know. Patty didn't offer an explanation."

"When did you talk to Patty?"

"Are you nuts? Last night. We discussed more than milk and cookies."

"Not cookies, Ben, pie! Poisoned pie!"

"Whatever."

"Do you..." I swallowed rocks for the third time in twelve hours. "Do you plan to stay at Patty's house?"

He shook his head. "I'm not an idiot. You're playing detective, and you believe Patty and I are lovers. Why would I stay there?"

"I didn't say you and Patty——"

"You didn't have to. Your expression this afternoon said it all."

Rats! Was I getting that transparent? I had trained myself to feign dispassion, exhibit frigidity. Indifference is a powerful aphrodisiac, especially in Hollywood. I had been awarded more than one assignment based on my lukewarm attitude, I'm not exactly sure why. Human nature, I guess.

Mother Nature was whipping up another thunderstorm. I could hear my window panes shudder. And Hitchcock, not the bravest mutt in town, was trying to wedge himself between Doris Day and the fireplace grate.

Glancing toward the window, I saw that there was a bee trapped between the screen and glass. "What," I murmured, "goes zub zub?"

"A bee flying backwards," said Ben.

"I thought you weren't good at riddles."

"I can spell."

"Okay, but you can't go outside in this weather," I pleaded. "Stay until morning. Please?"

Ben hesitated.

Then I blew it.

"What happened at the precinct, Ben? Why did you ask for an attorney? Does Miller honestly think you had something to do with Wylie's murder? It couldn't be the jacket alone; that's too circumstantial. What other evidence have they collected? Anything that pinpoints sweet, innocent Patty-Cakes?"

"Riddle yourself to sleep, Ingrid." His icy eyes melted a smidgen. "I'll be at the Broadmoor. Call if you need me."

"Ben," I called, "I need you."

But the bang of the front door smothered my cry.

I sank onto the couch like a slo-mo deep sea diver. Hitchcock sensed my mood. Tail between his legs, he pressed his fuzzy muzzle between my knees.

"Did you know you're a daddy?" I scratched his ears. "The bitch next door had pups. Don't love them too much, baby, because they won't stick around for long."

Hitchcock whined and burrowed closer while I thought of two things. First, Jimi Hendrix had said that the story of love is hello and good-bye... and hello again. Second, the Broadmoor hotel was only a few short blocks from Patty Jamestone's house.

I shifted positions on the couch. That way my gaze could wander toward the window and I could see Ben return if he changed his mind. I pictured him bursting into my family room, arms extended, his mouth forming the words "I'm sorry." My mind conjured up background music. Something romantic, something Sleepless-in-Seattle, something Barbra Streisand and Neil Diamond.

There was a small hole in the window screen. The bee buzzed frantically, failing to catch the hole. He reminded me of me. Watching the bee, my hand drifted under one poofy couch cushion, whereupon I encountered a lump surrounded by cellophane.

The missing fortune cookie!

Its wrapper had a tiny printed name——The Four Leaf Clover Company——plus an address that included the words Clear Lake City, Texas. Its strip of paper read: "A peace rally is as much of a misnomer as a slumber party."

I slumbered on the couch, waking once to scarf down a huge bowl of banana-garnished Cheerios, twice to use the bathroom, and three times to check on the bee's progress. Finally, as the sun ventured to rise through left-over storm clouds, I struggled to open my stubborn window, then unhinge the screen. Ben had fitted the window with an old closet-stored screen while I was in the hospital. Did that mean he believed my kill Ingrid supposition? Or was he merely being considerate? Probably the latter.

Just like Ben, the bee winged his way toward a more receptive environment, still buzzing up a storm.

It was too early to call Texas, so I brewed coffee, avidly consumed a thick peanut-butter-banana sandwich, showered, dumped a ton of laundry into my washer, and fed Hitchcock. Just for grins, I checked the credit limit on my last Visa statement, shook my head, then reached for my American Express card—don't leave home without it.

I glanced at my ersatz Coca-Cola clock, the kitchen phone extension, the clock, the phone again. Then, after stuffing my laundry into the dryer, I touch-toned 1-713-555-1212.

"The Four Leaf Clover Company," I said, feeling dumb.

The operator's computerized tape recorder actually had a number, only the business was based in Houston.

Strike one.

I was positive Wylie's sister knew the answer to my fortune cookie conundrum. She lived in Clear Lake City, not Houston proper. But to Patty, who believed that Brooklyn Heights was a spit away from Long Island, Clear Lake City and Houston were the same. They weren't, of course. It would be like saying that Disneyland was an L.A. suburb.

I had once visited my friend Charlie Daniels, who was singing his devil-went-down-to-Georgia song for the movie *Urban Cowboy*, filmed in Pasadena Texas, truly a spit away from Clear Lake City. During that visit, I had fallen madly in lust with John Travolta and "done lunch" with Diane Jamestone.

Searching my memory bank, I tried to recollect everything I knew about Wylie's sister. Diane "Woody" Jamestone looked like Woody Allen with breasts. While Wylie's resemblance to Allen had been charismatic, Diane's had been catastrophic. For reasons known only to her, and possibly Wylie, she had never opted for plastic surgery and/or marriage. She worked as a paste-up artist for the local telephone directory.

Information had her number. Woody's machine answered. Her recorded voice was brusque and to the point. "If your call's important," she said, "leave your name and number at the sound of the beep. If you're calling about Wylie Jamestone, fuck off."

Strike two!

"Hello, Woody, are you there?" I waited; no response. "This is Ingrid Beaumont. I'm not calling about Wylie. Well, in a way I guess I am. This is stupid. Look, I'm flying to Houston and I have your address, at least I think I do. Please let me talk to you. It's important. I've got a message from Wylie, something he said the night before he was killed."

Then I hung up. I didn't care to overstate my case and I wanted to pique Woody's curiosity.

I spread the last of my peanut butter between two slices of bread. The bananas were depleted, but not my curiosity. Ben would probably call it meddling, or, considering that he was a veterinarian, he might call it mousing.

"Curiosity killed the cat," I told Hitchcock.

His ears twitched at the word cat, yet he remained by my side. Maybe he wanted to catch a few crumbs from my sandwich. Maybe he sensed my pending departure and wanted a few crumbs of affection.

I knew exactly how he felt.

Mesa's tiny plane hop-scotched mountains, all the way to Denver. Fortunately, the Continental pilot was in a solicitous mood. Heading toward Texas, he flew above the clouds, even managed to avoid turbulence. Which was more than I could say for my choppy mentality.

Why was I wasting my time on this ridiculous odyssey? In all likelihood, the fortune cookies had nothing to do with Wylie's murder. Yes, they did. Forget woman's intuition. I've known men who have more intuition in their genitalia than a woman has in her little finger. But I couldn't forget that Wylie had recommended the take-out restaurant. He had mentioned it during Alice's Cheyenne Mountain Resort cocktail party, and his manner had been... urgent. Typical Wylie. He couldn't just say: "If perchance I get my bald pate pulverized, there's this fortune cookie clue."

Damn! I was acting squirrelly again. Rather than winging my way toward Houston, I should have been searching for the perfect way to trap perfect Patty. And I should have been mourning the loss of the only man I've ever loved.

However, truthfully, I was beginning to experience relief. Ben made me feel too dependent, too Hitchcockian. Sit, Ingrid! Stay, Ingrid! Chase the cat rather than a killer, Ingrid!

Also, Ben was assuming Hitchcock's persona—the director, not my dog. Ready, action, cut! Stop behaving like such a smartass, Ingrid. This scene plays better if your audience suspects foul play while you act unaware. Remember *Notorious*? Remember Bergman's performance? Remember how the audience knew she'd been poisoned long before she did?

In other words, Patty Jamestone was *friend*. She didn't kill Wylie. How can we be so sure? Easy. She said so.

Yeah. Right. Allow the audience to suspect Patty. Then, later, Ben can come to my rescue, just like Cary Grant. But first Ben has to come to his senses. Which might be difficult since he's probably buffing Patty.

Did I say choppy mentality? A better word might be tumultuous. Because I began to play a game called "What If."

What if Ben wasn't boffing Patty? What if Patty wasn't guilty? What if there was a simple explanation for her lie about Ben's jacket, just like the creme, milk, and pie? What if Stewie had returned from Nam? What if Tad had fabricated that story about Alice and Wylie? What if she hadn't, and Dwight found out, and Dwight killed Wylie? What if Wylie had met Alice tomorrow-- Sunday morning—and insisted they quit messing around? What if the Continental pilot had forgotten to take his No-Doze and the plane crashed?

It didn't. We landed safely.

"Have a nice day," said the clean-cut discount car rental lad, as he handed me my receipt and a map.

He didn't have any discount jeeps handy so I settled for a nondescript blue compact, totally devoid of personality. Except it coughed a lot when I keyed its ignition. The ashtray was filled with cigarette butts so the car probably suffered from second-hand smoke inhalation.

Have a nice *day*? My plane had landed at 5:24 P.M. and by the time I reached Clear Lake City it was eight-thirty. Due to incredible rush-hour traffic snarls, plus an automotive marathon led by several mechanized tortoises, I had established a rapport with my rental car. For instance, I knew that her steering wheel pulled to the left, her seat belt chafed, and her radio was stuck on Kenny Rogers.

I gassed up and washed the bugs off my windshield while Texas-style humidity bathed me in sweat.

According to my mental Colorado clock it was only seven-thirty, a respectable hour to visit. Should I eat something first? Was Woody a night person or a morning person? I'm a morning person, which means my wits are razor sharp around dawn.

Unfortunately, my return flight took off at 10:58 A.M. Which might limit my mousing. Rats! I was procrastinating.

Street lights and house lights helped me decipher Have A Nice Day's map. The address inside my purse—which didn't match my boots, laundered jeans, or gray PROPERTY OF THE BRONCOS sweatshirt—was The Four Leaf Clover Company's address. But the name on the mailbox read Diane Jamestone.

Home run!

A brand new yellow Prelude squatted inside Woody's carport, and her mailbox was illuminated by a street lamp. But her house was as darkly ambiguous as Ben Cassidy's eyes. Could Woody hit the sheets when the moon extinguished the sun's lightbulb? Some people did. My mother did.

Never visit without phoning first, my mother insists. And never visit someone's house without toting a token gift.

I didn't have a gift, I didn't have a phone handy, and I didn't have the nerve to knock on Woody's door and piss her off. Anyway, if she had reacted in a positive manner to my answering machine message, wouldn't she be anxiously awaiting my arrival?

I was procrastinating again, bathed in sweat again. What the hell had happened to Mickey... Spillane, not Mouse?

She was hungry, thirsty, exhausted, that's all.

A motel was the obvious solution. Dinner, sleep, an early wake-up call.

I drove to the nearest motel, dumped my one piece of carry-on luggage atop the room's double bed, yanked the paper strip from the toilet seat, flushed, ran a comb through my tangled hair, locked the door, then found a corner table inside the motel's pseudo-western restaurant, which, thank God, had a bartender. And a piano. And a fifty-ish piano player, who glanced toward my table.

"Jesus Christ!" he shouted. "I'll be damned! You're Rose Stewart!" Which was pretty ballsy, considering that I was seated near a contingency of Bible-toting Southern Baptists.

He attempted an off-key rendition of *Clowns* while all eyes turned in my direction, and I had a feeling the Baptists were muttering: "Who the heck is Rose Stewart?"

The lounge entertainer's loud voice prodded the lounging waitress. She scurried to my side.

"What can I getcha, Miz Stewart?"

"A steak," I replied. "Very rare, almost mooing. And a double vodka on the rocks."

She returned a few minutes later with two double vodkas. Happy hour?

"Buddy," she said, nodding toward the piano player, "told me to bring you this here second drink, his treat."

"Give Buddy my thanks."

The first drink soothed. The second anesthetized every butterfly inside my stomach. By the time my burnt-to-a-crisp steak arrived, I had consumed another vodka, purchased by a lounger who apparently knew who the heck Rose Stewart was.

The lumpy baked potato looked as mushy as The Beaver's friend, Lumpy. Tempted to send the whole meal back, I simply ordered one more drink, lots of olives please. After all, I desperately needed food, and a balanced diet included vegetables.

"Pimientos are really sweet peppers," I told Buddy, who toted my drink. "And sweet peppers are veggies, right?"

"What the hell are you doing here, Rose? Slumming?"

"What do you mean?"

"This motel ain't exactly the Ritz."

"It's better than a jail cell."

"How many jail cells have you visited recently?" he asked belligerently.

"None. Ben almost went to jail, though."

"Who's Ben?"

I felt the vodka slosh inside my cranium, above the bridge of my nose. "Ben's a vet," I explained.

Buddy misunderstood. "Me, too," he said bitterly. "I had myself a nice concert career started before they shipped me off to

Nam." He held out his hand, missing two fingers. "Landed near a land mine, but I was lucky. Could have lost more than fingers, if you get my drift."

Now I understood the belligerence. I had encountered it many times before. After all, I had protested the war while my buddies had fought for freedom, apple pie, John Wayne, the IRS, and robinhood.

Not robinhood. Motherhood. I was definitely feeling the vodka. "Hey, did you meet Stewie over there?" I slurred.

"Who's Stewie?"

"Rain."

"Yeah, I remember rain. And mud. Jesus, the mud!"

"I think Stewie died but maybe he didn't."

"Lots of guys died, Rose."

"We all die by bits and pieces, Buddy."

I had by-passed uninhibited and reached maudlin. Maybe I hadn't by-passed uninhibited. Buddy was looking real good. His leg muscles bunched beneath his butt-tight denims, and his mustache reminded me of Tom Selleck's. Although I had often fantasized sleeping with Selleck, I didn't want to boff Buddy. Yet, I wanted hugs. From a stranger? Buddy wasn't a stranger. After all, he'd known me as Rose Stewart for twenty-plus years.

Buddy sensed my need, probably because I had moved my chair closer to his and was resting my dizzy head against his blue button-down-collar shirt. No dummy, Buddy. His hand explored beneath my sweatshirt, and I soon discovered that a man didn't need five fingers to caress a woman's nipple. One thumb did nicely. I tried to stifle my moan.

"Let's get out of here," he said.

I didn't want to get out of here with Buddy, but I had obviously responded to his touch. Bothered, I said the first thing that came to mind. "Don't you have to play the piano?"

"Who's gonna' listen?"

I glanced around. The room was empty. Even the bartender and waitress had vanished. "Where'd they go, Buddy?"

"It's Wednesday, Rosie. We don't get crowds until the weekend."

"I meant the bartender and waitress."

"They hit the kitchen. Chow time."

Buddy's thumb continued stroking, and I had the insane notion that I was being unfaithful to Ben, who was probably at this very moment boffing Patty. Shaking myself free from Buddy, staggering upright, I realized that everything was out of focus, and it wasn't just the vodka. Tears blurred my vision. If Ben and Patty were having an affair, would screwing Buddy even the score? I flipped an imaginary coin. Heads, I'd sleep alone. Tails, we'd chow down inside my room. The imaginary coin spun, landed. "Goodnight, Buddy!" I said emphatically.

"I have condoms, Rosie."

"I love you, too."

Laughter dried my tears, until I reached for my purse.

"Where's my purse? Damn! I left it in my room. How can I pay for that overcooked steak and lumpy potato?"

"They'll put it on my tab, Rosie." Circling my waist with his good hand, Buddy's fingers patted my bulging front pocket. He fished the room key out, then winked. "Gonna take a sentimental journey," he sang. "Gonna fly you to the moon."

I remembered Bingo's long-ago accusation and my denial. I remembered the Vegas piano player who had sung about sentimental journeys and flying to the moon. In other words, why worry about Ben when I was still married to Bingo?

Overcome by another laughing fit, I let Buddy guide me to my room, insert the key, kick open the door, then flick the wall's light switch.

I screamed. Granted, my scream wasn't a piercing scream. However, it was loud enough for Hitchcock to chow down some butt, if he'd been there. Except Hitchcock would have barked, growled, frightened the intruder away before he or she could search my one piece of luggage, pull drawers from their runners, smash the bedside lamp, slash the mattress, and empty my purse. Before she could leave her lipstick-printed message across the mirror; a rather cryptic message that read: IT'S TIME TO STRAY

Why she? Because, although my purse and luggage had been ransacked, this aging hippie didn't wear lipstick. So the officious intruder was a woman.

Or a clown.

Chapter Twelve

My head no longer sloshed with vodka. Instead, it sloshed with the alternative rock theme I had created for last year's macho detective, and the hoe-down I had written for his sidekick, a country-western singer making his film debut.

After giving the movie two thumbs down—-way down—-S & E had praised the score, which had led to my present assignment.

How I wished that my Clear Lake City cops were Danny Glover and Mel Gibson, but God was playing one of his/her practical jokes again. *My* cops were an old crusty buffalo named Butler and a young buck-toothed rabbit named Morgan.

Butler couldn't care less about my trashed motel room, especially after Buddy introduced me as Rose Stewart.

"Ingrid Beaumont," I corrected, staring at the broken lamp and ruined shade with its dumb depiction of Roy Rogers and Trigger. Once upon a time, I had carried Roy to school. He was on my lunch box, strumming his guitar, singing an anthem to my mother's peanut-butter-banana sandwiches. Later, older, I toted a plain olive-green lunch box, shaped like a meatloaf. Patty toted Elvis. Often we traded—-sandwiches, not lunch pails.

My thoughts wandered because I was scared. In fact, the echo of my scream still rested between my throat and my tongue.

"I'm sorry you were frightened, Miz Beaumont," said Morgan, who, except for his buck teeth, could have doubled for my car rental lad.

"Damn Jane Fonda!" Butler shouted. He was approaching retirement age and apparently recognized my name if not my face. "Damn all you Jane Fondas!"

Was he putting me in the same league as Jane? I was flattered. I was also puzzled. Why would somebody scribble it's time to stray across my mirror. What did it mean?

Was the message a sexual innuendo? But how could the intruder know that I'd be tempted to stray? Had Ben followed me and discovered my lounge tete-a-tete? Had Bingo flown to Texas, then flown into one of his jealous rages? Neither theory made any sense. Ben and I were finished. Bingo and I had been finished for years. Why turn my motel room upside down? Where did the lipstick come from?

Who wore red lipstick? Patty. Alice. Tad. Cee-Cee. And millions of other women. But would millions of other women write that message?

No. Because it suddenly occurred to me that the message wasn't necessarily a sexual innuendo. It might have come from the Clover's theme song. *Farewell every old familiar face. It's time to stray... it's time to stray.*

So that narrowed the field considerably. Patty. Ben. And Alice, who knew the song like the back of her ring-laden hand. Any one of them could have disguised themselves, trailed me to the Colorado Springs airport, then boarded my plane... planes. I was so consumed with turbulent thoughts, I hadn't noticed the other passengers. It would be difficult to make connections so spur of the moment, but not impossible.

Furthermore, I was in the tourist section while Ben, Patty, and Alice could easily afford first class.

What about Dwight, our newest Clover? *Stupid, Beaumont!* I would have noticed Dwight's wheelchair. You can't disguise a wheelchair with hats and wigs and nondescript clothing. In any case, Dwight needed a special gizmo on his dash or he couldn't drive. So he couldn't possibly have followed me from Houston to Clear Lake city.

Dwight didn't wear lipstick. Neither did Ben.

And yet some sneaky individual had trailed me like a goddamn bloodhound, pillaged my room, and written the message. Why? The answer was obvious. Wylie's murderer didn't want me to decipher Wylie's clues.

"Maybe it's a code," said Butler, staring at the mirror. "That message could mean you skipped town with the goods."

"What goods?"

"Drugs."

He glared at me as if my luggage had been searched because I might have hidden ludes, smack, or worse inside my emergency Tampax. At which point, the motel manager burst into my room.

"Dear lord above," she said, raising her eyes toward the ceiling, where a water stain that resembled Zorro's logo graced the cheap, off-white paint. "I run a respectable motel, Miz Beaumont, not some sleazy dive. I should have guessed when you checked in, but the American Express card fooled me. Whores don't usually carry 'em."

"Yes, they do," I said dryly. "Also *Master*-card, *Diner's* Club, and *Discover*."

It went way above her head, like a hail-Mary pass.

"Well," she huffed, "I'll just put these here damages on your bill."

"What? Are you crazy? I had nothing to do with this conglomeration of luminary splinters and foam rubber. I was in your restaurant when the thief——"

"Can you prove it?"

"Certainly. The waitress and bartender——"

"Have gone home. It's well after midnight, Miz Beaumont."

"Look, I ordered a rare steak, which came burnt to a crisp, and a couple of drinks. Vodka."

"Did you pay with cash or credit card?"

"Neither. Bud..." I swallowed the rest of my explanation, aware that her eyes shot daggers toward Buddy, who looked guilty. "Buddy," I pleaded, "tell her."

"Tell her what?"

Oh, God! Like a bolt from the blue, I realized that Buddy's sensitive thumb had tweaked more than one nipple. I also understood why he was allowed to play the piano, even though he had mangled *Clowns,* not to mention *Feelings.*

"I heard your screams and came running," said Buddy. "You were hysterical. You yelled something about a fight with your boyfriend and how he'd threatened to kill you. I calmed you down, then called the police."

"Why didn't you tell us all this before, Buddy?" asked Morgan, who fortunately had more than a modified crew cut between his wet-behind-the-ears ears. "And," he added, "how did Miz Beaumont know your name?"

"She was scared, out of her mind, didn't trust me, wouldn't have trusted any man. I had to tell her who I was, repeat my name over and over, especially when she threatened to kill *me*."

"With what? Her fingernails?"

Buddy pointed toward a knife that lay on the floor, its blade almost hidden by the slashed mattress.

Butler retrieved the weapon, and I understood why, at his advanced age, he had remained a beat cop.

"If there were any fingerprints," I said with a groan, "you've smudged them."

"They were probably yours," he muttered. His eyes sought his partner's and his expression seemed to suggest that he was only months away from his retirement pension.

"How could that knife be mine, you bumbling, hobnailed idiot? There's my plane ticket receipt and my rental car receipt, right there on top of that pseudo-western bureau. How could I carry a knife onto the plane? Do you think I smuggled it through security?"

"Now just a minute, lady! You coulda' bought the knife after you arrived here with your boyfriend."

"I don't have a boyfriend. And I'm not responsible for your stupid screw-up, you provincial, chawbacon lummox."

I took a deep breath, which didn't help. "The intruder bought that knife. Look at its handle; cheap wood, shaped like a guitar. The lobby has a souvenir counter. This is a one-story motel, and the window's wide open. Somebody was ransacking my stuff when she heard Buddy sing. Buddy was planning to fly me to the moon, but first he had to insert my key. So she... the intruder... dropped her knife, then hit the happy trails to you until we meet again, thanks a lot Roy Rogers."

I received four different reactions to my outburst.

Butler looked as if he wanted to thrust the guitar-handled knife between my ribs and claim self defense.

Morgan, lost, said, "What has Roy Rogers got to do with anything?"

Buddy placed his arm around the motel manager's bony shoulders. "Don't let her upset you, sweetheart," he said. "Christ, she drank two double vodkas and two single shots, so she's not exactly sober."

The motel manager shook him off. "How did you know the exact amount Miz Beaumont drank? You're fired, Buddy boy."

Oh, what a baddog! I watched Buddy boy slink from the room. If he had possessed Hitchcock's tail, it would have been tucked between his legs.

The motel manager turned toward me. "I'm still gonna' put the damages on your credit card if your story don't check out."

"Credit cards! Oh, no!" I raced over to my open purse. My return plane ticket lay in the mess of spilled items. So did my wallet. Which, I quickly discovered, was minus twenty-seven dollars, my useless Visa, and my American Express card.

Morgan retrieved a small spiral notebook from his pocket. "Anything missing, Miz Beaumont?"

"Yes. My credit cards and my sanity. Happy trails. Until we meet again. What if the damn thief meant to slash *me?* What if she comes back?" I gathered the spilled items, including a package of matches, and stuffed everything back inside my purse. "How about some protective custody?"

Butler laughed.

"Okay, forget protective custody. Aren't you going to check out the souvenir counter and see who bought that knife?"

Before he could reply, the motel manager said, "After you arrived, Miz Beaumont, I stood behind the counter."

"Did you sell any knives?"

"Yep. One."

"Can you describe the woman who bought it?"

"Nope."

"You can't or you won't?"

"Can't. A *man* bought the knife."

"What did *he* look like?"

"A cowboy."

"Could you be a tad more specific?"

"He was standing in front of the counter. I saw him from the waist up. He wore a black Stetson and paid cash. That's all I remember."

"Thanks. Would you give me a different room, please?"

"Sorry," she said smugly, "no vacancies."

"But my credit cards were stolen, so I can't check into another motel." I stared at the slashed mattress, then shifted my gaze toward Butler. "How can I sleep? Where can I sleep?"

"Don't sleep," he said.

I didn't.

Once upon a time, I had watched a *Sixty Minutes* segment about divorced, homeless society ladies who lived in their cars. They had not only adjusted to discomfort, but they looked as fresh as the proverbial daisy. Not me. I looked like skunk cabbage.

Just before leaving Clear Lake City's version of the Norman Bates Motel, I had called the Broadmoor and asked for Ben. I didn't really expect him to be there, but he was.

"You said to call if I needed you, Cassidy."

"What's wrong, Ingrid? Where are you?"

I told him about Woody and the fortune cookie, then fibbed about the loss of my credit cards. Pride, I guess. Mickey Spillane wouldn't have left his purse in the room.

"Could you wire me some money, Ben? I'll pay you back, I promise, and the mugger didn't steal my return ticket, so——"

"When do you return?"

"Tomorrow. One-forty-five-ish, Colorado time."

"Do you want me to meet your plane?"

"No. My jeep's parked at the airport, thanks anyway. I just need some money for emergencies, like, well, food." The scream in my throat had become a lump.

"Jesus, Ingrid, do you have a local phone book handy?"

"Yes."

"Look up the nearest Western Union office."

"Hold on." I flipped through pages. "They don't seem to have one, Ben."

"Give me your number. I'll call you right back."

Right back took thirteen minutes.

"I contacted Western Union," said Ben, "but there's no outlet in Clear Lake City. You'll have to knock on Woody's door and wake her up. Okay? Okay, Ingrid? Answer me."

"I'll play it by ear."

"Don't you always?"

"What do you mean by that? My music? Our on-again, off-again relationship? Sorry, Ben, I'm hungry, exhausted, frightened—-"

"Frightened? Ingrid, you said the mugger grabbed your purse outside the motel then ran away. Did he hurt you?"

"No. Honest. The elephant probably stole my credit cards to keep me from charging. I'm sorry I bothered you, Ben."

Then I hung up.

Now I was hanging out. Once upon a time, we used to hang out at the football field during practice sessions. We prayed that we'd catch Dwight Cooper's eye, Junior Hartsel's eye. We wanted their fame to rub off on us, and we silently suggested that they rub against our tight cardigan sweaters, buttoned down the back, emphasizing our pointy Maidenformed breasts. We used to hang out at the drugstore, scrutinizing boys around the soda fountain, scrutinizing the makeup counter, checking our reflections in our mirrored compacts.

My rented compact sat on its rubbery haunches alongside Woody's curb, and my game plan was to wait until sunrise then punt. Driving to Woody's, I had scanned my rearview mirror, but, as Old Mother Hubbard might say, the streets were bare, and I had a feeling the intruder had done her job by frightening me. Even her knife had been a scare tactic. Why would she kill me and leave a mirror message that might be traced back to the Clovers?

As the hands on my watch crept toward three, I tried to forget tonight's events. Yeah. Right. Sing, sing a song.

Cowboy. The intruder might have disguised herself as a cowboy, hiding her hair beneath a black Stetson, scorning makeup, donning a loose shirt and vest. Tad could never disguise her big breasts, but she wasn't really a viable suspect. Would Patty scorn makeup? Not in a million years. Unless she played a role; the quintessential actress.

Alice could play a man. She didn't have a jutting bosom, she could hide her platinum Q-tip hair beneath the Stetson, and she possessed the kind of face that melted into a crowd. If Alice masterminded a crime, witnesses wouldn't be able to describe her features. "She's medium," they'd say.

And wasn't the guitar-handled knife an Alice weapon?

I tried to doze. But my brain scrambled, like quarterback John Elway looking for an open receiver. Why did I leave the motel, as if I were some spineless mouse? Why had I called Ben? What had happened to Ingrid Independent? After I solved the riddle of Wylie's death and the riddle of Bingo's reappearance, I'd have to get my act together.

The dashboard clock didn't work and my watch had stopped at three-ten. I figured it was now around three-fifty-ish. For the first time in a long time, I desperately wanted a cigarette. But cigarettes cost money, the real reason why I'd quit. My gaze strayed toward the car's ashtray. Most of the butts had been smoked down to their filters. However, one survived. Pressing the lighter into the dash, I lovingly smoothed out the ciggie's crumpled tip.

The lighter didn't work. I wasn't surprised.

Then I remembered the motel matches. "Thank you, God," I whispered, fumbling inside my purse.

Half the matches were missing, probably because the cheap-spirited motel manager didn't bother replacing used matchbooks with new. Curious, I extended my hand toward the car's window, catching the street lamp's glow. What dopey western motif had she used on the cover? Gene Autry? Champion?

Not even close. The matchbook was discreet... a white cover with black lettering... THE PALMER HOUSE HILTON.

My *Killer Shrink!* buddy-cop movie had used the Palmer House Hilton's magnificent lobby for one scene, a la *Beverly Hills Cop*. The Palmer House was located in Chicago.

Focusing my mind on the motel room, I remembered the toilet seat's paper strip. A maid had changed the sheets and cleaned the room. She would have discarded the matches if they had been left by a previous guest. Which meant, of course, that they had been left by the intruder.

Chicago. According to lounge entertainers, I had the time of my life. Obviously, those loungers hadn't been with me when I visited Richard Daley's city for the 1968 Democratic National Convention. I never saw a man dance with his wife, but I did see police dance with protesters. They rocked, rolled, swayed, swung, whirled, twirled, and, in general, tripped the nightlife fantastic. My most prominent Chicago testimonial was a scar on my forehead, which I covered with my bangs.

Chicago. I had been very dissonant, very dissident, very visible. Was there a pro-Vietnam activist stalking? Avenging? But why would she wait twenty-plus years, then follow me to Texas and trash my motel room? That made even less sense than my Bingo jealousy theory.

My hands were trembling. I struck three matches before one ignited. Finally, I drew stale nicotine into my lungs.

Dear God! The rush! My head practically exploded while my bladder demanded instant discharge. In other words, I had to pee. Badly. And if I pissed off Woody, too bad.

The Sixty Minutes ladies had toted portable potties. I was parked in a residential neighborhood, and seriously doubted that I could make it to the nearest gas station in time. So I really had no choice. Gathering my courage and resolve, I staggered toward Woody's front door and rang her bell until she answered.

She wore a brown terry bathrobe, minus belt. Her nightgown was red flannel. Her short mussed hair matched her robe. Her eyes matched her nightie. She had been crying. Or maybe she had some sort of allergy.

Yup. She did. Woody was allergic to me.

"Go 'way, Ingrid," she said, and began to shut the door.

"Bathroom," I gasped. "Please."

Her mouth twisted into a scowl. "Hey, I'm not stupid."

"Hey, I'm not kidding. If you don't let me inside, I'll pull down my jeans and squat on your doorstep."

Her scowl became a lopsided grin. "I'll just bet you would. Wylie..." Her grin vanished. "Wylie told me about the coach's office. Prom night."

"That was a mail slot," I said between clenched teeth, "and I didn't pee, I—wait a sec! How did Wylie know about the coach's office?"

"Wylie knew everything."

"Woody, please! I'll leave after I use your bathroom, cross my heart."

"Okay, Ingrid." She opened the door wide and stepped aside. From the tiny vestibule, I could discern a living room on my left, a dining room on my right. They were both furnished, but the walls were white, empty; not one picture, not even a clock.

"You look like shit," Woody said kindly.

The bathroom's fluorescent lighting did nothing to contradict her comment. The bloom was definitely fading from the Rose, and I wondered why Buddy had initiated his seduction. Perhaps his eyesight was failing, along with his better judgment. And why did men tend to age with grace while women just tended to age?

Ben was even better looking now than he had been thirty years ago, and Wylie hadn't really needed his fame or fortune to attract groupies. Despite his scorn for jocks, Wylie had matured into a shorter, whiter, skinnier Michael Jordan.

Dwight Cooper, always a hunk, was graceless below the waist. But above his belt, he still resembled Steve Reeves, that non-acting actor who had played all those marvelous "Hercules on a Fuckin' Rampage" roles. Dwight's eyes had appeared zombie-ish during the reunion dance, but usually they shined with intelligence. Once upon a time, he had been a virtual blur on the football field. Now he sold insurance with the same whiz-bang proficiency.

Even Buddy boy, disillusioned, disenchanted, not to mention dishonorable, had presented a tempting facade.

Only Junior Hartsel and Patty Jamestone broke the mold. Patty because she had aged with grace, and Junior because he hadn't.

What about Bingo? Well, if he exercised and paid the barber a visit, he'd pass muster.

My hair looked drab, a magnified version of the skunk cabbage's cowl-shaped spathe. For the first time in my life, I wished that I possessed Alice Shaw Cooper's expertise with a comb and bleach bottle. Alice had aged neatly. But then Alice had always looked fifteen going on fifty.

On the other hand, Tad was trying to reconstruct those wonderful days of yesteryear when she had mooned her butt at the drop of a hat.

I heard a knock on the bathroom door. "Are you asleep, Ingrid?" Woody asked. "Or did you fall in?"

"I'm asleep."

She actually chuckled. "I could brew some coffee. That might wake you up."

"I'd love a cup of coffee, Woody, thanks."

"Why were you parked outside my house?"

I sighed. "It's a long story."

"Okay. You can start by telling me what Wylie said the night before he was killed."

Chapter Thirteen

"Wylie's last words were a riddle?"

"Yes."

"How do you make a statue of an elephant? That's what he said?"

"Yes." Seated at Woody's kitchen table, I sipped her strong black coffee and sighed with pleasure. "Wylie left the dance in a hurry, and was killed before he could give me an answer. I don't suppose you know the answer."

Woody's eyes looked like Fourth of July firecrackers—red, white, blue, and sizzling. "Damn you, Ingrid! I thought from your message that Wylie's last words were about *me*."

"Well, he didn't exactly know his riddle might turn out to be his last words. I mean, they weren't really his last... I assume he said something between the dance and... okay, my message was tacky, but I needed to see you."

"Why?"

"This." I reached for the cookie wrapper, which fortunately I had kept in my back pocket. Otherwise the thief might have added it to her stash of goodies. "Tell me about The Four Leaf Clover Company."

"Would you like something to eat?"

"Sure. Thanks. Have you ever heard of a company called The Four Leaf—"

"No."

"No?" My eyebrow skimmed my bangs as I crinkled cellophane between my fingers.

"Maybe Wylie mentioned it," Woody said reluctantly.

"Mentioned it or created it?"

She opened the refrigerator door. "I have some left-over chicken, liverwurst, and three hard boiled eggs."

"Do you have any egg rolls? I love Chinese food. During the reunion, Wylie recommended a local Chinese restaurant. I think he wanted me to read your cookies."

"What do you mean *my* cookies?"

"Your address is on the cellophane. How do you think I found your house?"

"I assumed you looked it up in the telephone directory."

"Shit! That never occurred to me. I'm digging a goddamn hole with a goddamn spoon."

"Ingrid," said Woody, slamming the refrigerator door shut, "what do you want from me?"

"Answers."

"It's none of your business!"

"I'm making it my business. Wylie made it my business. He told me a riddle that may or may not have something to do with his murder. He left me a painting of Doris Day. *Doris Day*, for Christ's sake. You've been very nice, and I feel like some goddamn parasite, but I really have no choice. I've been poisoned, abandoned by my lover, robbed——"

"Calm down."

Gasping for breath, I pounded on the table with both fists. "Somebody owes me an explanation!"

Woody walked over to an old-fashioned bread box, opened it, and retrieved three slices from a loaf of seeded rye. I could sense the wheels in her head spinning.

"Since Wylie named you his parasitic beneficiary, so to speak, I'll explain what I can," she finally said. "But first you must understand one thing. Wylie and I hated each other."

"Why?"

"Politics. Ideologies. Sexual preferences."

I stared at her. "You're——"

"Happy with my lifestyle. No regrets. No guilt."

Well, that certainly explained Wylie's reaction to my Peter Pan is always played by a woman remark.

"Despite his repugnance and repudiation," Woody continued, "Wylie always confided in me, don't ask me why."

"Please sit down."

"At first Wylie savored his success," she said, ignoring my plea to sit. "It brought him money and power and Patty. Pretty Patty. She couldn't spend my brother's money fast enough. He encouraged her, laughed when she bought their mansion on Long Island, their status cars, jewelry. But she desperately wanted a movie career, which he wouldn't buy her."

"Why not?"

"I think the deal was that she could only perform for him. Tit for tat. Patty's tit for tattered dreams."

God, what a great line! Maybe I could write it into my Bonnie Raitt song, the one about doormats. I'd have to make tit a bird or something, but I could call my song *Tattered Dreams.*

"Remember how Patty starred in almost every Colorado Springs Community Theatre production?" Woody asked.

I nodded.

"Well, I think she married Wylie because he was accumulating mega-bucks and he planned to move to New York. Broadway beckoned. But Wylie wouldn't let her audition. He was always so damn stubborn."

"I know. Once he got an idea into his head, you couldn't change his mind. He'd simply manipulate—-"

"Mustard or mayo?"

"What?"

"I'm fixing you a club sandwich, Ingrid, with chicken, liverwurst, and eggs."

"Mustard. Just chicken and eggs, please. Kill the wurst. So what happened to rock the boat?"

"Patty had an affair."

"With who? Whom?"

"Someone who lives in Colorado Springs."

"You're kidding! When did Patty visit the Springs? And why didn't Alice spread the news?"

"Are you kidding? Why would Patty broadcast her visits when she was having an affair?"

"Yeah. Right. Good point." I felt my cheeks bake. "How did Wylie find out? Private detective?"

"I don't know. But Wylie knew. And he threatened Patty with divorce."

"Why didn't she take him up on it? With her settlement she could have financed her own play, or even a small movie."

"Patty signed a pre-nuptial agreement. If they divorced, she'd get practically zero. Here's your sandwich, Ingrid."

"Thanks. Why would Patty sign a pre-nuptial agreement? I thought Wylie wanted his Somebody-I-Adore very badly. He was nuts about her."

"He was nuts about you." Having served the sandwich, Woody finally sat.

"Me? That's crazy. He never even gave one hint——"

"Wylie couldn't handle rejection, and you would have rejected him. You were in love with Ben Cassidy. Wylie told me intimate details about you and Ben."

"The prom! Wylie must have spied on Ben and me. That's how he knew about the coach's mail slot. Then there was Stewie's wake... marathon sex. Ohmigod! New York!"

"New York?"

"I rejected him, and he couldn't deal with that. Never mind. Snagged pantyhose." Ignoring Woody's puzzled expression, I stood and leaned against the table. "I assume Patty promised to clean up her act."

"Correct."

"That doesn't explain the fortune cookies."

"Enter Junior Hartsel."

"Junior? I don't understand."

"Eat your sandwich and let me talk."

"Sorry." I plopped my tush onto the chair again. It was a comfortable chair, the white cushions patterned with those adorable Jewish ducks who wore kerchiefs on their heads and looked like they quacked in Yiddish.

"Junior had this brilliant advertising scheme," said Woody. "He wanted to produce fortune cookies with ads inside. For example, the strip of paper might read 'A single rose for the living is better than a costly wreath at the grave.' On the back it would say So-and-So's Flower Boutique, address and phone number. Junior wanted my brother to invest."

"But the cookies I saw didn't——"

"Let me finish."

"Sorry."

"I was involved because of my P.R. background. Before I went into layout and composition, I used to sell ads. Anyway, Wylie thought the idea stupid, but he led poor Junior on a merry chase. They flew to Houston and met with me to discuss details. Junior had computer print-outs, showing labor costs, profit margins, test markets, even a name for the corporation. Coyote's Cookies. Wylie suggested Acme."

"Of course. Roadrunner cartoons. Wylie always loved 'em."

"Junior was ecstatic. Then, after weeks of procrastination, my brother reneged."

"Why would Wylie do that to Junior?"

"His thing about jocks. Remember?"

"Yes."

My sandwich tasted like sawdust as I suddenly realized that Wylie had spiked the prom punch on purpose, challenged Dwight on purpose, even if it placed all of us in danger. Wylie had always been intuitive. He knew that Dwight, drunk or sober, wouldn't let anybody drive his new convertible. Had the top been down? Yes. Wylie had sat on the folded-down top, his legs dangling around Alice. Patty had sat in Stewie's lap while I had sat in Ben's. Tad had perched up front, next to Dwight, so that he could cop a feel every now and then. And nobody had suspected Wylie's ingenuity. Or his duplicity.

"Wylie," Woody said, "took it one step further. Using Junior's computer print-out, he established The Four Leaf Clover Company. Then he began to test market his own cookies."

"But I thought he thought the idea was stupid."

"Wylie didn't care if he lost money. You see, my brother no longer savored success, don't ask me why."

I didn't have to ask. I knew why. Wylie honestly believed he'd sold out, and the price of his success wasn't happiness, or even self-fulfillment. He hadn't gone from nothing to something, except financially. He hadn't developed that God-given talent, merely exploited it. Which in my book, and Horatio Alger's book, was okay. Except Horatio Alger preached hard work and resistance to temptation. In the beginning, Wylie had tempted resisters with his satirical anti-war lampoons. Then he had tempted investors.

Finally, inevitably, he had succumbed to temptation.

Had it led to his death?

He must have known death was a possibility, 'else why the treasure hunt? Why leave the painting to me?

Because once upon a time we were kindred spirits?

Because, according to Woody, Wylie was nuts about me?

Had perfect Patty known that Wylie was nuts about me? Could her motive be jealousy? *Nah,* to quote Kim O'Connor. I wasn't nuts about Wylie. Besides, according to Patty, her husband had been screwing around for years. Why kill him now?

Or had Junior killed Wylie?

Maybe they were working together. Patty for her freedom, Junior for vindication.

On the other hand, who gave a rat's spit? After my prom revelation, did I really want to identify Wylie's killer?

Of couse I did. Because the killer was now after *me.*

A contemplative Woody refilled my coffee mug. Sipping through steam, I asked, "Why did Wylie put your address on the cookie wrappers?"

"I don't know."

"Yes, you do."

"I suppose Wylie sensed his mortality and felt familial. He bought me a brand new Honda for my birthday last summer, and his card read 'Sell it or drive it, I don't care. Love Wylie.' Love Wylie. There was no comma. I was supposed to love him..." She paused and shrugged.

I didn't mention that her Prelude still squatted in her carport. Or that her eyes had been very red when I knocked on her door. Truthfully, Woody and Wylie's love-hate relationship was none of my business. Unless she had traveled to Colorado Springs and bopped her brother over the head. Unless she had seen my rental car earlier, followed me, written it's time to stray on my motel mirror, stolen my credit cards, and slashed my mattress with a stupid guitar-handled knife.

"Your address," I prompted.

"Before he started test marketing cookies, Wylie put the company in my name. He wanted any profits to go to me, his pet charity. You see, I would never take a penny from him." She tried to shrug again, but her shoulders were still humped from the first shrug. "My attorney is dissolving all assets even as we speak."

"Are there any assets?"

"Yes. Wylie didn't take a bank loan or private loan to pay for his new business. He dissolved his own assets, and paid cash for everything. Bakery equipment, a fleet of trucks... it was like that Richard Pryor movie."

"'Brewster's Millions.' The premise was to spend millions of dollars within a certain time limit. Pryor's film was a re-make. When we were kids, Patty and I watched the original on TV, and we would type up long lists determining how we'd spend the money. Does Patty know about the fortune cookies?"

"I guess. Why?"

"She might have planned Wylie's murder to stop his wild spending."

Woody looked startled, and my guess was that she suspected Junior Hartsel.

As if she'd read my mind, she said, "I thought about turning the company over to Junior, I really did, but I wasn't sure Wylie would approve."

"How could he approve or disapprove? He's dead."

"I know. But Wylie always promised he'd resurrect, a Stephen King corpse." This time her shrug was emphatic.

"Woody," I said, "your walls are so... well, unadorned. How come you don't have any Wylie Jamestone paintings prominently displayed? Every home I've entered recently sports at least one."

"I own one, but I keep it upstairs, inside the guest room closet."

"Why?"

"I don't like it. Art should be pretty."

Rising, she approached the kitchen counter, grabbed a pad and pencil, then returned to her chair. Within minutes she had sketched a truly remarkable representation of Woody Allen. Or was it Wylie? No. It was Allen. The face on the pad wore glasses, and he wasn't bald. His bubbled blurb read: THE LION AND THE CALF SHALL LIE DOWN TOGETHER BUT THE CALF WON'T GET MUCH SLEEP.

"Woody, that's great."

"No big deal."

"Who's the calf?"

Her lopsided grin appeared. "I underestimated your intelligence, Ingrid. Patty's the lion."

"But you seemed startled when I suggested that Patty might have killed your brother."

"True. Then I remembered what you said before, when we first began this inquisition. You said that Wylie had left you a painting of Doris Day."

"So?"

"Patty always wanted to emulate Doris Day, or Debbie Reynolds, or Sandra Dee. Audrey Hepburn came in fourth."

"No, first. Wait a sec! Wylie never made his clues that easy. And if, in this case he did, why would Patty hand over the painting?"

"The police had already seen it so she couldn't pretend it didn't exist."

"The police didn't believe it meant anything. They thought Wylie was playing one of his dumb treasure hunts." Woody started to speak, but I held up my hand like a school crossing guard. "Okay, your brother was never dumb. But why didn't Patty simply give me a different painting?"

"I don't know, Ingrid. Maybe she wasn't thinking straight. Even if she planned Wylie's murder, she'd still be agitated."

"I saw her the day after the murder. She was very calm." I remembered Patty's Breakfast-at-Tiffany crying jag. "I guess she wasn't all that calm." The Houston sun was beginning to spike the foggy foggy dew. "Maybe Patty thought I couldn't decipher Wylie's painting. After all, the virgin clue's a tad obtuse."

"What virgin clue?"

I told Woody about Doris and Rock. "Who did we know before she was a virgin?"

"You. Patty."

"Who else?"

"Alice Cooper."

"How long has Wylie been sleeping with Alice?"

Woody looked startled again. "How the hell did you know that?"

"Long story. Answer my question. Please?"

"It started when he learned about Patty's affair."

"Why Alice?"

"I think Wylie thought Alice would tell the world, or at least print it in one of her chatty newsletters. Guess what, folks? I boffed Wylie Jamestone."

"Buffed."

"What?"

"Alice says buffed for boffed."

"For the first time in her life," Woody murmured, "Alice kept her mouth shut."

"An ironic twist of fate!"

"Wylie wanted Patty to feel embarrassed, maybe even mortified. Revenge."

"Dammit, Wylie was courting death, like a moth drawn to a flame." I had a sudden thought. "How recent is the painting you've hidden away upstairs?"

"Very. It was on the front seat of my birthday car."

"Could I see it?"

"Sure. Why not?"

Woody led the way up a short flight of shag-carpeted steps, entered a standard guest room, then flicked a light switch—unnecessary, since the sun was now spreading across the sky like soft butter. Opening the closet door, reaching inside, she pulled out the painting. It was un-framed, gathering dust.

I scrutinized the portrait.

Long black hair, tons of makeup, and a nose the size of Texas. Well, maybe New Mexico. Alice Cooper! His blurb read: THE FUN THING ABOUT BEING SOBER IS MEETING ALL THE FRIENDS I'VE HAD FOR YEARS—ESPECIALLY THE ONE'S I'VE NEVER MET.

Was Woody's painting another clue? Could Wylie have meant that Alice was planning to murder him? No. Much too obvious!

Or was it? Wylie had been sleeping with Alice before the reunion, which explained why he had arrived a few days early. That way he could secretly meet and buff Alice.

Meeting all the friends I've had for years.

Woody had celebrated her birthday last summer. But Alice had touted our fun reunion months ahead of time.

The fun thing about being sober.

I drank. Wylie drank. So did Ben. And Tad. And Junior. Dwight didn't drink, not since the senior prom. Patty didn't drink either, for the same reason. Yes, she did. The bloody Bloody Marys. Bingo drank. Lots. Stoli neat. Stoli not so neat, especially after he'd downed a few doubles.

Especially the one's I've never met.

Had Wylie ever met Bingo? Not that I could recall.

I glanced toward Woody's open closet. Was Alice a closet alcoholic? She was definitely a closet nymphomaniac. Rats! She had been our friend for years, but we'd never really met her.

Re-focusing on Woody, I saw something I had never seen before. Though mussed, her hair looked as soft as a duck's downy butt. Her eyes, no longer red-rimmed, were very blue, fringed by thick lashes. She was beautiful, and I had a sudden gut-wrench, ashamed of the nickname we had bestowed upon her. Woody wasn't a Woody. She was a Diane. No, Diana. Goddess of the forest.

My gaze darted back to Wylie's painting. It had to mean something. Our reunion was too coincidental.

Woody apparently agreed. "Ingrid," she said, "I think you should pay your friend Alice Shaw Cooper a visit."

Chapter Fourteen

My return flight encountered turbulence. I was so scared my spit just about dried up, but saliva deprivation wasn't caused by my fear that we might crash. It was caused by the mirror message, Wylie's cruel rejection of Junior, Wylie's prom duplicity, and Woody's Alice Cooper painting.

The plot sickened.

Mesmerized by my fasten-your-seatbelt sign, I thought about trivialities. Like how I would have to call the credit card companies, apply for a new driver's license, and—-damn! If the thief wasn't a Clover, she now knew my address.

I had discovered the loss of my license early this morning. Worming my way toward Houston, spying a police cruiser, I had instinctively opened my purse and groped for my license. Habit.

Last night Butler had accepted Buddy's introduction and my subsequent correction without proof, probably because I wasn't chained to some recruitment center gate.

Had the thief appropriated my house/car keys?

Yup. Fortunately, I kept a spare in one of those miniature magnetized boxes that stick to your fender. I squirreled cash inside Jeep's glove compartment, so I could pay for parking. Also, I knew how to pry open my kitchen window from the outside.

I didn't have to pry.

Scrunching Jeep's tires close to my curb, I glimpsed a tall shadowy figure pacing up and down my family room.

The mirror message kleptomaniac?

If yes, why wasn't Hitchcock barking? Because it was probably Barry Isaac Nicholas Gregory Oates, that's why. And he had probably crept inside my house, just like Kim O'Connor crept inside Patty's borrowed house. By butt-crawling through Hitchcock's humongous doggie door.

Walking toward the front porch, I heard music. Martha and the Vandellas. *My Baby Won't Come Back.*

Bingo! It had to be Bingo, trespassing bastard!

It wasn't. It was Ben. And he hadn't butt-squirmed through the doggie door because he still had his key.

"There's stew simmering in your crock pot," he said, turning off the stereo, "and some freshly brewed coffee. Or, considering your disheveled appearance, would you prefer a shot of vodka?"

"No, thanks. The fun thing about being sober is meeting old friends," I paraphrased.

"What?"

"Everybody keeps telling me I look like shit."

"I didn't say you looked like shit."

"Where's your car?"

"Parked up the block, across the street."

"Why?"

"When I arrived, there was some sort of party next door. My guess would be a baby shower."

"Good guess. My neighbor's daughter got pregnant around the same time as her Collie. Oh, God! I keep forgetting that normal things happen while I play hide and seek."

"Kick the can, not hide and seek."

"What do you mean?"

"You can kick *my* can, babe."

"I don't understand." Wearily, I ran my fingers through my bangs, then rubbed my eyes. "Ben, what are you doing here?"

"Waiting."

"Right," I said patiently, my tone the same one I employed when a producer insisted that he wanted his slasher flick to plagiarize the theme from another movie, *Jaws* for instance. "May I ask why you're waiting?"

Ben plopped down on the couch and absently patted Hitchcock's rump, which still rotated counter-clockwise from excitement at my return. *It's a miracle,* Hitchcock's tail seemed to semaphore. On the other hand, Hitchcock sensed that I was in a baddog mood, so he didn't jump, knead, or cleanse my face.

Finally Ben said, "I was worried about you."

"Not to worry. They say flying's safer than driving, and after Houston I really believe that."

"Come on, Ingrid, don't play dumb. I'm bothered by your obsessive need to solve Wylie's murder."

"It's not obsessive. It's compulsive."

"What's the difference?"

"An obsession is an unreasonable preoccupation. A compulsion is an irresistible impulse."

"An impulse to perform an irrational act."

"I couldn't be more rational, Ben."

"Ingrid, the last thing you said to me on the phone was something about an elephant stealing your credit cards. That's rational?"

I fumed silently, brushed the travel dust from my jeans and sweatshirt, then murmured, "I'm not your responsibility."

"Yes, you are. Remember that Chinese bit about saving somebody's life?"

"You're Irish and Cherokee, Ben. I don't think there's one Chinese leaf on your family tree."

"I was making a point, damn it!"

"I assume your point is Patty's poison. Look, I've seen 'Notorious' at least a dozen times and I've always tried to imagine what happened afterwards. I mean, after Cary Grant rescued Ingrid Bergman, did he hug and kiss her? Or screw her brains out? Realistically, he probably stuck his finger down her throat and watched her gastric lavage all over her slippers. Or, if you want to get even more pragmatic, Cary probably said, 'Tally-ho, Miss Bergman,' then left the set."

"What's *your* point?"

"Once the ambulance toted me to the hospital and the doctors pumped out baneberries, your responsibility ended."

"Oh, I see. Ingrid Beaumont doesn't want hugs and kisses. It's not in the script, right?"

"There is no script!"

"Then what are we arguing about?"

I felt as though I had something wedged inside my throat, Cary Grant's finger maybe. Cary Grant's *bony* finger, since, sadly, Cary had tally-hoed to that vast Hollywood set in the sky.

God, I really missed Cary Grant. Which was probably why tears blurred my vision and I began to heave great gulping sobs.

Hitchcock and Ben reacted simultaneously. Hitchcock whined and wriggled his body toward my boots while Ben rushed to my side and pressed my face against his shoulder.

"Cary was so charismatic," I gasped. "Even his stupid movies, like that one set in Spain, awful dialogue, but nobody cared, because Cary was Cinemascoped larger than life, and a woman could come just by watching his lips move. God, I miss him."

"Poor baby," Ben soothed, maneuvering me toward the couch. My whole body shook. No doubt I looked as though I belonged in one of those end-of-coitus Madonna videos.

"He will live forever in his films," Ben said, sitting and pulling me into his lap.

Did Ben honestly believe I was crying over Cary Grant? It didn't matter. Ben was petting me like a lover, not an animal doctor, and that led to fresh tears. You might even say it opened the floodgates.

"It *was* rape," I sobbed, trying to make myself a small blob in the middle of Ben's lap. "And I'm happy he's dead. Happy, happy, happy."

"Okay, baby, it's gonna' be okay."

"Woody said Wylie t-told her things about us, in-intimate details, so he knew..."

Fresh sobs overwhelmed me as I pictured my Manhattan hotel room. One humongous bed. Lamps. A mirrored dresser. An escritoire decorated with liquor bottles, including a bottle of vodka, which is half empty or half full, depending, I suppose, on your point of view.

Wylie wants to get me uninhibited, but I've detoured down the road toward Maudlin City. Hiding his impatience, he listens to my marital woes and hands me a few tissues along with quite a few vodka refills.

"Ingrid," he says, "have you ever heard that old joke about the elephant and the circus parade?"

"I don't think so."

"Eb says, 'I'm in the circus parade, but I don't know how to

lead the elephant.' Flo says, 'It's simple. Just tie a rope around her neck, take hold of the other end, then ask her where she wants to go.' Where do you want to go, my love?"

"Back," I murmur, "before the prom."

"Though I dance at a ball," says Wylie, "I am nothing at all. What am I?"

"That's too easy. You're a shadow."

"Very good. Come sit on the bed. A red dancer dances in a red room with white chairs set all around. What am I?"

"The tongue, mouth, and teeth."

"Fantastic! Give me one."

Give me one sounds like you show me yours and I'll show you mine, but I'm intrigued. "Okay, Wylie, here's a hard one. I'm a bottomless barrel, shaped like a hive, filled with flesh, and the flesh is alive. What am I?"

"You're right, darling, that's a hard one." He places my hand across the bulge between his thighs. "You want to feel hard? Feel this."

"I'm a thimble!" I yell, delighted to have fooled him.

Wylie's flesh is alive. Swiftly, he removes my hand and unzips his fly so I can see his flesh. Substantial. Circumcised. His hand captures the nape of my neck and he begins to push my face toward his energetic flesh.

"Stop it!" I shout.

But he doesn't stop. "Red and blue and purple and green," he says, "and no one can reach it, not even a queen. What am I?"

"Dammit, Wylie!" I wrench my head free. "Patty!"

"Wrong, Ingrid, rainbow. I'm a rainbow."

"I meant——"

"Come to think of it, Patty's not such a bad answer."

Then he lunges.

Sobbing my story into Ben's shoulder, I repeated my first sentence, even finished it. "He knew how to manipulate me."

"Okay. Now I understand." Ben stroked the tangled hair away from my hot brow and blotchy cheeks. "Hush, baby, I'm here, and I won't let anyone ever hurt you again."

I couldn't hush. The snagged pantyhose spilled from my drawer like slithering snakes, their reinforced toes and heels hissing. "You have that stuff for dogs, Ace Promazine," I said. "Wylie tried to tranquilize me with vodka and true riddles. That's what they're called, Ben, true riddles, invented thousands of years ago by some unknown person who enjoyed working with words. Just like me. Just like Wylie. *True bastard!*"

Ben didn't need a whole lot of words. Three sufficed. "I love you," he said.

My shoulders relaxed and I heaved a deep sigh.

Shifting me onto a couch cushion, Ben walked toward Doris Day, turned, then said, "I'm sorry, Ingrid. After we talked on the phone last night, I began to ponder your Lieutenant Miller reaction. Ordinarily you'd never suspect that I had anything to do with Wylie's murder. But circumstantial became circumspect, cagey, and I can't really blame you."

At the word cagey, I had a blurry thought, a memory prod, but intuition told me to let Ben keep talking.

"I guess manipulation is contagious, like the measles," he continued. "Patty pulled strings, too. She used the oldest ploy of all. Helplessness. Patty's not exactly emancipated."

"A butterfly trapped inside a rainbow," I murmured. "Is that what you meant before when you said I could kick your can?"

"Yes."

"But it's such a nice can. Why would I want to kick it?"

"Because I was way off base. For instance, I kept wondering why Patty lied about my jacket. Fear? Jealousy?"

"Jealousy?"

Ben's neck turned ruddy. "Ingrid, I'm not Robert Redford, but I'm not Casper Milquetoast either. When Patty instigated her seduction, I was flattered."

"Don't you mean tempted?"

"No. Flattered. I tried to explain that my love for you was a stumbling block. A roadblock, actually."

"So she puked."

"She was drunk."

"She was frustrated. That scene did come from a movie script, Ben. Patty was playing Scarlett. As God is my witness, I'll never be rejected again. Weren't you tempted to play Rhett?"

"On my word of honor, Ingrid, nothing happened."

"Wylie happened."

"And you thought Patty and I planned his murder."

I opened my mouth to deny, then snapped it shut. Because Ben was on target, on the nose, on the dot.

Crossing the room, he knelt, targeted my nose, and dotted it with kisses. "I couldn't really blame you for coming to that conclusion," he murmured.

Blame! What had Ben said three nights ago? Something about the smart guilties. I had toted guilt for years, like a backpack filled with heavy bricks. If I had insisted that Ben drive Dwight's convertible. If I had kept Stewie from enlisting in the Marines, written one post-prom song to make him cringe. If I had married Ben, rather than screwing up, screwing around, screwing every demonstrator who displayed lively flesh. If I had responded to Bingo's cry for love, or at least security. If I hadn't let Wylie inside my hotel room—no! I couldn't blame myself for Wylie. In fact, I couldn't blame myself for all those other ifs. It was fate, astral influences, whatever.

Then why did I still have the guilties? Because Wylie had entrusted me with a mission, the bastard, and I hadn't fulfilled his trust.

I felt like crying again. Instead, I sang, "Ain't no river wide enough to keep me away from you."

"Ain't no mountain high enough." Rising, Ben stretched his cramped leg muscles.

"Mountain. We're supposed to toss Wylie's ashes and watch him pollute Cripple Creek. But first..."

"You want to solve his murder."

"Yes. I have to."

"You don't have to. Let sleeping dogs lie."

I leaned forward and gave Hitchcock a few ear scratches. He lay with his muzzle across one rather drool-soaked boot. "Listen, Ben, I don't need another ghost inside my head. If I don't solve his murder, Wylie will haunt me."

"Bullshit!"

"It's not bullshit. I can't allow Wylie's death to become another pair of snagged pantyhose."

"Pantyhose?"

"For example, I might be scoring a movie and hear Wylie's voice. Why do girl elephants wear angora sweaters? How do you talk to an eleph—damn! I'm so stupid."

"Why? What's the matter?"

"How do you talk to an elephant? Use big words. Kim O'Connor!" I told Ben about Kim. "Before, when you used the word cagey, I had a memory nudge. Kim said she felt caged. Honestly, honey, Kim sounds very young and very old at the same time. I mean, she's extremely perceptive, but she's definitely a kid."

"So?"

"So a kid would be tuned into the latest wisecracks, but she'd also remember nonsense stuff, like knock-knock jokes and elephant jokes."

"That's true. I played knock-knock with my daughter until she reached puberty. What's your point?"

Ignoring Ben's question and my own cramped muscles, I raced toward the gate-legged table and reached for my trusty U.S. West directory. Let your fingers do the talking.

"Rats," I muttered. "There's one listing for John, but it's the wrong street. No Mary, no Kimberly. Maybe we should call your daughter, Ben. Wait a sec! Here it is. O'Connor, Tonto. Clever Mary. She didn't want to pay for an unlisted number, so she used her dog's name."

"I assume you plan to ask Kim if she knows the answer to Wylie's elephant-statue riddle."

"Yes. Are you going to get angry again?"

"No. But I'm going to leave again. I have an appointment with my attorney. By the way, thanks. She's great. Reminds me of Debra Winger."

"God, Ben, you've never told me what happened at the police station."

"I'm a viable suspect, Ingrid. However, my jacket's not enough. Debra Winger says—"

"Your lawyer's name is Debra Winger?"

"No. Susan Goldstein. I tease her with Debra. She says they have to prove opportunity, motive, maybe even find an eye witness who—"

"Why the appointment?"

"Debra... Susan phoned the Broadmoor this morning while I was jogging, and she left a message to meet her around four o'clock. She said it was urgent but I shouldn't worry."

"That sounds like lawyer-speak."

Ben walked over to the spinet and picked up a small vase that held one ceramic rose. "I think you're right, Ingrid. I think Patty killed Wylie. You see, I've been trying to reach her. I pounded on her door twice last night. She wasn't there, or wouldn't respond. I've called at least a dozen times and left messages on her answering machine. I don't understand why she's acting this way unless she murdered him. Remember when I told Miller that anyone could have left the Dew Drop and returned very quickly, very quietly?"

"Yes. I said Patty could have slipped away. But how could she, Ben? In what?"

"My rental car."

His eyes looked mournful, as if a trustworthy bitch had nipped his ankle, and I recalled an old Ben habit. He would leave his keys in the ignition. Because, he used to say, who'd want to steal this piece of junk? But that was thirty years ago!

"Ben, did you leave your keys in the car?"

"Yes."

"So Patty could have driven it."

"Yes."

"And the police might have found somebody who saw your car and jotted down the license number."

"Yes."

"Okay. Let's not panic, and let's not jump to conclusions." I joined him at the spinet, removed the vase from his tight grip, then clasped his hands in mine. "I'm almost positive Wylie meant to lead me to his virgin clue, which specifies Alice. So does the clarinet and Woody's painting." I told Ben about the clarinet and Woody's painting. "After the murder, when I called Alice, she said she was at the Dew Drop Inn. Was she?"

"Absolutely."

"How did she behave? Subdued? Agitated?"

"Neither. She was whooping it up."

"Define 'whooping.'"

"You know Alice. She was collecting tidbits for her next newsletter, and she kept insisting that Dwight regale us with his old football stories."

"Speaking of old football stories, was Junior there?"

"Very there. He and Tad were practically doing it under the table. Then Junior dumped Tad... literally... she was sprawled across his lap... and began to hustle Patty. I heard him say something about making it real."

"Making what real?"

"I don't know. Patty shook her head. 'That's the way the cookie crumbles,' she said. Junior promptly shut up. Then he joined Tad, who was crying."

"I'm beginning to feel sorry for Tad."

"Don't bother. Soon she and Junior were doing it again. But those were all isolated instances, babe. The Dew Drop was packed. Anybody could have slipped away and returned without drawing attention." Ben twisted our hands and glanced down at his watch. "Damn! Now I'm running late."

"Where's your luggage?"

"In the car. I wanted to patch things up."

"Consider them patched."

"Before I leave, please tell me one thing."

"What?" I asked suspiciously.

"Why do girl elephants wear angora sweaters?"

"Huh?"

"Before, when you talked about Wylie haunting you, you said—"

"Oh. Right. Girl elephants wear angora sweaters to tell them apart from boy elephants."

"I'm sorry I asked." Ben untangled our hands, gave me a kiss that virtually seared my lips, then raced toward the door.

I was exhausted, both emotionally and physically, but I had to solve a murder. Fast. Forget Wylie haunting me. Ben was now my prime concern. So I reached for the phone to call Tonto O'Connor, changed my mind, glanced down at my utilities envelope, and called Aspen.

"Apparently Ben threatened Wylie," Cee-Cee said after we had exchanged hello-how-are-yous. "I mean, that's what Bill told me the last time we talked on the phone. But he said Miller sounded kind of desperate because Wylie was so famous and all the tabloids... well, you know."

Did Cee-Cee sound a tad hesitant? I remembered a portion of my dialogue with Miller. *What makes you think the police arrived after Jamestone was killed? Patty mentioned it.* Yeah. Right. I should have said Sinead-the-cat mentioned it. I should have kept my mouth shut.

"Ceese, did I get you in hot water with Bill?"

She sighed. "Bill's an old-fashioned teeter-totter, Ingrid. One moment he's telling me I have a logical mind, the next he's telling me to mind my own business. That's one of the reasons we got divorced. Apparently Miller shares with Bill. Everyone confesses to Bill, even criminals. He's kind of priest-like."

Except in bed! "I'm sorry, Ceese."

"It's not your fault."

Yes, it is. "How's your Canine Companion doing?"

"Great. I should be home soon." She sighed again. "Dwight Cooper heard Ben say something about burying a hatchet in Wylie's balls."

"That was during the dance, Ceese, and it was a figure of speech. Christ, if I had a nickel for every time I've cussed out a producer or musician, not to mention my ex. Remember what I told you at breakfast? I threatened to bash Wylie's head in."

"Take it easy. Obviously Ben's taunt isn't enough to indict, but it does make him—-"

"A viable suspect. I've really got to touch base with Miller, Ceese, because I've discovered that Junior Hartsel, the ex jock, has a motive, and according to Kim O'Connor he visited Patty, and he was at the Dew Drop, and he said something to Patty about making it real. She said, 'That's the way the cookie crumbles.' Do you think they planned Wylie's murder together, and making it real meant making it happen? Also, a mysterious woman threatened me last night, and... well, it's a long story, but Ben said Patty wasn't home last night."

"Yikes, Ingrid! Contact Miller. I think he's set his sights on your doctor."

"Which is probably why Ben's talking to Susan Goldstein. By

the way, Ben says thanks."

"Have you met Susan? She looks like Debra Winger."

"No, I haven't met her, but she sounds wonderful. Come home soon, Tiger."

"As soon as I can. I'm missing all the... action."

I could have sworn Cee-Cee had been about to say fun, just before she remembered my threat comment. Hanging up, I stared at the phone, then took a deep breath, prepared to do battle with Mary O'Connor. But it wasn't necessary.

"O'Connor residence," said a young voice. "Mr. and Mrs. O'Connor ain't here right now."

"Kim? This is Ingrid Beaumont."

"Hi, Grid. Did you call about the Hollywood trip? I've already asked Mom, and she said ask your father. So I did, and he said ask your mother. So it's practically in the bag. All I have to do is tell Daddy that Mom said okay, then tell Mom that Daddy said okay."

"Honey, it's only been a couple of days. I'll talk to your parents and make arrangements, I promise. I called because..." I paused, as a new thought occurred. "Kim, this is very important. When you found Mr. Jamestone, did you see a sheepskin jacket? The same one that grossed you out?"

"No. Yes. No."

"The truth, honey."

"I took the jacket from the kitchen and covered Mr. Jamestone's body. He looked cold. Then I thought maybe I shouldn't have touched the jacket, like maybe I was fooling around with evidence, so I put it back. Am I in big trouble?"

"You're probably in never do anything like that again trouble. But you'll have to tell Lieutenant Miller. The police think Ben... the Indian might have killed Mr. Jamestone."

"I'm sorry, Grid. You like the Indian a lot, don't you? I can hear it in your voice."

"Yes, I like him. A lot." I took a moment to admire her teenage sagacity. "Kim, did you tell elephant jokes when you were little?"

"Nah. But my sister did. She thought they were funny. I thought they were stupid."

"Okay. Here's a real stupid one. How do you make a statue

of an elephant?"

"Heck, that's easy. Find a big piece of stone then cut away everything that doesn't look like an elephant."

Chapter Fifteen

"Damn you, Wylie," I swore, after saying good-bye to Kim. "Cut away everything that doesn't look like an elephant? What the hell does that mean?"

I gazed toward the fireplace and stared suspiciously at my legacy painting. It was becoming a permanent floor fixture, and, thanks to Hitchcock, looked like the Leaning Tower of Day. "Do you know the answer to the answer, Doris?"

Her painted lips seemed to form three words: *Que serra, serra.* What will be will be. The answer's not there to see. Wrong! The answer was there, if I could only figure it out, with a little help from my friends.

Which meant that a long overdue Alice visit was in order.

But first I had to take care of trivialities. So I called the VISA twenty-four-hour number, punched the button that would give me a service rep, and was put on terminal hold.

My family room felt eerie, like the eye of a hurricane, and I wished that Ben had been able to stick around. Forget Ingrid Independent. For one thing, the Palmer House matchbook cover still bothered me. Chicago. Had my left-winged past caught up to my right-winged present? *Damn Jane Fonda. Damn all you Jane Fondas.* Come to think of it, Jane had changed too. She had hit the jackpot by exploiting what Wylie might have called "the abdomophobias of weighty Wendy-ites and potbellied Peter Pans."

I glanced toward Hitchcock. He was chasing cats in his sleep, and I was grateful for his comforting presence, not to mention his sharp canines.

The credit card company's recorded voice kept announcing that my call was important, hang on, so I hung up.

Fortunately, my local locksmith was a friend. I had once written him a freebie, an advertising jingle. "Keys get lost, but never Joe, call 555-KEYS, and I'm ready to go." Simplistic? Sure. Effective? Very. As Sara Lee might say, nobody never forgot 555-KEYS.

Joe said he'd change my locks right away, but I said first thing tomorrow morning might be better. Hitchcock could play watchdog, I had a few miles to go before I slept, and Ben might wonder why his key didn't fit. He might even believe that I had changed my mind about patching.

Should I try the credit card companies again, or should I shower? No riddle there! How could I face immaculate Alice when I resembled Wylie's famous painting of Mick Jagger?

Wylie had titled his portrait *Ferae Naturae*. Jagger's blurb stated: I SHOUTED OUT "WHO KILLED THE KENNEDYS?" WHEN AFTER ALL, IT WAS YOU AND ME.

Who killed the Kennedys? Who killed Wylie Jamestone? The answer's not there to see. Oh, yeah? I'm gonna' see it. After all, *me* didn't kill Wylie. And you was probably Patty and/or Junior. But how could I prove it? First, I'd have to find a big piece of stone and chisel.

I had a feeling my elephant stone lay hidden inside Alice's house. Or was it hidden inside Alice's head? If she was Wylie's murderer, it was hidden inside her heart.

How do you chisel a heart? Easy. Easy as pie. Easy as baneberry pie. Just press your TV remote, find a country-western station, and watch videos. Eventually, someone will sing about chiseling.

I didn't have time to watch country-western videos.

Instead, I showered, subdued my hair with a blo-dryer, donned a robe, then began to scarf down Ben's stew.

Naturally, the phone rang. I've rarely made it through a meal without the telephone's intrusive summons, and I couldn't allow my machine to get it because the right coast is two hours ahead while the left coast is one hour behind, and the call might mean big bucks. Or at least an opportunity to earn a few bucks. Hesitate and you've lost your movie soundtrack.

"Hello," I said, "this is Ingrid Beaumont."

"Ingrid Beaumont Oates. We're not divorced yet."

Bingo!

I tried to keep my voice on an even keel. "Why did you disappear again, Bingo? And what did you mean by trouble?"

"Not now. Your phone might be bugged."

"Are you crazy? Who would bug my phone?"

"Meet me at the top of Pikes Peak, near the cascade, half an hour. Be sure to bring your checkbook and pen, Rose."

Then he hung up.

The Pikes Peak Highway has a scenic route that makes one catch one's breath. Driving to the top is pure pleasure, unless it's cold and dark, and one has the feeling that one is being spied upon. Maybe I should lasso Hitchcock, toss him inside Jeep, ask him to play bodyguard rather than watchdog. Good old Hitchcock. No. Good young Hitchcock. Because he wasn't too old to learn new tricks and—rats! What should you know before you teach a dog new tricks? You should know more than the dog. Bingo, sly bastard, had assumed I'd know more than the dog. His entire message was a riddle, easy to decipher, unless you happened to be a bugger. I should have guessed right away when he called me Rose and told me to bring a pen.

Meet me at the top of Pikes Peak, near the cascade.

The Pikes Peak Penrose Library was located downtown, on Cascade Avenue.

Half an hour.

Which meant I had at least forty-five minutes.

One didn't need one's best glad rags to meet one's ex-ex at the library, so I donned clean jeans and a white sweatshirt with the words KILLER SHRINK! printed on the front—a gift from my ex agent.

I contemplated leaving Ben a note, but I wanted to retain at least one shred of independence. Then I had second thoughts. Alice might be the murderer and I planned to hit her house after my Bingo rendezvous. So I scribbled: "The answer to Wylie's riddle is cut away everything that doesn't look like an elephant. Ponder that while I visit Alice. Love Ingrid."

Just like Wylie, I had forgotten to add a comma.

Accidentally on purpose?

The Penrose Library closed at nine. It was five-thirty and the parking lot was full. An ancient VW bug maneuvered around my jeep, capturing the last empty space.

Eyes half shut, I hummed Canned Heat's *On The Road Again*. At the same time, I visualized somebody exiting the library, entering a car, and driving away.

It worked. Somebody did. A young man smoking a cigarette. God, how I wanted a cigarette. But Jeep's ashtray was buttless, clean as a whistle.

The young man whistled through his fingers. "It's all yours," he shouted, gunning his motor.

Jeep gunned back, and stalled. Desperate, I pressed the accelerator pedal and flooded the motor. After counting slowly to one hundred twice, I turned my ignition key, then my steering wheel. By the time my boots finally found the pavement, a Boy Scout could have helped several old ladies across the street.

Not exactly an auspicious beginning.

Meet me at the top.

The library's top floor includes the children's book section and the historical research area. Bearing in mind those wonderful Olive Garden balloon kids, I headed for those wonderful days of yesteryear.

Bingo! Trying not to look like Bingo. His silver-blond hair had been dyed brown.

Patty had once said, somewhat critically, that a person should always dress like a million bucks. Bingo had followed Patty's advice. His suit was green and wrinkled. Good Will? Salvation Army? Or, like his hair, another half-assed disguise?

To my knowledge, Bingo didn't own a suit. Never had. His new boots shined and his feet looked like they belonged to someone else. He slumped in a chair, pretending to read a book, an upside-down book. As I approached his table, he whispered, "You're late, Ingrid."

"And you look ridiculous, Bingo. Anybody would be able to recognize you, except your mother."

"Please keep your voice down."

"Why? Are you afraid *they* bugged the library?"

"I don't want to draw attention to us."

"Dammit, Bingo, there's nobody here except one librarian and one old lady who's asleep, snoring."

"Okay, Ingrid, forget it."

"Don't you dare leave. I'll scream my head off. Speaking of which, did you crush Wylie Jamestone's head?"

"Why would you think that?"

"You said you were in trouble and you stole his picture."

"I didn't steal it. I flushed it down the toilet."

"Where did you go after you flushed?"

"Chicago."

I pictured envelopes and addresses. Mrs. Nicholas Oates. Herbert Oates. Stanley Oates. Beatrice. Chicago, Illinois.

"Did you finally collect your inheritance, Bingo?"

His mouth twisted. Some might call it a smile, but I knew better. "Herb and Stan paid me ten thousand dollars to shut me up," he said. "I signed some legal forms, but that's all water under the bridge."

I was so angry, I felt like blasting his bridge with dynamite. "You had money, you son of a bitch, and you couldn't send me a few dollars to help pay off your debts?"

"What debts?"

"Your lawyer and your health club contract and your department store charges and..." I paused, breathing hard. "By any chance did the Oates mini-fortune cure your impotence?"

The moment I said it, I wished I hadn't. But for the first time in my life I understood how a person could squeeze a trigger or thrust a knife or bash someone's head in.

Surprisingly, Bingo laughed. The librarian glanced our way. The snoring woman twitched.

"I'd love to prove my potency, Ing," he said, "but your clothes don't turn me on. I prefer the girl who used to wear hip-huggers, the girl whose belly-button beckoned. No wonder the cops always roughed you up. They wanted a free feel. Did you happen to glance at yourself in the mirror? Why wear that idiotic killer shrink sweatshirt? Did your tits shrink? I remember sweaty undershirts. God, Ing, your nipples——"

"That's enough, Bingo!" Tit for tat. Tit for tattered dreams. "This time *I'm* leaving, and I don't give a rat's spit if you're in trouble or..." I swallowed the rest of my words. Chicago. The matchbook cover. Was Bingo's trouble my trouble?

He sensed my uncertainty. "I need money," he said.

"What happened to your ten thousand?"

"I bet it all on sports. Baseball, basketball, football. At first I won, then I lost everything. Three weeks ago, I bet a bundle against Denver. Your Broncos were playing the Kansas City Chiefs. The odds were two to one and the spread—-"

"How much?"

"How much was the spread?"

"No. How much money did you bet?"

"Five thousand. I wanted to win back what I lost."

"But the Broncos didn't lose," I said smugly. "How could you bet money you didn't have, Bingo? Bookies?"

"Of course."

"Legal?"

"Are you serious?"

"So now you owe them five thousand dollars?"

"Well, not exactly. I bet another five on the Giant game." He shrugged.

"I've never been good at math, Bingo, but I think five and five equals ten."

"If I don't pay, they'll kill me."

"Aren't you being a tad dramatic?"

"No. They've already roughed me up once. It happened just before I flew to the Springs."

"Where did you get the money to fly here?"

"I closed a deal with a friend. He wired me an advance."

Close cover before striking. The matches.

"Bingo, did you follow me to Texas?"

"Why would I follow you?"

"To trash my motel room and write it's time to stray on the mirror, which is very Barry Isaac Nicholas Gregory Oates, considering your jealous streak. Then you could steal my credit cards and make the whole thing look as if it had something to do with Wylie's murder. What's the limit on American Express, Bingo? I'm not certain they'd go for ten thousand, but they might advance five, and five would keep your bookies at bay."

"I don't know what the hell you're talking about."

"Answer me, Bingo! Yes or no? Did you trail me to Houston? Did you steal my credit cards?"

"Listen to yourself, Ingrid. Have you totally lost it? If I had your credit cards, why would we be meeting like this? I'd be long gone."

"True." I took a deep breath. "Why did you arrange this cloak and dagger rendezvous? You can't honestly believe I'd bail you out."

"Please, Ing, you loved me once, and I'm sure you don't want to see me dead."

"Don't be so sure."

He gave me a sincere smile, not a twisty one, and I realized that my armadillo's armor was wearing thin.

"Spillane, not mouse, Spillane, not mouse," I said, chanting the words like a mantra. "Spillane, not mouse."

"What the hell does that mean?"

"It means *ciao,* Bingo."

"No. Wait. Don't leave. Please. Listen. There's this woman named Charlene. They call her Charlie Bronson. She's a hit woman, and she's after me."

"You've got to be kidding. Try again, Bingo."

"I'm not kidding. God, I shouldn't have come here."

"The library?"

"No. Colorado Springs. Please listen. I saw Killer Shrink! on video store shelves; it's very popular in Chicago. They changed the name, but it was your movie, your music. We were still together when you wrote it. Anyway, it occurred to me that you might have collected residuals and— -"

"I was paid a flat fee, you bastard!"

My heart pounded. It felt as though thousands of feet were stomping the concrete floor at Denver's Mile High Stadium. I wanted nothing more than to leap from my chair, tackle Bingo, and pound his head against the library's wooden floor boards.

"I'm sorry," he said. "I guess maybe I've placed you in danger, too."

"Bullshit! They wouldn't kill someone who'd reneged on a measly ten grand. That doesn't make any sense."

"Yes, it does. Charlie trained with the FBI before she hooked up with my Chicago bookies. I think she wants to kill me, make her bones, or whatever they call it. But she can't if I pay the bookies what I owe them."

I still didn't believe him. Then, inside my head, I heard that marvelous soundtrack from *The Sting* and pictured Redford's hit woman. "What does Charlie look like, Bingo?"

"I've never actually seen her face."

"Is she young? Old? Black? White?"

I glanced toward the old lady. Didn't her snores sound a tad contrived? Picturing a cartoon chainsaw buzzing through animated wood, I began to compose background music. Something Scott Joplin, something Submarine Sandwich, something organ grinder's genetically-altered monkey.

A carpetbag satchel flopped across the old lady's sensible shoes and support hose. It was large enough to carry knitting needles. And a gun.

"Whoa," I said. "How do you know anybody's gunning for you, Bingo? By the very nature of their profession, a hit person would be sneaky."

"Charlie was at the Olive Garden, Ingrid, the night I met you there. I think she was told to scare me, so she left her calling card. Remember when I went to the bar for my drink?"

"Of course."

"A woman bumped into me. I didn't get a look at her face, it happened much too quickly. But she pressed an empty wine glass into my hand."

"Oh, I get it. Charlie Bronson's calling card is a wine glass."

"Don't be such a smartass. Charlie left an obvious lipstick smudge on the glass. Her trademark is purple lipstick."

Purple lipstick! The mirror message! Had Charlie Bronson followed me to Texas? But why? Anyway, the mirror message had been printed with red lipstick.

"Bingo," I said, "how did your so-called hit woman know you planned to meet me at the Olive Garden?"

"She bugged your phone."

"She did not."

"It's the only way, Ingrid. I'm hiding out at my friend's house, the one who sent me the advance, and I'm positive Charlie didn't follow me there..." he swallowed "...or I'd be dead already. Sleeping with the sharks."

"Fishes." I had a sudden thought. My phone hadn't worked after Patty's frantic call, the one about the prowler. Ben had blamed it on the storm. But somebody could have cut the line, then arrived the next morning while I was in the hospital. She could have fixed my phone, and, at the same time, bugged it.

During my Kim O'Connor visit, both Bingo and Ben had left messages on my answering machine. Which meant what?

Which meant that Ben had recorded a new leave your name and number and—wait a sec!

"How did Charlie know where I lived, Bingo?"

"I told you, Ingrid, they roughed me up."

"So you mentioned your rich wife?"

"I didn't exactly say rich."

"What exactly did you say?"

"Famous."

"They told you about Charlie Bronson, and you said you'd get the money from me. Then you gave them my name and address, right? Answer me, you bastard!"

"Ingrid, they threatened to break my arm."

"Better yours than mine. How can I be rich and famous if I can't write music?"

"I'm sorry."

"Yeah. I'll bet."

"If that's a joke, it's not funny."

"What's not funny is your hasty exit from the restaurant. Charlie couldn't follow you so she kept bugging me."

"Please loan me the money, Ingrid. Please?"

"I don't have it, I swear."

"Then I'm dead."

"Turn yourself over to the police, Bingo. It's your only chance."

"Rose Stewart wants me to trust cops?"

"*Rose Stewart* is dead! She died a long time ago!"

Nervously, I glanced up and down the rows of empty tables. I had that eerie feeling again, the same feeling I had felt inside my family room, that eye of the hurricane feeling.

Bingo watched me survey the room. "What are you looking for,

Ing?"

"A woman with a smudged wineglass," I replied, trying for sarcasm. But my voice must have sounded scared stiff.

"Don't worry. Charlie's probably halfway to Pikes Peak by now. It's a long drive and—-"

"Holy shit, Bingo! I can't believe you're so stupid. Even if Charlie had studied her FBI manuals very carefully, bugged my phone, then honed in on our conversation, she'd simply follow me. She doesn't know the area, and she'd never waste her time trying to figure out some goddamn map." I felt sweaty centipedes creep down my spine as I pictured an ancient Volkswagen capturing what should have been my parking space. "How long has that old lady been here? The one at the table next to ours. The one who's supposedly snoozing."

"I don't know. Before you arrived, I had my head buried in a book."

"Reading?"

"No. Thinking."

"About what? Sweaty undershirts?"

I sneaked a peak at the old lady again. Her gray hair could be a wig. Her pooching stomach could be padded. Her wrinkled face could be the result of clever cosmetic application.

Cosmetics! The old lady didn't wear purple lipstick.

But the librarian did.

"Oh dear," I said inadequately. "I think we're about to be button-holed, Bingo. If your hit woman has been eavesdropping on our conversation, she now knows that I don't have any money and you're still broke."

"For Christ's sake, Ingrid, Charlie's—-"

"Standing over there by the desk. No! Don't look!"

"Don't panic," murmured Bingo. His face was as white as a sheet, and his whole body shook like an Aspen. "The one thing we must not do is run around like some friggin' chicken with its head cut off."

"Two friggin' chickens. If she kills you, she'll have to kill me. Wait a sec! The old lady. We can write her a message and jostle her awake. She can pass the message on to a real librarian who can call the police. The precinct's just a few blocks from here."

My throat hurt from keeping my voice low.

"Police? No way!"

"I want a cop, Bingo, and you might consider trading information for protection. Unless, of course, you prefer death."

"Cold-hearted bitch," he whispered.

"Self-serving bastard!" I shouted. "Okay, you win. I'll give you the money."

Bingo almost fell off his chair.

The old lady blinked open her eyes. "Hush, my dear," she warned. "You're inside a liberry."

I yanked open my purse, retrieved my checkbook and pen, hunched over, then scribbled madly. "The man sitting next to me wants lots of money," I told the old lady, "or he won't give me a divorce. I'll have to sell my house. Just look how much he wants." Rising, I stomped toward her and thrust the checkbook directly under her nose. "Can you believe that?"

"It's hard to believe," she said.

"Well, I'm not kidding." I slammed the checkbook against her table. "Would you care to look again, ma'am? Did you see the amount?"

"I saw," she said. "Lordy, it's way past suppertime. I've got to get home. My grandchildren worry. I tell them not to worry. What could happen inside a liberry? They always say you could fall and break a hip, Granny. I say I'm old, but I'm not senile. Worrywarts, the whole lot of 'em." Rising, she clutched her satchel. "That's too much money for a divorce, my dear, unless you're Joan Collins or Roseanne whatever-her-name-is-now."

After watching the old lady amble toward the stairs, I slid my tush atop my chair, ripped out the check, then handed it over to Bingo. "This is postdated, you rat-bastard. Dwight Cooper once offered to buy my house. It's prime real estate, and he knows how destitute I've been. But you've got to give me a chance to contact Dwight and——"

"A postdated check won't fly." Bingo tore the check in half, then fourths. "I need cash, Ingrid. No cash, no divorce."

The librarian was inching forward, listening hard. Her purple lipstick glistened. Stall, I thought. Give Granny a chance to do her thing.

"Bingo, what the hell do you want from me?"

"I want cash, Ing, ten thousand dollars. Borrow it. Patty Jamestone has plenty, and soon she'll have more."

"I imagine Patty's assets are frozen until they find Wylie's murderer."

"Alice Cooper's assets aren't frozen," he said slyly.

"Why on earth would Alice lend me ten thousand dollars?"

"Not lend, Ingrid, pay. Just ask her where she happened to be the afternoon Wylie Jamestone was killed."

"She was at the Dew Drop Inn."

"She was visiting Wylie."

"You saw her?"

"I saw her car."

"How would you know her car? Since you've been gone, she's changed cars."

"Alice never changes. She used to plaster her cars with paraphernalia, and she still does. For instance, Alice sells Mary Kay cosmetics, right?"

"Jesus, Bingo, everybody sells Mary Kay."

"Everybody does not have a handicap sticker. Everybody does not have a flag-waving Fourth of July Garfield suctioned to their window. Everybody does not have a friggin' slinky toy, blinking its red eyes when you step on the brakes. And everybody does not have a bumper sticker that reads Tipper Gore For Vice."

I almost laughed. Under different circumstances, I would have. Alice's bumper sticker had read TIPPER GORE FOR VICE PRESIDENT. Until some joker ripped off the President.

"What were *you* doing outside Wylie's house?" Before Bingo could reply, I whispered, "Never mind. Tell me later. I think your hit woman is planning to make her move."

"What makes you think——"

"Don't argue. I've been snatching glimpses. I have a sneaky suspicion Charlie Bronson might get a bang out of killing people, even if they owed ten dollars rather than ten thousand."

I took a deep breath and released it slowly. "Okay, Bingo, try and act natural. Stand up, push your chair back, then run like hell."

Chapter Sixteen

According to my TV's digital clock, it was 7:20 P.M.

"You've lost me, babe," said Ben. "Take a deep breath and start again."

My significant lover's dark eyes were filled with compassion. However, he had sensed that physical contact would be inappropriate, and he was right. I felt like a tiny Chihuahua. If Ben stroked me, I'd shiver. If he hugged me, I'd shatter into a million pieces. God, I felt so fragile.

The police had offered to drive me home, but Mickey—Spillane, not Mouse—had insisted that she felt fine and would drive home by her lonesome, even though her jeep swerved a few times along the way. Bumps, I told myself. Potholes. The tires needed air. I needed air.

Now Ben and I stood in the middle of my family room, at arm's length, facing each other. A bottle of Courvoisier perched on top of the spinet, next to my ceramic rose. Aware that yet another thunderstorm drew nigh, Hitchcock had wedged himself between Doris Day and the fireplace grate.

"Start with Bingo's phone call," Ben suggested.

Clutching my snifter, I began all over again. Soon my snifter was empty. Ben replenished it.

"The old lady's name is Shirley," I continued, "and she's not senile, not by a long shot. Her relatives should be shot for even hinting that Granny might be in her dotage. She managed to evacuate the whole 'liberry,' starting with the childrens' section. Shirley promised them bubble gum if they marched like little soldiers and zipped their mouths shut."

"Unzip your mouth and swallow," Ben said softly. "Your face looks bleached, almost as white as your sweatshirt."

Instinctively obeying, I felt the cognac stain my cheeks pink and deliver a few tears to my aching eyeballs.

"Bingo insisted that Alice was blackmailable, Ben. Is that a word? Blackmailable?"

"Let's assume it is."

"So I asked Bingo what he was doing outside Wylie's house. Before he could answer, Charlie Bronson lifted the hem of her skirt. I surmised that she was either planning to entertain us with a striptease, or she just might have a gun hidden beneath her undies. Bingo and I stood up, pushed our chairs in her direction, then ran like hell. I ran faster. Bingo has gained weight and his new boots aren't broken in yet so they hurt his feet. Anyway, I raced down the stairs and practically fell into Lieutenant Miller's arms."

"A propitious landing."

"Bingo and Charlie weren't so lucky. They got met by cops. Charlie immediately professed innocence. I was so pissed, I stepped forward and pulled her skirt down to her ankles. It had an elastic waistband and she wasn't wearing a slip. She wasn't wearing undies, either. The cops just watched, mesmerized. Sure enough, there was a small g-gun t-tucked into her pa-pantyhose."

Ben propelled me toward the couch, sat me down, then helped me lift the snifter to my lips. "Take it easy, babe," he said. "I can't tell whether you're about to laugh or cry."

"Neither. Sneeze. Never mind, my sneeze went away. One cop handcuffed Char... *ah-chew.*"

"God bless you."

"Thanks. Rats! Almost forgot." Rising, I placed my snifter on the coffee table, raced over to the telephone table, then picked up the phone's receiver. Cautiously, as if somebody had handed me a live rattlesnake, I began to unscrew its mouthpiece. Sensing Ben's approach, I turned and thrust the receiver toward him.

"Clever," he said. "Bingo's hit woman planted an F.M. transmitter made in the form of a telephone microphone. She substituted this drop-in for the original microphone, and was drawing D.C. power from the phone company's central batteries. I'd guess the range is about two hundred and fifty feet."

"I knew somebody was watching the house. I felt it. By any chance did a repairman show up here last Tuesday morning while

I was in the hospital?"

"Not a repair *man*," Ben said ruefully.

"She wore purple lipstick, right?"

"Yup. Also jeans, thick-soled boots, a stocking cap, and a heavy tool belt. She looked very authentic. She fiddled around outside, then tested the phone. Hitchcock went nuts. I had to lock him inside your bedroom. So Charlie probably did her thing while I was upstairs with Hitchcock. I'm sorry, Ingrid."

"Why? You couldn't have known. Even if you had mentioned a repair woman, I wouldn't have suspected anything. Did you record a new answering machine message?"

"Yup." Ben screwed the mouthpiece back on, then hung up the bugged receiver.

"No wonder Bingo sounded so abrasive. He heard a man's voice and——"

"Speaking of Bingo, what did the police do with him?"

"They took him into custody. I think they plan to ship him back to Chicago and notify the FBI. Bingo gushed like a broken water faucet. His bookies are part of a mob, Mafia, whatever they call it nowadays. Prostitution, drugs, gambling, the whole enchilada. Bingo promised to confess everything and identify everybody, *if* he can join the government's witness protection program. He has nothing to lose and he's always hated his nickname."

"Your divorce."

"What?"

"Did you ask Bingo about signing the divorce papers?"

"Ben, that was the last thing on my mind."

"What was the first thing on your mind? As if I didn't know."

"Long story," I mumbled, returning to the couch and my Courvoisier.

"We have time." Ben crossed the room and stood in front of me. "You're not going anywhere."

"I wanted to pay Alice a visit."

"Not tonight, honey. Enough is enough. We'll go tomorrow. The first thing on your mind was Wylie, right? Tell me how Bingo knew about Alice."

"Lieutenant Miller was very nice for a cop. He gave me a few minutes alone with my ex-ex so I could say, 'Good-bye, you bas-

tard, good luck.'" I took a deep breath. "Bingo was staying with
an old friend, an ex-con named Jefferson Price. That's how come
Bingo had access to a car and phone. Jeff was into drugs, and he
had recently lost his job. His former employer migrates to Arizona every winter, and takes his watchdog along. Are you getting
the picture, Ben?"

"No. Yes. The klutzy thief."

"Correct. Jefferson and Bingo plotted the robbery together. Bingo didn't know Wylie was staying there. The game plan was simple, even though it required two people. Bingo would back a small
van up the driveway and they'd tote everything out through the
garage. Police patrol that posh neighborhood at night, and people walk their dogs. Since it was Sunday afternoon, Jeff figured
everyone would be watching football. But he didn't figure Alice's
car would be parked in the driveway. He and Bingo couldn't stick
around; it would look too suspicious, especially if someone glanced
out a window. So they drove away, scarfed down some Taco Bell,
smoked a joint or three, then returned. Alice's car was gone. Jeff
entered through the front door. Bingo says it was wide open."

"When did Price feed the cat?"

"Almost immediately. Jeff headed toward the kitchen, looking
for munchies. Remember, he was stoned. Bingo says Sinead
rubbed against Jeff's legs. Jeff was sincerely touched. He reckoned
it was puppy love, or pussy love. So he pried open the milk carton, then couldn't find the cat's dish. Trailing Sinead, he entered
the studio and sloshed milk into her bowl. He was higher than a
kite, completely focused on the cat. When he finally discovered
Wylie's dead body, he stumbled into the kitchen, tossed the carton
back inside the refrigerator, pocketed his gloves, then ran outside."

"But first he tried to mop up the spill with my jacket, right?"

"Wrong. Kim O'Connor was responsible for the blood stains.
Poor kid thought Wylie looked cold."

"Does Miller know about Kim's conscientiousness?"

"Of course. I told him."

"Is the thief still incarcerated?"

"Nope. His poor old mother bailed him out. Jeff will be tried
for breaking and entering, but the cops couldn't make a murder
charge stick. That's why they've been hounding you. I told Miller

about The Four Leaf Clover Company, and Junior, and Patty, but I don't think he took me seriously. Cops have never taken me seriously. I really need to visit Alice. She's the missing link."

"Tomorrow we'll visit Alice together, just a social call. If anything looks or sounds suspicious, we'll notify Miller. Okay?"

"Sure." The potent brandy had propelled me into stage one, uninhibited. Every nerve end tingled with desire. I felt as if I might come should Ben's finger brush my fly.

Standing, I wound my arms around his shoulders and snuggled my head beneath his craggy chin. My hair, no longer subdued, tickled his nose. He sneezed. "God bless," I murmured. "I wonder if we're both coming down with colds."

The back of his hand stroked my forehead, then my cheekbones. "You do feel feverish," he said, unwinding my arms. "Isn't it time you curled up with a comfy pillow?"

"I'd rather curl up with a comfy vet."

"You need sleep."

"You don't want me?"

"I don't want you getting sick. Do you think you can swallow some aspirin?"

"I'd rather swallow—"

"Bed, Ingrid. I'm not kidding."

"What's blue, has four legs, and goes bah, bah, bah?"

"A blue elephant singing the Whiffenpoof song?"

"Wrong. A very sad, very lost lamb."

"Aha! Now we're mawkish. Do you feel like crying? That would be a perfectly normal reaction."

"Is it my sweatshirt?"

"Is what your sweatshirt?"

"Bingo said my sweatshirt didn't turn him on. He said I looked idiotic."

"You look fine. Bingo's the idiot."

"Fine means straight teeth, Ben. Fine means a good personality. Fine means—"

"Beautiful." He crushed me against his chest. Then his hand crept between my thighs. "I want you, Ingrid, I'll always want you," he murmured passionately, squeezing gently.

I reached to squeeze him back, but sneezed instead.

Lifting my sweatshirt, his warm lips nuzzled my breasts.

I sneezed again. And again. And again.

Vaguely, I wondered if perfect Patty had ever sneezed during a climax.

By midnight, my stuffy nose dripped, my throat was raw, and my face burned like a Girl Scout's marshmallow. I didn't feel mawkish anymore, but I did feel sorry for myself. It wasn't fair. I had survived poison, Texas, and Charlie Bronson's booby-trapped pantyhose. Could I possibly allow myself to be felled by the twenty four hour flu?

No way! Twelve hours at the max. Because I planned to visit Alice, with or without Ben, come hell or high water.

High water didn't come, but hell did... with a vengeance. My body blazed and my brain sizzled like bacon. I could hear the devil laughing up a storm outside my window. How I wished it would rain inside my bedroom. A soothing shower.

Ben apparently had the same thought. Maybe not. Forget soothing showers. He filled my tub with cold tap water, ice cubes, and me.

"Poke this thermometer under your tongue," he said. "Open your mouth, honey."

I couldn't open my mouth. Unless I gritted my teeth, they chattered like those wind-up dentures they sell in novelty shops.

I preferred hell to my bathtub, I really did.

It wasn't fair.

When I awoke the next morning, the sun was shining. My nose was still stuffy and my throat felt like I had swallowed rusty razor blades, but my fever had gone down the drain, along with several melting ice cubes.

Ben clutched his pillow. I guess at one point he had clutched me, and I guess it felt good to be cradled by strong arms, yet I deplored my weakness. The weak don't inherit anything except debts, and they don't solve murder mysteries.

I walked downstairs, called Joe, and postponed the lock-changing appointment. Hitchcock would have roused Ben, and Ben needed sleep. Re-entering the bedroom, I noticed how exhausted he looked. His dark lashes didn't quite hide the smudges under his eyes, and he breathed deeply, like a little boy after a rough and tumble day at the amusement park.

Speaking of which, my slasher movie soundtrack was due. If I didn't finish it soon, I would miss my deadline. Most of the background stuff had already been completed, but the producer wanted a scary theme for his killer, an amusement park fun house proprietor who was badly scarred. Therein lay my problem. Everything I composed sounded like Andrew Lloyd Webber. I mean, it didn't just sound like Andrew Lloyd, it was Andrew Lloyd. Maybe after Texas and the library, I could conjure up some original notes. All I had to do was remember how I felt when I saw Charlie's purple lipstick, and how I felt when I saw the lipstick-printed words on the mirror.

Avoiding my mirror, positive my eye-smudges duplicated Ben's, I donned clean jeans and my freshly laundered, lucky orange sweatshirt. Was it still lucky? After all, I had been poisoned while wearing it. But I had worn it inside out and backwards, so the luck might have been hidden.

Justification achieved, I tugged on my comfy cowboy boots and tiptoed downstairs again.

Hitchcock looked mournful.

"Did I forget to feed you last night? Bad Ingrid!"

I filled his dish with kibble, added several large biscuits, then remembered how Wylie loved to chomp dog biscuits. "After all, I was born in the year of the Dog," he had teased.

Bingo had been addicted to Kentucky Fried Chicken. He was a Cock, and roosters peck other birds, or so I've heard.

Why was I playing this ridiculous Chinese zodiac game? Why was I obsessing over food? Because I was hungry, that's why. I couldn't cook, but I could boil water. Hot tea would soothe my sore throat. Ramen Noodle Soup would give me strength.

Toting a mug of tea in one hand, a spoon-masted Styrofoam cup of soup in the other, I finally sat down at my piano.

But I couldn't concentrate. My first finger kept plunking "my dog has fleas" while the words "cut away an el'fant" pushed everything else from my brain. Dum, dum, dum, *dum*. Cut away an *el'fant*.

Wait a sec! The answer to Wylie's riddle wasn't cut away an elephant. It was cut away everything that doesn't look like an elephant.

Okay. Think loud. Think strong. What does an elephant look like? An elephant has big ears. Did any of my suspects have big ears? Nope. Patty didn't even wear big earrings.

Elephants are thickset, nearly hairless. Junior was nearly hairless, but he couldn't be called thickset, not by any stretch of the imagination. Unless you counted his butt. Maybe Wylie had counted Junior's butt. Tad was thickset, if you counted her breasts. And Tad had tusks, or at least incisors. But would an aging cheerleader shout eat shit and die, then bop her provoker over the head the very next day? It would be a tad obvious.

Anyway, everybody yelled stuff they didn't mean. If Wylie's balls had been severed by a hatchet, Ben would be on death row.

Patty and Alice weren't thickset, quite the contrary.

Elephants have muscular trunks.

Abandoning my piano bench, I raced toward the family room, retrieved my dictionary, then took a few moments to study Doris Day. I'd have to frame and hang her soon, even though she didn't seem to mind the floor. Well, hell, she reclined against comfy pillows, didn't she?

"What's the deal, Doris? You witnessed Wylie's murder. Was it Junior? Alice? Tad? Dwight? Patty?"

Did Lady Day's smile expand when I mentioned Patty?

Perched atop my piano bench again, I thumbed through the dictionary. Truncheon. Trundle. Trunk. The main stem of a tree. A large rigid piece of luggage. The proboscis of an elephant. Men's shorts worn chiefly for sports. Aha! Sports! Junior? Dwight? Farfetched! Looking down at the dictionary, I murmured the last definition out loud. "The body apart from the head and appendages: torso."

Who possessed a muscular torso? Stewie and Dwight and Ben. But I had to believe that Ben was innocent. Why? Because he said so. And because I loved him.

I couldn't really believe that Stewie had returned from the dead; talk about farfetched. Unless, of course, Wylie's comment about resurrecting as a Stephen King corpse had some deeper meaning. Rats! If I honestly believed that theory, I'd be sitting inside the local loony bin, clunking my Chicago-scarred forehead against a padded wall.

That left Dwight Eisenhower Cooper. Assuming Dwight had caught Wylie unaware, reclining like Doris Day, what would be his motive? The jock thing? The drinking contest? The car crash? Jealousy?

Could Dwight truly be jealous? When I visited Alice, I'd have to view her through objective eyes. Rich Alice. Thin, bony Alice. Neat-as-a-pin Alice. And, until recent revelations, virginal Alice.

I was ignoring my soundtrack. Perhaps a logical interpretation for Wylie's riddle would occur, unbidden, while I composed the bad guy music for *Phantom of the Amusement Park*.

After approximately forty-five minutes and three cups of tea, I realized that my bad guy's theme still sounded like Andrew Lloyd Webber, diluted by instant soup.

Since my creative caretaker played hide and seek, I really had no good reason to stay home.

Should I wake Ben?

I didn't want to wake Ben. He was on vacation. He needed sleep. Also, I had the gut feeling he wasn't a team player.

In other words, he wouldn't let me carry the ball. And he'd probably punt on third down. Would that be so bad? Yes. I wasn't a mystery solver, but I had to solve this particular mystery. My pride was at stake, not to mention my life.

Maybe I should lasso Hitchcock, toss him inside Jeep, and take him along as my watchdog- bodyguard. That way Ben wouldn't worry.

He might not worry but he'd definitely feel the urge to rattle my bones.

Unless Wylie's killer rattled my bones first.

Standing, I nudged my piano bench backwards with my tush, hit one last discordant chord, then searched high and low for Hitchcock's choke collar. And finally found it, outside the doggie door, along with my TV remote.

"Great balls of fire, Hitchcock!"

My ganglionic mutt looked both guilty and smug.

So did I.

Chapter Seventeen

Hitchcock and Jeep have a love-hate relationship. Jeep stalls with less frequency when Hitchcock balances himself on her front seat, yet her transmission seems to shudder when Hitchcock lifts his leg and pees across her tires. Hitchcock hates the smell of exhaust fumes, yet he loves to poke his head outside Jeep's window and capture air between his teeth.

Sometimes Hitchcock barks at shadows while Jeep revs loudly. On those occasions, my imagination kicks in. I can almost hear Jeep shout: "Look, Hitch, there's a cat! Chase the cat!" And I can almost hear Hitchcock growl: "Jeeze, Jeep, why don't you honk your horn? Maybe Cat'll run under your tires, the ones I peed on."

Usually I was amused by the antics of my mutt and car. But today I anxiously anticipated a conversation with Alice Shaw Cooper, a woman I had known since childhood, a woman I wanted to meet again for the first time.

Soon we all arrived at Alice's house, which looked, at least to me, as if it had been built by Frank Lloyd Wright on steroids. The structure possessed the broad low roofs and horizontal lines that were the hallmark of Wright's prairie houses, yet it bulged every now and then with diminutive Gothicism.

Alice's new-old 1991 granite silver BMW 525I blocked the driveway. Her manicured lawn was bordered by tree stems. I hitched Hitch to a stem.

"Stay, Hitchcock! Good dog."

The sun had disappeared, and I felt winter color my cheeks crimson. How cold was it? It was so cold, the snowman made a down payment on a house.

"Dammit, Wylie," I said between clenched teeth. "Once I solve your murder, will you stop haunting me? No more dumb jokes. No more riddles."

It suddenly occurred to me that Hitchcock wouldn't be much protection, tied to a tree trunk. I knew, however, that Alice would never let me enter her immaculate domain with a shaggy-haired mutt by my side. Except for her marbled vestibule and fired-clay-tile kitchen, Alice's rooms were carpeted. White carpeting. Correction. The formal dining room had off-white carpeting, but it was plush.

I tapped my fingernail against her ornamental doorbell.

She answered on the first ring, as if she had been peering through her stained glass window, the one with all those goofy, frolicking unicorns.

"Well," she said, "it's about time. I was wondering when you'd finally show up."

"Why on earth would I 'show up'?"

"Ingrid, it's proper to make a condolence call."

"I did make a condolence call. I condoled Patty. Why should I condole you?"

"Wylie was my fiancee."

"That was thirty years ago."

"Better late than never."

"What?"

"Better late than——"

"Never mind. Look, Alice, I'm sorry Wylie was struck down in his prime. He had so much to give the world. He will live in our hearts forever. On our walls, too. Everybody collected Wylie. Everybody loved him."

Except Patty, Junior, Dwight, Tad, Woody, and Ben.

As I continued mouthing my standard, albeit caustic cliches, I tried to study Alice through Wylie's eyes, any man's eyes. She wasn't tall or short. She was thin rather than slender. Her clavicle knobbed and her hipbones jutted. Her breasts were practically nonexistent. Maybe she had great nipples, but I didn't know for sure. I had never seen her naked, not even inside the locker room or during our multiple pajama parties. She scorned tight clothes, and she always wore full slips.

Alice had moved to Colorado Springs in 1959. Although she

couldn't carry a tune, she knew all the words to *Purple People Eater.* She could sing *The Chipmunk Song,* and sounded just like Alvin. We clasped her to our budding bosoms.

The early sixties embraced us. Two of our favorite things were *The Sound of Music* and Billy Gray (Bud) in *Father Knows Best.* Even after Our Gang's female members had switched to straight skirts with kick pleats, Alice flaunted full skirts over forty-'leven petticoats. That was Patty's word, forty-'leven, but I used it in one of my protest songs. "Forty-'leven soldiers, marching 'cross the sea."

The seventies arrived with a bang. Kent State. Four student demonstrators killed. My mother sent me a letter that began: "Dear Ingrid, are you happy now?" Alice's newsletter, black-bordered, listed all of our classmates who were wounded, dead, or missing in action. It was the first time her chatty gossip sheet had mentioned Vietnam.

The eighties emerged. John Lennon gave an autograph and signed his life away. Wylie's painting of John—AS USUAL, THERE'S A GREAT WOMAN BEHIND EVERY MAN—was sold to Yoko for an undisclosed amount; some said six figures. Wylie's painting of Ronald Reagan—IF YOU'VE SEEN ONE REDWOOD, YOU'VE SEEN THEM ALL—was purchased by Arnold Schwarzenegger; some said he destroyed it. Alice began to clothe herself in black and white. Black for John Lennon, white to celebrate Reagan's White House victory.

The eighties segued into the non-noncomformist nineties. Kids sported perforated faces and bodies, and soon they'd all look like human cribbage boards. Alice didn't even possess pierced ears. If God had wanted her to wear holes in her ears, Alice was fond of saying, he would have needled her lobes from the git-go.

Opening the door wide, she gestured me inside. "I hope they catch the S.O.B. who killed Wylie," she stated angrily.

"Maybe it was a D.O.B." I shed my camel's hair jacket, handed it to Alice, and vaguely noticed that her vestibule was decorated with a hat rack. Which included a couple of orange and blue Denver Bronco stocking caps, a black Stetson, an old-fashioned Easter bonnet, and one Beatles poor boy cap.

"What's a D.O.B.?" she asked, hanging my jacket inside the

front hall closet.

"Daughter of a bitch."

"Ingrid, you're such a wisecracker. Shall we go into the living room?"

I glanced down at my mud-encrusted cowboy boots. "How about the kitchen, Alice?"

"Okay," she said somewhat reluctantly, "but you'll have to excuse the mess. We're redecorating, raising the cabinets."

"Why raise them? Dwight won't be able to reach——"

"He's better, Ingrid. It's a miracle. Remember when Dwight went away last summer?"

I didn't, but I nodded.

"He heard about this midwestern preacher who cures through touch and prayer," Alice continued, her brown eyes aglow.

Touch and prayer? It sounded like a new long distance telephone company. Sprint, MCI, AT&T, T&P.

"Alice," I said skeptically, "are you telling me that Dwight's cured?"

"No. But he's improved."

"Define 'improved.'"

"He can stand. I mean, he can't walk or even move away from his chair yet, but it's a start."

I pictured Dwight sprinting across the football field while Tad and her fellow cheerleaders hollered two bits, four bits, six bits, a dollar, and my heart ached.

"Maybe," I said sarcastically, "Dwight's preacher can cure my songwriter's block."

"You couldn't afford him," Alice shot back. "He charges a fortune. But he gives most of his money to charity."

"What's his name? Elmer Gantry? Jimmy Swigert? Tammy Faye Bakker?"

"No, Ingrid. His name is Starbuck."

Holy shit! Starbuck! The leading character in *The Rainmaker*, one of Patty and my all-time favorite movies.

"Yup," I said, "it's a miracle. I wonder if Starbuck's paid the Springs a visit. We've had so much rain recently."

"Better rain than snow." Alice glanced toward the kitchen window, where icy blasts had begun to rattle the insulated glass. Then she nodded toward what her parents had called "The Breakfast Nook." Alice had inherited her house from her folks, so Our Gang had clustered around that antique oak table many times. Wylie always called it the breakfast nooky.

Gingerly, I slid my tush onto the wooden seat of a ladder-back chair. "Where's Dwight, Alice? I didn't see his van."

"Gosh, Ingrid, he's selling insurance. During the reunion, Dwight had appointments day and night. Then, after Wylie's death, everybody suddenly wanted extended coverage, new policies. Dwight takes them out to breakfast, lunch, supper. Sometimes he doesn't get home until dawn. He looks so tired, but he's in hog heaven. Dwight would be walking on air, if he could walk, and he will walk some day, thanks to Preacher Starbuck."

"I just got over the flu," I said lamely, as if Dwight's insurance might be providential and Preacher Starbuck had missed his big chance by a somewhat narrow margin.

"Gee whiz, you poor thing." Alice metamorphosed into Mother Hen rather than Mother Goose. "Here, sit on my cushioned chair. Are you hot? Cold? Would you like a cup of tea?"

I was already caffeinated to the max, so I said, "Do you have any vodka handy?"

"Wisecracker! Dwight and I don't drink. Well, I've sipped a little sherry now and again, for very special occasions."

"What about Wylie?"

"What do you mean what about Wylie?"

"Maybe you keep a bottle of booze handy, just in case your lover arrives unexpectedly."

"Lover?"

"Don't play dumb, kiddo. Tad confessed."

"Oh, dear. Wylie thought Tad saw us, but she was sound asleep when he left." Alice slid her rump onto my abandoned chair, arranged her black pleated skirt beneath her knees, picked imaginary lint from her white blouse, then raised her chin. "After Elvis died," she said, "women came out of the woodwork. He loved me. No, me. No, me. Remember?"

"Yes."

"Well, Wylie loved me."

"Apparently he loved me, too."

"Bullshit!"

Instinctively, I glanced around to see if anybody else had shouted that word. A ventriloquist, maybe.

Alice's smile was complacent. "Did Wylie play games with you?"

"What do you mean by games?"

"Obviously he didn't."

"What kind of games?"

"Do you promise to keep it a secret, Ingrid? Cross your heart and hope to die?"

"Sure."

"Wylie played elephant charging. First he'd tie my wrists to the bed, then he'd charge."

"Why don't they allow elephants on the beach?" I said dryly.

"Because they can't keep their trunks up." Alice giggled. "That was one of Wylie's favorites. Here's another one."

I thought she meant another riddle, but she meant another game. As I listened, astonished, Alice described Wylie's favorite jollifications. Most of his horseplay had nothing whatsoever to do with elephants, although a few... shall we say amusements?... involved animal positions.

Alice bragged on and on, and, at long last, I began to compose a viable theme for my scarred amusement park proprietor. The producer wanted scary, but wicked innocence was scarier than pure evil. So I'd set my music to the sound of shattered glass. No. Wind chimes.

"Don't forget," said Alice, "you crossed your heart and hoped to die. Remember how you and Patty used to say that all the time? Patty truly believed she'd drop dead if she was fibbing. So did you, Ingrid."

Alice had shocked me. Now it was my turn to shock her, maybe even shock her into telling the truth. "Speaking of dead, Alice, why did you kill Wylie?"

"That's not funny, Ingrid." She stared at my face. "Hey, you're not kidding. What makes you think I killed Wylie?"

"Your car was parked in his driveway."

"When?"

"Sunday afternoon."

"No, it wasn't."

"Yes, it was. Somebody saw it."

"Then somebody needs glasses," she said indignantly. "Or somebody saw somebody else's car."

"Right. There must be at least a dozen people who drive a silver BMW with a handicap sticker, Mary Kay, Garfield, and Tipper Gore for Vice."

"I didn't see Wylie that afternoon, Ingrid, I swear to God. I saw him that morning."

"Where?"

"The El Paso Perrera Club. We met for brunch. Eggs and bacon and fresh seafood and champa- —"

"Baloney, Alice! They don't allow Jews."

"Wylie didn't sign the tab. I did."

"They wouldn't let a woman join their sacred circle either," I said. It was a sore point. The Perrera Club met downtown, inside an old brick building that people swore was haunted. The club had been around forever. My small group of high school dissenters had contemplated picketing, but we were already staging so many other protests, the Perrera Club kind of got lost in the shuffle.

"My daddy belonged," Alice said smugly, "and my grandfather was one of the original roundtable members. I'm a legacy. I don't pay dues or anything, but I can eat there."

"Why would Wylie eat there? He hated ethnic and/or sexist bigotry."

She giggled again. "Wylie was such a hoot. He wore that little Jewish cap."

"Yarmulke?"

"Yes. He treated the whole thing as a big joke. Snubbed the members, even though quite a few came up to shake his hand, Wylie being so famous and all. He asked the club director if the food was kosher, then made up an elephant joke, right there on the spot. How do you tell the difference between Jewish elephants and Christian elephants? Jewish elephants have bigger noses, I mean trunks. Gosh-darn, I loused it up."

"Okay, Alice, you met at the club. Did you argue?"

"No! I swear to God!"

"Did you eat and run, or did you eat and screw?"

"Ingrid! Watch your mouth!"

Instead, I watched hers. She blotted her lips with imaginary tissue. Which meant that she was agitated. Which meant that she and Wylie had eaten each other. Where? One of the haunted Perrera Club nooks? There went my breaking up is hard to do theory.

"What time did you leave the club, Alice?"

"Shortly before the football game. I drove to the Dew Drop Inn and parked near Dwight's van."

"Who borrowed your car keys during the game?"

"What?"

"You heard me."

She hesitated, then blurted, "Ben Cassidy. I'm sorry, Ingrid. I didn't tell the police, but I might have mentioned it to Dwight, and he might have told them."

"No. He told them about balls."

"Whose balls?"

"Wylie's balls. Why would Ben borrow your keys, Alice? That doesn't make any sense. He had his own car."

"Patty actually borrowed my keys. She said Ben's car was running on fumes. She said she was allergic to cats, and the cat next door kept sneaking inside, and she needed more sinus medicine. She said that Ben had offered to drive to the drugstore. Since it was almost half-time, she didn't want Ben to stop, fill his car with gas, and miss the third quarter."

"Damn! It's so obvious. Patty invented that convenient story, drove home, killed Wylie, then drove back."

"No, she didn't. During half-time we finally crowned her Queen. She was supposed to be Queen of the Reunion, but she left the dance so abruptly Saturday night, we decided to hold her coronation on Sunday. It was Dwight's idea. Tad Mallard played the piano while I crowned Patty. Then Patty sang 'Moon River' and danced on top of the bar. Junior Hartsel shot a video. The third quarter began, but nobody cared. Patty was magic. She shined like a bright star. Then she went to the bathroom."

"How long was she inside the bathroom?"

"Seven or eight minutes, maybe less. Then she returned my keys and sat down next to Ben."

"Think carefully, Alice. Are you absolutely certain that Patty was only gone seven or eight minutes?"

"I'm positive. Dwight kept asking me the time."

"Why?"

"He had an appointment, a new prospect. That's one reason why we drove separate cars. You know the other reason, Ingrid, but you crossed your heart and—-"

"Dwight left before the game ended?"

"No. The Broncos started scoring, catching up, so he called and canceled his appointment."

I pictured Dwight's muscular forearm and the watch he sported so proudly. It was an expensive watch, the kind with multiple time zones, a gift from Our Gang, purchased after the car crash. "Why did Dwight ask you the time, Alice? Is his watch broken?"

"No. He scratched his wrist, poor thing, so he couldn't wear it. The band buckle hurt. He said it felt funny on his other wrist. You know men, Ingrid. They're such babies, even Wylie. Wylie cried the first time we did it, last year, in New York. He said it was such a beautiful experience, almost mythical, like the unicorns on my window. I flew to Manhattan once a month and had my hair done. That way I could meet Wy—-"

"How did Dwight scratch his wrist?" The question came from nowhere, but I didn't want to hear any more about The Adventures of Alice and Wylie. Enough is enough, to quote Ben.

"Dwight said he gashed it on one of our new cabinets. They aren't sandpapered yet. I caught a splinter myself, ouch, ouch. That reminds me. The workmen are due back from their lunch break, so we'll have to leave the kitchen soon." She blotted her lips again. "Dwight never loved me, Ingrid. He married me for my money."

"Why did you marry him?"

"I was scared to have sex. Isn't that silly? I mean, once I had done it..." For the first time, she blushed. "We should leave the kitchen now."

"One more question, Alice, a Wylie riddle. How do you make a statue of an elephant?"

"Oh, that's easy. Cut away everything that doesn't look like an elephant."

Rats! I should have called Alice immediately and saved myself a lot of wondering. But I had called. She had hung up, sick to her stomach. Delayed reaction? Had she bopped Wylie over the head and blocked it out, just like her first-floor suicide leap? No way! Why kill the man who had dropped his trunks and removed her panties, not to mention her fear of sex?

Which brought me back to step one, the afternoon of the murder. If Patty borrowed Alice's car keys, then stuck around to get herself crowned Queen, who the hell did she hand the keys over to? Tad was playing the piano. Junior was shooting a video. Thanks to Preacher Starbuck, Dwight could stand, but he couldn't walk, or drive Alice's BMW. Dwight's van didn't have pedals. Everything was located on the dash or steering column.

That left Ben.

Maybe Patty really was allergic to Sinead. Maybe Ben really did drive to the drugstore. So how come Alice's car ended up in Wylie's driveway?

Suppose Patty gave the keys to someone who wasn't on my suspect list? Woody said that Wylie said that Patty committed adultery. Right here in good old Colorado Springs. And that starts with C and that rhymes with P and that stands for paramour. Suppose Mr. P was at the Dew Drop Inn? There was only one way to find out.

"Alice, may I use your phone?"

"Of course." She nodded toward her wall extension, an authentic reproduction of a nineteen- sixty-something Corvette. "I ordered my phone from Home Shopping. Isn't it cute? Ingrid, watch out! Gosh-darn, I warned you."

"Rats!" I stared down at my hand, which had brushed against a cabinet. One humongous splinter almost crucified my palm.

"I'll fetch my tweezers," said Alice. "Don't move."

Moving quickly, I yanked out the splinter, then ran to the phone. *Telephone number, telephone number,* I thought. *I can't remember the goddamn telephone number.*

A pad dangled from the Corvette's base. On the pad, underlined, was Patty Jamestone's phone number. At least, in that respect, Alice was predictable. Miss Organized.

Patty answered on the second ring, as if she had been expecting an important call.

"I'm driving over right now," I said, "so don't you dare leave."

"Why would I leave? I'm glad you're coming. I could use some help. This Wylie memorial thing is getting complicated. I've invited so many celebs, Ingrid, and I can't find hotel or motel accommodations for them. There's some sort of bicycle competition at the Olympic Center, and most of the reunion gang stayed for Wylie's service, or to mingle with celebs, who knows? Anyway, I've been going nuts." She sneezed. "That goddamn cat keeps sneaking inside. I boarded up the doggie door, but she's found another entrance. The basement has an open window. It's stuck. Hold on. I need some Kleenex."

Okay, so maybe she was allergic.

"I've decided to sing 'Moon River,'" Patty continued between nose-blows, "so you can sing Janis."

"No, I can't."

"Your Stewie bullshit? Don't be stupid, Ing. You sang at the reunion dance."

"I've had the flu, Patty, and my throat's raw."

"Oh, I'm sorry. Please hurry over. I'll be waiting."

"See you later, alligator."

"After a while, crocodile."

"Never smile at a crocodile," I said automatically, then pumped the Corvette's cradle.

Alice returned while I was talking into my machine, leaving a message for Ben. Where was he? Sleeping? Jogging?

"I finally found the tweezers," said Alice. "Gosh, Ingrid, your hand is bleeding. Would you like a bandage?"

"No, thanks." Cautiously, I approached the sink and ran cold water over my scratch. "See? All better."

"Why don't you stay for supper? Dwight probably won't get home until late. We can watch TV, Home Shopping. We can buy stuff at a discount and put everything on our credit cards."

"My credit cards were stolen."

"They were? Bummer. Who stole them?"

"I don't know. If I did, I'd get them back."

"Maybe they got lost, Ingrid. I thought I lost mine, but Dwight found them beneath the car's floor mat. I guess they fell out of my purse when I hit my brakes last Sunday, on the way to the Dew Drop Inn. A stupid cat darted across the street, and my purse fell off the seat. Remember the bumper sticker I had on my last car? I brake for Unicorns? Gosh, it was cute."

"My credit cards weren't lost, Alice, and that's a fact."

I watched her reaction. If she blotted her lips on invisible tissue, it would express guilt. But she didn't blot.

"You can charge stuff to Dwight and pay him back," she said enthusiastically. "I've done that before, charged stuff to Dwight, so they have his credit card number on file. Even if they don't, I have it written down some place. Please stay."

"I'd love to stay, really, but I have to help Patty with Wylie's memorial service. Anyway, that shopping club's a scam. They offer bargain prices, then charge for postage and handling."

"Fair is fair, Ingrid. They can't send things for free."

"It's the handling, Alice. They can charge whatever they damn well please for handling."

"Oh. That never occurred to me."

It occurred to *me* that Alice was very lonely, and I was glad she had finally consummated with Wylie. After all, he hadn't charged her for handling.

Or had he?

Wylie played elephant charging. First he'd tie my wrists to the bed, then he'd charge.

I felt sick to my stomach, and it didn't have anything to do with elephants charging. It was Wylie's mythical comment. Mythical, like Alice's unicorns. Wylie had made fun of their love affair, but Alice hadn't caught the joke.

Or had she?

Chapter Eighteen

See you later, alligator. After a while, crocodile. Never smile at a crock—*Wylie's treasure hunt was a crock!*

His clues had deliberately led me to Alice, there was no doubt in my mind. But why?

Hitchcock barked. Jeep swerved and I grasped the steering wheel for dear life. Hitchcock settled down. Jeep straightened out. My thoughts didn't.

Why would Wylie lead me to Alice? Because he had surmised, correctly, that Alice would brag about their affair. Which would lead me, in a roundabout way, to Patty's affair. But why didn't Wylie simply clue me in on Mr. Paramour?

Because he didn't know Mr. P's identity!

How could he not know? Easy as baneberry pie. Patty had been very sneaky, just like Kim's cat. Wylie had demanded that Patty clean up her act. In a sense, he had boarded up the doggie door. But Patty had found a new entrance. Which probably meant that she was still boffing Mr. P.

Sing sing a song. Think loud. Think strong. Think of good things. Raggedy Ann gives good head. So does the merry widow. Kim had sneaked inside and watched. Watched who? Dex the Chauffeur. But Kim had seen others, at least from the outside. A guy in a wheelchair, a balding nerd who wore a high school jock jack, an Indian.

Doctor Ben.

I remembered telling Cee-Cee that doctors heal sick animals, and I heard her reply, clear as a dog's bark. "Doctors kill."

Could Dr. B be Mr. P? Or was Mr. P Mr. D?

Mister Dex, that is.

Dex seemed the type to eat and run, unless he found himself a tasty, expensive morsel. Dex was blonde, arrogant, Hitler's youth. Patty was addicted to youth, especially her own. Could she have talked Dex into killing Wylie? It was possible. It happened all the time. Just watch TV. This movie is based on a true story, inspired by a true event. It's about a beautiful older woman who talks her young lover into killing her rich, successful husband. Starring Farrah and Leonardo.

Starring Patty and Dex?

The wheelchair guy and balding nerd had motives, too, especially the balding nerd. What about the Indian? A Vegas gambler would put all his chips on Ben, if Ben had boffed pretty Patty. Come seven, come eleven, come Cassidy.

With that last thought, I turned into Patty's driveway. The media crowd had vanished. Nasty weather? Or were they accumulating juicy tidbits from other sources?

Hitchcock looked mournful.

"All right, you dumb mutt. Patty might bitch, but she doesn't have white carpeting, and if you behave, she might let you stay. Heel!"

Hitchcock didn't know my heel from a hole in the ground, but he trotted by my side. I thunked the brass door knocker and heard Tonto's frenetic back-yard-bark. Hitchcock barked back.

Patty answered on the third thunk. She wore black tailored slacks and a pale pink turtleneck sweater. Her feet were bare, except for the toenail polish that matched her lipstick and sweater. "Hi, Ing," she said cheerfully. "Long time, no see."

"Speaking of long-time-no-see, where did all those noxious newshounds go?"

"They're staked out at the Broadmoor. My celebs have begun to arrive. Dylan, Joanne Woodward, and three Pauls; Newman, McCartney and Simon. Remember Wylie's portrait of Paul Simon?"

"Sure."

Wylie had painted Simon sitting on a pony. Strands from the pony's mane fanned backwards until they became guitar strings. The canvas was titled *Slow Down, You Move Too Fast*, and Paul's blurb stated: THE PUBLIC HUNGERS TO SEE TALENTED YOUNG PEOPLE KILL THEMSELVES.

Entering the foyer, I heard Hitchcock's nails click. They needed pruning badly.

"Speaking of hounds," said Patty, "why did you bring yours?"

"I've been neglecting him lately. Besides, you didn't seem to mind when your so-called prowler lurked."

"What do you mean so-called?"

"Why beat around the bush, Patty?" I hung my jacket inside the closet, next to her mink coat. "There was no prowler."

Her cheerful facade evaporated. "I see that your sweatshirt is outside-in this time, pet. You're the only person I know who wears sweatshirts and jeans for all occasions."

"This isn't exactly an occasion."

"I hope you wear something dressier for Wylie's memorial service. A dress, maybe."

"Dammit, Patty, you sound like my mother!"

Unperturbed by the unflattering comparison, she glanced toward Hitchcock. "If he barks, he's history. If you bark, you're history. I'm in no mood to play scavenger hunt."

"Treasure hunt."

"Whatever. Wylie's *so-called* clues led you to me, right?"

"Did you kill him, Patty?"

"No," she said as we entered the kitchen. "I was at the Dew Drop, and I can prove it."

"Did you follow me to Texas last Wednesday?"

"What were you doing in Texas?"

"Mousing. Somebody trailed me to Clear Lake City, Texas, then left a knife and... never mind. All I know is that you weren't here. Ben tried to get in touch with you."

"Why would I follow you, Ingrid?"

I gazed at her pink lipstick. But she had other shades. Peach. Mauve. Light red. Medium red. Dark red.

"Maybe you wanted to scare me, Patty. Maybe you felt that I was on the verge of solving Wylie's murder."

"Maybe I spent last Wednesday with Alice."

"Did you?"

"Yes. Dwight was gone on business. Alice and I watched some stupid home shopping show on TV. Oh God, you've raised your eyebrow, and I know what that means. Look, I spent Wednesday night with Alice, cross my heart and hope to die."

I believed her. Patty had changed a lot, but she wouldn't cross her heart and hope to die without fearing repercussions. Her childhood rite was sacred. Besides, it would be such a simple matter to verify her story. One phone call. "Did you spend last Wednesday night with Patty, Alice?" "Yes, I did, Ingrid. Why do you ask?"

So Patty had spent the night with Alice, and that eliminated Alice. Dwight was confined to a wheelchair, and Ben was at the Broadmoor. There were no more leaves on my clover.

It's time to stray, it's time to stray. The words reverberated inside my skull. Maybe the Chicago matchbook didn't mean anything. Maybe Patty had simply enticed an admirer to follow me, scare me.

Who?

Junior Hartsel?

Dex the Chauffeur?

I recalled something Ben had said yesterday——was it only yesterday? Ben had said that Patty possessed Junior's telephone number, inside a purse-sized directory. Why would perfect Patty carry a mediocre man's number around? Ben's number, yes. Mel Gibsons's number, definitely. Why Junior Hartsel?

Ask her! No. Maybe she'd let something slip, although, truthfully, Patty never let her slips show. They always reached the hem of her skirts, then stopped, and she had never bunched the waistbands beneath her belt. Patty always looked like a million bucks. From hat to shoes, everything matched.

I had another memory nudge, like a pinprick, like the one I had felt with Ben; the nudge that eventually led to Kim and caged. But I couldn't get a clear picture. It had something to do with everything matched.

Patty's kitchen table was paved with sympathy cards and telegrams. Plants, blooms, nosegays, and stuffed elephants perched atop every surface. The flora was traditional. The elephants were probably from people who had known Wylie well. Which precipitated my next question.

"This isn't a bark, Patty, but how did Wylie know about your lover?"

"He didn't."

"Baloney! Wylie——"

"Didn't know who he was."

I walked over to the refrigerator. If I opened it, would I find footprints in the butter? What kind of prints? Chauffeur shoes? Football cleats? Nikes?

"Patty," I said, "aren't you mildly curious? I mean, you didn't even blink when I mentioned——"

"My affair?" She shrugged. "Haven't you read the stats, Ing? Everyone screws around. Didn't you cheat on Bingo?"

Sarcasm, always close to the surface, escalated. "I thought about it, but most of the time I was just too damn tired."

"Yeah. It must be exhausting to sit at your piano and doodle songs."

Doodle songs? Ouch! "It must be even more exhausting to shop for jewelry and dead minks, Patty."

"Not exhausting, Ingrid, tedious. So I shopped for a lover, instead."

"Wylie discovered your affair, that's a fact. But how come he didn't discover your afairee?"

She laughed. "I suppose I'm the afairer."

"How come, Patty?"

"I covered my doo-doo, Ing, like a cat in a litter box."

Hitchcock's ears levitated at the word cat. Since it wasn't preceded by chase the, he flopped down with his head between his paws.

"Defined 'covered,'" I said.

"Wylie's private eye was a woman. Equal opportunity and all that shit. She must do very well, since she opted to lease a brand new Cadillac and dined at the Briarhurst Manor."

"Jesus Christ! Hit ladies and women detectives! Mickey Spillane is definitely an ambulatory anachronism."

"What?"

"Nothing. Go on."

"It's really quite simple. I dined at the Briarhurst, too, and made certain that Wylie's bird dog, or rather bird bitch, saw me rub against the wrong man. And please don't ask me to define wrong man."

"Junior Hartsel."

Patty finally looked startled. Brushing a few stray cards from a chair, she sat. "How did you know?"

"Ben heard Junior say something about making it real. He was hustling you at the time and—-"

"Wasn't Wylie stupid? As if I could sleep with that chickenshit has-been."

"Which chickenshit has-been did you sleep with, Patty?"

"That's a bark, pet."

I strolled over to a window and glanced through the glass at the gray poplars and green firs. Last Monday, clutching Doris Day, I had felt branches whip my face, but I couldn't see the forest for the trees. Now it was time to chop down some tree stems.

"Patty, how do you make a statue of an elephant?"

"Find a big piece of stone, then cut away everything that doesn't look like an elephant. Why?"

"Wylie told me that riddle Saturday night. I thought it might be a clue."

"Big deal, Ingrid. Wylie always told idiotic elephant jokes." She nodded toward a few stuffed animals. "He simply refused to grow up."

I pictured Wylie's Doris Day. The frightening thing about middle-age is the knowledge that you'll outgrow it. Okay, who didn't want to grow up?

Wylie, but he was the deadee, so he didn't count.

Patty wanted to grow, but she didn't want to age. There's a big difference.

Junior was still living in those wonderful days of yesteryear, when he had scored big, especially with girls.

What about Dwight? Had he really adjusted or did he still picture himself as the swift-footed football hero? Leading the Broncos to their umpteenth Superbowl championship?

And let's not forget Tad. When she glanced into a mirror, did she see the quintessential cheerleader? Then, after Wylie had shattered her illusions, did she reciprocate by shattering Wylie's skull?

Alice had been a grownup before we'd all caught up. Yet, conversely, she had always been extremely childish, almost goose-silly. She had even called Wylie's apartment a beatnik pad, long after beatniks had evolved into hippies.

Holy shit! Wylie's apartment!

A light bulb materialized above my head. I could actually see it. I could also see the naked bulb attached to a chain that had swung down from Wylie's ceiling. We used to call it his Film Noire bulb, because it captured the wispy waves from our cigarette and dope smoke, and because it cast nifty shadows across Wylie's old, shabby furniture.

His wall cracks had been covered by posters. One stated that war was unhealthy for children and other living things. Behind each poster lived roaches, the cock kind, not the clip kind.

Why would Wylie rent a roach-infested, dilapidated rattrap? Because, he said, it was cheap and still possessed its original fireplace. Above the fireplace was a mantel. On the mantel perched a statue. A statue of an elephant?

Nope.

A statue of Patty.

In our senior year, Wylie had tried his hand at sculpting. An artist, he said, should be able to work in any medium. I disagreed. I couldn't create an opera, I said. But Wylie was always so damn stubborn. He wouldn't accept reasonable doubt, and chose to sculpt The Four Leaf Clovers for his first project. It was ambitious. It was dreadful. Mainly because he had taken a piece of stone and cut away everything that didn't look like a Clover.

Undaunted, Wylie cast a mold. Better, but no cigar.

Frustrated, he chopped off Sunshine, then Rain, then Rose, until all that remained was adorable Patty.

A more mature, adorable Patty sat on the edge of her chair. Her expression was difficult to decipher, but I felt as though she wanted to feed me honey vanilla Haagen Dazs atop a slice of baneberry pie. Finally she said, "Cat got your tongue, Ingrid?"

Hitchcock lifted his head and glanced my way.

"Good dog," I said, watching his tail sweep croissant crumbs toward a nearby trash can. "Patty, remember Wylie's first and only attempt at statuary?"

"Sure. Wylie molded you, Ben, and Stewie from scratch. For me, he cheated and covered a Barbie doll with plaster of Paris."

"No wonder you looked perfect while the rest of us looked like blobby creatures from that old sci-fi flick." I took a deep breath. "Why did you hire somebody to kill Wylie?"

"I didn't."

"Yes, you did. The painting. The riddle. The statue. It had to be you, wonderful you."

"That's a nasty bark, Ing. Get out of my house."

"It's not your house. The fortune cookies, right?"

"What fortune cookies?"

"I know all about Wylie's fortune cookie company." I *tsked* my tongue against the roof of my mouth. "Wylie was throwing his money down the drain and you must have been royally pissed."

"The truth? I was more than pissed."

She scowled, and I watched, amazed, as her features merged into a butterfly's elongated larva. Patty looked like a caterpillar trapped inside a rainbow-colored flame, and I sincerely doubted that anybody in their right mind would crown her queen of anything.

Correction. They'd crown her Queen of the Moths.

Wylie was courting death, like a moth drawn to a flame.

"If you didn't act quickly," I said, "there'd be no money left to launch your goddamn movie career."

Rising, she walked toward the refrigerator, opened it, and retrieved a plastic-wrapped plate. I expected to see butter filled with footprints, I really did, but Patty extended her arm, and I saw tortellini.

Her scowl twisted into a smile. "How do you kill tortellini, Ingrid?"

"I don't know. How?"

"Spray them with pasta-cide."

"God, that's terrible. Another Wylie riddle?"

"Of course." Patty fed the plate to the refrigerator and slammed its door. "My late husband was a pest, and I'm not talking nuisance. I'm talking plague. Let's just say that I needed a pesticide, an agent to destroy—"

"Who was your agent? Junior Hartsel?"

"Are you serious? Junior couldn't kill a fly. He hasn't got the guts. I promised Junior the cookie company if he would pretend to be my lover. I told him I would divorce Wylie and ask for the company as part of my settlement."

"But you signed a prenuptial agreement."

"How the hell do you know that?"

"Woody Jamestone. The reason why I flew to Texas."

"My goodness, pet, you have been a busy bee."

Something snapped. Something inside my head zubbed. Busy bee? I had been manipulated by a master puppeteer, a *dead* puppeteer no less. I had put my life on hold, when all I wanted to do was hold Ben, love Ben, and doodle songs.

"Yes!" I shouted. "Wylie led me on a merry chase, which finally ended with the merry widow."

My boots were made for walking. They stomped toward Patty.

She retreated, until her back pressed against the refrigerator door.

"Okay," I said. "You're right, of course. Junior hasn't got the guts. Who was your agent, Patty? Dex?"

"What's a Dex?"

She looked agitated. No, frightened.

"Don't play dumb," I said. "Hitler's youth, the boy next door, Kim's chauffeur. Kim sneaked through the doggie door and saw you with Dex. What were her exact words? Oh yes, I remember. 'Raggedy gives good head. So does the merry widow.'"

"I d-don't know wh-what you're t-talking about," Patty stammered.

"It doesn't matter. I'm tired of playing sleuth. I didn't want the job in the first place. I hate mysteries. I don't even like riddles any more. So I think I'll let the police tie up loose ends."

She shook her thick braid. "Fiddle-de-dee, as Scarlett would say. A painting of Doris Day? An elephant joke? An old Barbie statue? The cops'll laugh. You haven't got one shred of proof, pet."

"Because you covered your doo-doo?"

"Exactly."

"Not exactly, *pet,* since you stupidly forgot to empty the litter box before taking another dump."

"Define 'dump,'" she mimicked.

"The fortune cookie fiasco. Your secret affair. Alice Shaw Cooper's car."

"What?"

"Bingo saw Alice's BMW parked in your driveway, just before Wylie was murdered. Alice said she loaned you her car keys, and I believe her."

"Bingo? When did Bingo hit the Springs? And what was he doing in this posh neighborhood?"

"Long story. Let's just say that Bingo has a rather intimate relationship with the police department and can be reached at a moment's notice. Meanwhile, the cops can question reunionites, discover exactly who was missing during your Dew Drop coronation. The crowning took place after you borrowed Alice's car keys, right? Junior shot a video. Maybe he captured your little key exchange on tape. Maybe someone saw you hand them over to the killer. That's a humongous dump, Patty."

"You're crazy. Junior didn't shoot his video until later, and everybody was watching the Broncos. It was their two-minute drill, just before half-time. The quarterback kept throwing the ball, completing passes. Nobody watched me."

"Wrong! Somebody always watches you. They can't help it. You have a certain mystique, Patty, like perfume, and football passes wouldn't mean shit to someone who was contemplating his own pass."

"Ingrid's right, you know."

I whirled about, then gasped.

While Patty and I had been busy snapping at each other, a man had entered the kitchen. His upper lip sneered and his eyes glittered with anger. He held a gun, but it was pointed at Patty, not me.

"Why did you fuck the chauffeur?" he asked.

"What chauffeur?"

"Knock it off. I've been sitting outside the kitchen door. Tell me why, Patty. You'd better make it quick, and you'd better make it good."

"I did it for you, darling."

"That's such a crock."

"No, really, listen!" she cried, desperation straining her perfect, swan-arched neck. "I thought I could talk Dex into killing Wylie, so you wouldn't have to."

Chapter Nineteen

It felt strange to be right and wrong at the same time. I had guessed correctly that Patty would try and talk Dex into killing Wylie. I hadn't guessed, however, that he'd say thanks but no thanks. Which was what Patty was telling the man who sat just inside the kitchen entrance.

Falling to her knees, she wrung her hands. "I did it for you, Dwight, honest."

He placed the gun in his lap and wheeled his chair forward. His legs were clad in jeans. His white shirt was rolled up above his muscular forearms. He halted to flex his fingers, and I could discern deep scratches. Cabinets, hell! Those scratches were caused by claws. Sinead.

Since I was bothered, to put it mildly, I said the first thing that popped into my head. "Why did the cat scratch your wrist, Dwight?"

"I was getting rid of fingerprints when I dropped the damn statue," he said ruefully. "It bounced off the cat. She hissed and clawed me when I tried to pick it up. She was a Stephen King cat, Ingrid, and that's no joke."

"Speaking of jokes, how does an elephant sink a submarine?" Dwight and Patty just stared at me. "He knocks on the door. You knocked on the door, Dwight. Wylie answered, then offered to show you his newest painting... Charles Manson. That sounds like Wylie. He wanted praise, or maybe he thought that you had found out about Alice and he wanted forgiveness."

"Alice? Forgiveness?"

"You entered the studio and saw the statue," I said quickly, hoping to cover my faux pas, although, at this stage of the game it didn't really matter. "What a great weapon, you thought, much better than a knife, or whatever you'd brought along. But how on earth did you manage to reach Wylie's head? Did he bend down or something?"

"No. I just—-"

"Dwight, shut up!"

"Why? You've already spilled the beans, Patty."

"Ingrid? She can't prove anything." Rising to her feet, Patty fastidiously brushed croissant crumbs from her slacks. "We were very careful, darling, remember? Nobody saw me drop the keys in your lap. Anyway, the cops have never believed Ingrid."

"I didn't mean Ingrid."

"Dex? He won't say boo. I promised to fly him to the coast and arrange an audition."

"Which coast? What kind of audition? Porn flicks?"

While they argued, I kept staring at the gun, probably the same gun Patty had mentioned on the phone while talking to Ben. If I grabbed the gun, Dwight couldn't chase me. He was confined to his chair. What about Patty? My size twelve body could handle Patty's size six body.

Darting forward, I grabbed the gun. It was almost too easy.

Patty laughed. "You don't scare me, pet," she said. "You're a pacifist."

"I've sold out and become a Republican. They adore guns."

"Wisecracker!"

We all turned our faces toward the back door. Alice entered. Before anybody could react, she had pried the gun from my hand.

"You're such a wisecracker, Ingrid," she said. "You're not a Republican, but I am. You couldn't shoot anyone, but I can. Do you know where Wylie's murder weapon came from, Dwight? You have three guesses."

"Alice..."

"That's right. Me. I gave Wylie the statue. I ordered it from home shopping. By the way, Ingrid, you're absolutely right. They charge too much for handling. But it was worth the expense. Wylie loved his statue. He said it reminded him of his sister, Woody."

Dwight's brow glistened with perspiration and his eyes looked stricken. "What are you doing here, Alice?"

"I was watching TV when I remembered something I told Ingrid. You found my credit cards inside the BMW last Sunday. But how could you, Dwight? We didn't drive any place together. So that meant you borrowed my car, after Patty borrowed my keys. My guess is that you asked someone to drive you during Patty's coronation. You probably said you planned to 'kidnap' Wylie. Why shouldn't he be at the Dew Drop with the rest of the gang? Then you killed him and told your driver Wylie wouldn't leave."

"That's a stupid guess," said Patty. "The police questioned the reunion participants, even the ones who returned home after Sunday's football game. You gave the police a detailed list, Alice. Remember?"

She chewed her bottom lip, uncertain, then said, "Ingrid left my house because she wanted to help you with Wylie's memorial service. But that's my forte. I can plan a celebration better than anybody."

"Celebration?" I asked, totally bemused by the sight of Alice comfortably holding the gun, as if she held her TV's remote control. At the same time, I silently cursed myself for missing the lost credit cards clue. "Celebration, Alice?"

"Wylie loved parties. The prom. Stewie's wake. The reunion dance."

"Wylie didn't love the reunion dance," I said dryly. "It reminded him of growing old."

"Now he doesn't have to grow old. Should we have a wake, Patty? I think we should have a wake. We can hang black and white streamers with black elephant cut-outs, and maybe we could hire one of those striptease dancers, costumed as Death."

I was beginning to enjoy Alice's vision because I had a feeling Wylie would have appreciated the decor, especially when Death stripped down to her panties and garter belt.

"What a shame Dwight and Patty can't attend your wake," I said. "They've both just admitted they planned Wylie's murder together. Did you hear them, Alice?"

She nodded.

"The cops might not believe me," I said smugly, "but they'll believe both of us."

220 / Denise Dietz

Patty pounded on the refrigerator with her fists. "Shit!" she shouted. "Everything's going wrong. It's not supposed to happen this way. Wylie is dead, and his paintings are worth a fortune, and the three Pauls are in town, not to mention a bunch of other celebs. Goldie and Kurt are driving down from Aspen, and I figured a movie was just around the corner. I wouldn't expect a starring role. I'm not greedy. Maybe a small but pivotal part..."

Despite Patty's histrionics, I heard Hitchcock growl. The growl wasn't threatening, more like puzzled. Hitchcock knew that Alice and Dwight were both friend. However, he didn't know the difference between a gun and gum, so the gun hadn't caused his growl.

Patty continued pounding. I was standing between Patty and Alice, watching Patty pound. Alice stood slightly behind me, clutching the gun, mesmerized by Patty.

With an effort, I drew my gaze away from Patty, glanced at Hitchcock, then followed Hitchcock's gaze.

An empty wheelchair, slowly gliding backwards, had caused the puzzled growl.

"Alice, watch out!"

Too late. Dwight had approached from behind, clasped his wife in a bear hug, and lifted her off the floor.

Alice dropped the gun. It fell, landing where her feet had been planted.

Dwight kicked the gun across the kitchen. I couldn't move. Surprised by Dwight's sudden recovery, I shouted the first thing that came to mind. "*Biscuit*, Hitchcock!"

Hitchcock eagerly bounded forward, skidded to a halt, sniffed, then lifted his fuzzy muzzle. His expression seemed to suggest that I was looney-tunes. Furthermore, he didn't care for the gun's odor.

"*Bone*, Hitchcock, bury the *bone!*" Absurdly, I began to explain. "There's a doggie door. No, dammit, the doggie door's been boarded up. Okay, there's an open window downstairs, in the base— "

"It's a miracle!" Alice's voice cut across my demented plea. "You can walk, Dwight."

"Of course he can walk," said Patty. Cautiously, she

approached Hitchcock, hunkered down, gave him a few tentative head taps, then retrieved the gun. "Dwight can do other things even better," she added sagaciously.

"Starbuck," breathed Alice, as Dwight finally released her.

"Fuck Starbuck! I may be an ex jock, but I'm not stupid. Do you honestly believe I'd spend mega-bucks on an evangelist?"

"Then how did you get cured?" asked Alice.

"Acupuncture."

"You're kidding," I said.

"No, I'm not." Liberating a Camel from the pack that rested between the folds of his shirt sleeve, he tapped his pockets as though searching for matches. Then he tossed his unlit cigarette toward the sink. "My brain had been bruised during the accident, and my injury was in that part of my brain that controlled my legs. All I had to do was energize my brain."

"I think I like Starbuck better," I murmured.

"You can't argue with success, Ingrid. The whole thing started when I made an appointment to sell an acupuncturist life insurance. He said he was pragmatic, but that theoretically it was possible to resolve my problem with acupuncture. I didn't believe him, until he told me stories about miraculous cures. He mentioned protons and electrons, and said the body was a magnet. He suggested I picture my brain as a spider's web with a hole in it. The hole had been repaired, but my vibrating apparatus was out of whack. To make a long story short, he promised to stimulate my brain."

"I guess it's like a woman stimulating a penis, right?"

"Only if she had needle-sharp teeth, Ing."

Dwight sounded like our old high school bud, the kid whose neck was too thick for button-down collars, the kid who was embarrassed to ace English and math because his teammates were barely passing, the kid who had carried me to an emergency room after I slipped on a patch of ice and broke my arm.

Now I knew why Dwight's eyes had appeared so zombie-ish during the reunion dance, why he "sulked." He had been contemplating Wylie's murder, due to take place the very next afternoon.

"Oh, God," I moaned. "Why did you ruin everything by killing

Wylie?"

Stupid question. I knew the answer. Somebody I adore.

Dwight had adored Patty. Ben was Sunshine and Stewie was Rain, but Dwight had been Nightfall, stygian gloom, the time when worms come out.

My elusive memory nudge pricked. I pictured Alice's vestibule, the hat rack with a black Stetson hanging from one rung. Looking down, I saw that the hat matched Dwight's black-tooled, leather boots. "Did you follow me to Texas and play cowboy, Dwight?"

"Don't say another word," Patty warned.

"Why? It's all over now." He shrugged. "I followed you, Ingrid. It was all her idea." He pointed toward a furious Patty. "I was supposed to ransack your house and leave that message on your bathroom mirror, a kind of Charles Manson bit. In fact, Patty got the idea from Wylie's painting." Dwight shrugged again. "I saw you leave with a suitcase, so I followed you to the Colorado Springs Airport, then called Patty. She said you'd never recognize me if I wore a cowboy hat and was very careful, because people never saw what they didn't expect to see, so you'd never see me without my wheelchair."

I glanced toward Patty. "You bitch!"

"I bought my hat at the airport," Dwight continued. "Then I flew to Houston, first class. I watched you rent a car, rented one of my own from the same discount agency, then trailed you to Clear Lake City. It was easy. The traffic crawled. I stayed a couple of car lengths behind, and didn't let anybody enter my lane. When you checked into that motel, I called Alice and spoke to Patty. She said to proceed with the original plan. Then I saw the souvenir counter..." He shrugged for the third time.

"Okay," I said thoughtfully. "The knife was your idea, but the lipstick was Patty's. True?"

"Of course. Christ, I don't carry lipstick around. I was supposed to use it on your bathroom mirror."

"Why write 'it's time to stray'?"

"The Clover's intro line means it's time to leave, but Wylie strayed. He was a goddamn wolf in sheep's clothing."

"He was not," Alice said indignantly.

We all ignored her. "The matchbook cover," I prodded.

"What matchbook cover?"

"You left matches behind, Dwight. They were from the Palmer House Hilton. Chicago."

"Oh. Did I? Patty and I met there. We both flew to Chicago and—"

"Wait a sec! How come Wylie's private eye didn't report your assignation?"

"We bribed her," Patty said smugly. "After she ratted on Junior and me, Dwight and I confronted her in Chicago. We wined and dined her, and offered her Starbuck's fee."

I remembered Alice's words. *Dwight went away last summer. He heard about this midwestern preacher.*

"When Stewie died," said Dwight, "I wanted to marry Patty. But what could I give her?"

"You could give her love," I said, then mentally kicked myself. What a pat answer. What a non-Patty answer.

"Wylie was a bastard," Dwight continued, sidestepping my love remark. "You have no idea, Ingrid. Wylie had his groupies and cheated on Patty at every opportunity."

I glanced at Alice. Groupie? She looked more like a guilty guppy.

"He abused her," said Dwight.

Patty had the grace to blush. Because, I thought wryly, Wylie's abuse probably consisted of his refusal to buy her that coveted movie career.

"Enough, darling." Patty nodded toward Alice and me. "They don't have to hear every detail."

But Dwight couldn't be stopped. It was as if he had energized his tongue as well as his legs.

"Patty said to keep my recovery a secret. That way nobody would suspect me. How could a crippled man kill Wylie?"

I had been partially right. Again. The perfect murder, masterminded by perfect Patty, committed by a paralyzed person rather than a dead one. In retrospect, my Stewie theory didn't sound so ridiculous any more.

"Alice caught me standing," Dwight continued, "so I made up that bit about Starbuck. Burt Lancaster played a con man in the movie... 'The Rainmaker' it was called. Patty and I once watched it on TV, after we made love."

Part brag, part groan, Dwight's last four words slipped out of his mouth like a greased pig at a state fair. Except Dwight's words and the image they evoked weren't laughable. I, for one, don't find greased pigs funny.

"You buffed Patty? There's no Starbuck?" Alice's voice sounded raspy. "Where did all the money go? Preacher Starbuck wouldn't accept personal checks or credit cards," she added unnecessarily.

"Wylie's detective," said Dwight, "and the acupuncturist. His services didn't come cheap."

I had a feeling the acupuncturist was just another Starbuck, but I mentally zipped my lips shut.

"I didn't think I'd have the courage to murder Wylie in cold blood," Dwight admitted somewhat dolefully, as if maybe it wasn't macho to acknowledge that particular flaw. "But then I learned about the prom." His eyes glittered. "Did you know that Wylie spiked the punch and challenged me to a drinking contest on purpose, hoping I'd crash my car?"

"Yes," I said.

"Bullshit!" Alice shouted. She had heard enough defamation and was defending her lover.

Due to my afternoon session with Alice, I was immune, but Dwight and Patty glanced around the kitchen, searching for a hidden ventriloquist.

With their attention temporarily diverted, I made a run for Patty's gun.

We wrestled. Dwight joined us. Alice didn't, and I felt my strength waning.

Then I saw it. Her. Sinead. Entering from the basement stairwell, sauntering across the kitchen, she headed straight for legs. Because she was hungry and the leg trick had worked before with Jeff-the-Thief. Cats are smart. They remember little things like that. Or maybe it was instinct. In any case, Sinead chose Dwight's legs.

"*Cat*, Hitchcock!" I screamed. "Chase the *cat!*"

Hitchcock didn't hesitate. Jeep had apparently taught him what a cat looked like, or maybe it was instinct. Hitchcock bounded toward us, a shaggy black avenger.

When the dust settled, a spiky-furred Sinead sat on top of the butcherblock counter, hiding behind a huge stuffed elephant. Hitchcock had his front paws on the counter. Patty looked dazed. Dwight was sprawled on the floor. And I held the gun.

"Alice," I said, "call the police."

She didn't have to. Lieutenant Peter Miller entered the kitchen, slightly *after* the nick of time. He was followed by his partner, Shannon LeJeune, and Ben.

"Did you just happen to be in Patty Jamestone's neighborhood?" I asked sarcastically, handing Miller the gun.

"Not exactly," he replied.

"Cee-Cee Sinclair phoned Bill from Aspen?"

"No."

"Then how—-"

"The police don't spend every minute hassling anti-war protesters," Miller interrupted with a gritty grin. "Sometimes we investigate a murder, especially when the murder weapon is conveniently found at the scene of the crime."

"But there were no fingerprints."

"The people who own this house didn't seem the type to buy authentic reproductions. They'd want the original Thinker. So we started checking out knick-knack stores, novelty shops, furniture stores, catalogues. Nothing." His eyes touched upon Shannon. "My partner said she was addicted to the House Shopping channel."

"Home shopping," I corrected.

"Right. I won't bore you with details, but it seems that Dwight Cooper bought one statue."

"I used your credit card, you son of a bitch," Alice hissed, her angry look directed toward Dwight. "After withdrawing enough instant cash for Preacher Starbuck, my credit cards were over the limit."

"We drove to the Cooper residence," Miller continued, "where we found Dr. Cassidy breaking a window."

"Oh, no!" screeched Alice. "Not my unicorns."

"Sorry." Ben grinned sheepishly. "I slept late, then jogged.

Ingrid and Hitchcock were missing, so I checked the answering machine. Ingrid said she was at Alice's house and planned to visit Patty. I tried Alice first. Her door was locked. When nobody answered the doorbell, I thought maybe Alice was the killer, so I picked up a rock and—"

"Killed Alice's goofy unicorns?"

"Not all of them, Ingrid. Lieutenant Miller arrived, and we drove over here. Are you all right, babe?"

"I will be if I can ask a few questions." My eyebrow skimmed my bangs as I stared at Miller.

"Be my guest," he said.

My gaze shifted to a handcuffed Patty. "Dwight drove Alice's BMW."

"No, Ing, he took a bus. Of course he drove Alice's car."

"That's a rhetorical question, Patty. Here's a real one. Are you allergic to cats?"

"Yes. Long-haired ones. Their fur make me sneeze. Why do you ask? The car keys?"

"No. Ben said you went inside the studio to kiss Wylie goodbye. But Wylie had already left the house. Kim... the kid next door saw him. When you emerged from the studio, your lipstick was smeared. Ben also said Mancini was on the stereo, which sounded odd since Wylie didn't particularly care for Mancini while you love him, but I didn't follow through. How come your lipstick was smudged? You kissed the cat, right?"

"Yuck! Why would I kiss a cat? I kissed a painting."

"Doris Day or Charles Manson?"

"Manson."

"That was sick, Patty."

She shrugged.

"Speaking of sick," I said, "what about the poisoned pie? Junior didn't buy it from a church lady."

"Is that another rhetorical question?"

"Yes. No."

"I looked up poisons in a book. Then I remembered reading a mystery series written by Diane Mott Davidson, a Colorado author. Her books include recipes, so I ferreted out her telephone number, called her, and said I wanted to write a mystery novel.

I asked her where one would find baneberries, and she told me. By the way, she's very nice. I asked her how a killer would bake a baneberry pie. Then I baked the pie and poured your creme de menthe into the potted plant so that Ben would think you were drunk. But I never meant to kill you, Ing, cross my heart and hope to die. I just wanted to frighten you."

"What about the milk?"

"There was no milk. The thief put an empty carton—-"

"Why did you lie about Ben's jacket?"

"I wanted the cops to suspect Ben. I knew he had threatened Wylie... Dwight heard him at the dance. I didn't think the cops could actually prove anything, but I figured the longer it took to solve Wylie's murder, the safer we'd be. Dwight and me. If it hadn't been for you and your damn dog..." She glared at Hitchcock, waggishly wagging his tail. Her angry gaze moved to the bristly, bewhiskered, bewildered cat, still atop the counter, and she issued forth a loud *ah-chew*.

Ben, Miller, Shannon, Dwight, and Alice all chorused: "Bless you." I didn't. It seemed wrong, somehow, to bless a murderer.

Last night I had wondered if Patty would sneeze during a climax. I guess that answered my question.

"Do you love Dwight?" I asked, curious. I thought maybe she did, even if she loved herself most of all.

"Love is hello and good-bye," she said.

"And hello again." I glanced toward Ben. "Hello."

"Hello."

"See you later, alligator," Patty chanted, as Shannon escorted her through the kitchen.

"After a while, crocodile," I replied automatically.

She smiled and a shiver ran up and down my spine. I didn't smile back, because one never smiles at a crocodile.